THE VAUGHN IDENTITY

TIM GAMBRELL

CANDY JAR BOOKS · CARDIFF
2024

The right of Tim Gambrell to be identified as the Authors of the Work has been asserted by him in accordance with the Copyright, Designs and Patents Act 1988.

Characters from 'The Web of Fear'
© Hannah Haisman & Henry Lincoln, 1968, 2024
*United Nations Intelligence Taskforce
and characters from* The Invasion © Kate Sherwin, 1969, 2024
UNIT: Blood & Thunder
© Andy Frankham-Allen & Shaun Russell, 2022, 2024
Doctor Who is © British Broadcasting Corporation, 1963, 2024

Range Editor: Tim Gambrell
Editors: Shaun Russell & Andy Frankham-Allen
Editorial: Keren Williams
Licensed by Hannah Haisman and Kate Sherwin
Cover by Martin Baines

ISBN: 978-1-917022-18-7

Printed and bound in the UK by
4edge, 22 Eldon Way, Hockley, Essex, SS5 4AD

Published by
Candy Jar Books
Mackintosh House
136 Newport Road, Cardiff, CF24 1DJ
www.candyjarbooks.co.uk

All rights reserved.
No part of this publication may be reproduced, stored in a retrieval system, or transmitted at any time or by any means, electronic, mechanical, photocopying, recording or otherwise without the prior permission of the copyright holder. This book is sold subject to the condition that it shall not by way of trade or otherwise be circulated without the publisher's prior consent in any form of binding or cover other than that in which it is published.

PROLOGUE

THE INVASION was over.

UNIT, with a little help from the Doctor and his friends, had put an end to Tobias Vaughn's collaboration with the Cybermen. Planet Earth was safe, Vaughn and his allies were dead, and their ship near the moon destroyed.

And yet, it wasn't as simple as that, thought Brigadier Lethbridge-Stewart, seated at his desk in UNIT HQ under Waterloo Station – affectionately termed *the Warren*, due to its endless concrete corridors. He pondered the sheet of paper in his left hand, while his right scooped up the ringing telephone. The caller didn't even give him time to announce himself. Fortunately, he recognised the voice immediately: Anne Travers.

'Brigadier, we've got a problem.'

'Yes,' he told her. 'I've got your Telex here. We've received similar figures from Geneva and the Met Office, too.' He understood the data enough to know that it was bad news.

'What did you expect, exploding an enormous bomb above the earth?'

He bristled at the implied criticism. 'Five thousand miles above, Anne.'

'Well, the particles aren't just sitting up there. Gravity doesn't pick and choose what it affects.'

'As I told Colonel Schrader in Geneva earlier, while the rest of the world slept, *we* had to think on our feet. If the damn thing had landed it would have destroyed everything.'

'A quick death. Unlike the slow, lingering one that awaits us if we can't do something about this potential fallout. Can I speak to the Doctor?'

The printout crumpled slightly as the Brigadier's grip

tightened. 'I only wish you could. Blasted fellow's gone! Captain Turner and Miss Watkins saw them all off without me knowing.'

'Isobel and your officer protégé, eh? Right little matchmaker you are.'

'If we could focus on the matter in hand?'

'Okay. Ted's got a suggestion. I think it's sound, but I was hoping to get the Doctor's opinion on it first.'

Both the Brigadier and Anne had been in similar situations after the London Event. They had to trust their own skill and judgment then, as now.

'Geneva haven't come up with a plan yet,' he told her. 'Your guidance, as always, would be invaluable.'

'Thank you.'

'Is your plan something that can be actioned from New York?'

'I think so. We're looking at induced ionisation of the particles.'

'I see.' He didn't, but that didn't matter. 'Any potential side-effects?'

'Unknown.'

'What if I have to sell it up the line? Say it's the lesser of two evils, I suppose.'

'Undoubtedly.'

Good God. 'All right. How will it work?'

'We've analysed some particles we collected from a weather balloon. It's a different kind of radiation to anything we've seen terrestrially. We've bombarded it with highly charged ions and that seems to have neutralised the threat. The challenge is to create enough charged ions over a wide enough area. And high enough in the atmosphere for it to be effective before the particles reach the surface.'

'I thought they already had?'

'Some have – hopefully harmless in their current concentration – but there's a greater quantity still to fall.'

'I see.' The Brigadier rubbed his chin. 'Rockets?'

'That would take too long. Ted thinks we can utilise the International Electromatics satellite network. They can be programmed to transmit a controlled pulse. This should stimulate adjacent particles and create a temporary ionised atmospheric layer.'

'Should?' he queried.

'Yes. *Should* is the best I can give you.'

2

'And I note the word "temporary". How temporary?'

'Difficult to say. We're effectively putting the satellites into fault mode to get them to perform outside their design parameters. If the effect wears off too soon there's a chance we could repeat it without totally destabilising the hardware...'

'That was an unspoken *but* if ever I've heard one.'

'Seat of the pants, Brigadier, seat of the pants,' said Anne, brightly. 'But if the irradiated particles pass through this manipulated layer and are rendered harmless—'

'The general public need never know.'

'Exactly. Except that international communications are likely to go down for some hours while the satellites are recalibrated.'

'How long before you and Ted can get your plan in motion?'

There was a slight pause at the other end and some muffled voices. 'About twenty minutes ago, I'm told. We may get cut off soon.'

Impulsive fellow, the Brigadier thought. *Just like her father.*

A knock at the door interrupted the conversation.

'Come.'

Sergeant Walters entered, a sheet of paper in his hand. 'Sorry, sir. Thought this might be important.' He handed over the printout. 'Met Office recording high levels of electrical ionisation in the upper atmosphere. Unknown cause. Wondering if it's anything to do with those spaceships we blew up, sir?'

'Thank you, Walters,' said the Brigadier. 'Nothing to worry about.'

'Very good, sir.' Walters came to attention before leaving.

The Brigadier spoke into the telephone again. 'Did you hear that, Anne?'

'I did, yes. Sounds like it's working already.'

'Are you able to monitor progress at your end?'

There was another slight pause.

'Captain Kramer tells us we have to. We're preparing another weather balloon now.'

'Good. Then we'll touch base again in twelve hours.'

'If we're all still alive...'

The Brigadier sighed inwardly. 'Try to look on the bright side.'

'I am, Brigadier, I am.' Anne's voice startled to crackle and break up.

The Brigadier replaced the handset. 'And let's hope there aren't any more unexpected developments.'

CHAPTER ONE

OF ALL the strange and wonderful things Corporal John Benton had seen so far in his secondment to UNIT, those silver giants had been by far the worst. He'd not been there long. He still remembered clearly the day Brigadier Lethbridge-Stewart had explained to him what it was that the United Nations Intelligence Taskforce did. Benton was a practical man; he had a job to do, and that job didn't include doubting one's commanding officers. It almost never entered his head to disbelieve. And by the time Benton might have done, he'd already seen sufficient evidence to assure him that the threats, outlandish though they may have seemed, were very real.

Dust had settled, wounds had been licked and cover stories had been issued – both nationally and internationally. Now it was time for the clean-up operation. Benton and his patrol were checking the windowless warehouses behind the London IE headquarters building. His eye was drawn to the logo on the wall. International Electromatics. The words turned his stomach. So much death and destruction lay at their feet – or rather the feet of their now-deceased managing director, Tobias Vaughn.

With a shudder, it occurred to Benton just how close the UK – in fact, the whole world – had come to a complete take-over, with the maniac Vaughn in charge at the head of a relentless cyber army. Only UNIT had stood in their way. And thankfully for the world, UNIT had succeeded. They'd lost some good lads, though. Benton didn't know any of the officers that well, but of one thing he was certain: Brigadier Lethbridge-Stewart would have felt the loss of every single one of them.

You could tell with some officers, and Benton was sure the Brig was one of the best…

'You hear that, Corp?'

Private O'Leary dragged Benton from the reverie he'd slipped into unawares.

'Hear what?'

The young private stopped and looked around, his rifle out before him. Benton secretly applauded the youngster's composure. He wasn't sure he'd have been so calm and collected when he was nineteen. But then, service had sharpened some of Benton's softer edges since then. He had a long way to measure up to someone like Captain Turner, but he was also a long way off Private O'Leary.

Benton hid his smirk. How many times had his stepdad told him, 'You'll never amount to anything, Johnny, if you keep comparing yourself to others. Be the best man you can be'…? More times than he could count. Benton had been lucky to have two strong role models growing up – his dad, who died when he was only a kid, and his stepdad, who'd been in his life almost as long as his dad had been dead.

'Corp?'

Benton chided himself. Always letting his mind wander. Another thing he had to work on if he was going to succeed in UNIT.

'I think it came from inside one of these crates here—'

The fist smashed through both the crate and O'Leary's skull just as Benton leaned in to listen. The body of the private simply crumpled to the warehouse floor, his rifle clattering to the side.

Benton took one look at his dead comrade, then with cold, measured anger he stepped back, aimed his rifle and fired over and over again into the body of the concealed attacker. The lid of the crate hinged outwards, spilling the attacker onto the floor, alongside poor O'Leary.

'What the…?'

Somehow it – whatever it was – was still holding on to life. A lad no older than O'Leary, his torso lacerated with metal protuberances. Benton hadn't seen anything like it in his life. He almost gagged on the smell. His free hand rose to cover his mouth, unintentionally causing his rifle to lower.

A mistake.

Immediately from an adjacent crate, another figure emerged. Similar, yet different enough to show that these weren't faceless adversaries. This new one was female for a start. And around the metal and plastic protuberances she wore… It looked like a canteen tabard, embroidered with the IE logo.

Benton made a quick assessment. He had a moral objection to attacking a woman, but he also had a moral objection to being killed. He backed away and reloaded his weapon. Whatever she was, like the still twitching figure on the floor, this ex-canteen girl was neither robot nor human anymore. Some sort of halfway point between the two; an interrupted conversion, maybe. Half of her face was a mask of metal, with one blank hollow for an eye. And the other half…

'Don't like the look of yours, much!' said a cheeky voice, startling Benton.

Jack Tracy.

Benton held up a cautionary hand to his fellow corporal. He was grateful for the company, but he wasn't going to lose another comrade if he could help it.

'What the hell's going on?' Any hint of levity had left Tracy's voice.

As if responding to Tracy's tone, the figure raised her head, with one good eye. Then, spasmodically, she lifted her arms. Benton noted how some of the fingers didn't look like bone and skin anymore. They flexed towards him.

Benton raised his rifle to fire.

But he was too slow.

Before he had a chance to register what had happened, the creature struck. Its left arm swept sideways, instantly knocking him to the floor.

It was fortunate that Tracy had arrived as backup. Benton looked up, partially dazed, expecting to have to fend off a further attack. Instead, he watched as the bullets from Tracy's rifle shredded the creature's exposed flesh, splattering blood through the air. It paused, as if reconsidering its actions, the weak light from above glinting off the metal of its exposed skull.

Tracy did the same. 'You okay, John?'

He didn't take his eyes from the still creature but reached out a hand for Benton to take if he needed it. Tracy always held his nerve well. He'd go far.

Benton staggered to his feet, noting that the first of the creatures was still twitching next to the shattered remains of Private O'Leary. Tracy must have followed his gaze, perhaps lulled into a false sense of security through the immobility of the female before them. As Benton reached for his radio, he found himself grabbed by the throat and lifted off the ground, his legs floundering uselessly. He was aware that Tracy was in the same predicament next to him. This creature – whatever she was – was immensely strong.

Benton stopped struggling as his vision started to darken at the edges. With a final burst of effort, he kicked out with the sole of his boot at the torso of the creature. Maybe he impacted with something important because she immediately released both corporals and doubled over, with a pained mechanical wheeze. As she stood upright again, a dribble of dark liquid trailed from the corner of her mouth.

Benton quickly pulled a grenade from his pocket, dropped it in the remains of the tabard pouch, and made a run for it, half dragging Tracy as he left. They scrambled from the room and flung themselves to the floor, just before the grenade exploded.

Benton remained there for a while, allowing the dust to settle on his uniform. His eyes were wide, and his hands shook.

'Thanks,' said Tracy, between ragged breaths.

Benton coughed and gave a half-smile. 'We need to R/T the Warren for backup. Something tells me this business isn't over after all.'

Elsewhere in London, Brigadier Lethbridge-Stewart strode through the hallowed halls of the Ministry of Defence. It was impossible not to get caught up in the pomp and splendour of such a place. Marbled floors, mahogany panelled walls, row upon row of framed portraits. He'd often told himself he'd hate to be posted there, at a remove from his calling, from the action, and from his men – *personnel*, he reminded himself. There were a number of female staff already seconded to UNIT and the figure was unlikely to decrease. But that was by-the-by.

Since he'd joined UNIT, the Brigadier had already spent far more time in Whitehall than ever before. And whatever he'd told himself in the past, he had to acknowledge that an eventual posting there, after another promotion or two, wouldn't be such a bad thing. It gave one a sense of national pride, of achievement.

The Brigadier slapped his own mental wrist again. National pride was one thing, but he had to maintain a duel focus these days, and satisfy two masters: one internal, the other at the United Nations. This was to be an era of embracing the brotherhood of man, not looking out only for oneself.

At least that was the plan.

A pin-striped mole of a man scuttled from an office ahead: the ministerial secretary. 'Ahh, Brigadier,' he said, avoiding eye contact. 'Go straight in. The minister's waiting.'

This was why he was here; why he was often here these days. Ministerial conferences. He'd have preferred to be allowed to get on with the job UNIT was set up for, but it wasn't that easy. On the one hand, the Government was willing; on the other hand, they were suspicious. How easy a ride UNIT had depended on which hand they held out to shake. After the recent shenanigans with International Electromatics and Major General Rutlidge taking a gun to himself, both the army's upper echelons and the Government had withdrawn to lick their wounds.

Things couldn't stay that way forever, though.

The Brigadier opened the door and entered. The late morning sun filtered in through heavily leaded windows. The ministerial suite was warm and stuffy, with the nauseating aroma of stale cigar smoke. The defence minister was seated behind an expansive, leather-topped desk. Seated before the desk, in one of the two chairs which had been set for the meeting, was a general. The Brigadier wasn't familiar with the officer. He stood as the Brigadier entered

'Lethbridge-Stewart,' said the minister, remaining seated. 'Glad you could make it.'

The Brigadier glanced slyly at the clock on the wall. Eleven. He was bang on time – as always. Unless he'd missed a memo along the way.

'You did say eleven hundred hours, Minister?'

'Quick session with you both, then I promised to attend a charity luncheon at my club.'

It didn't answer the Brigadier's question, but it seemed to be the closest he'd get to a yes.

The minister continued. 'Do you know General Ffowlkes-

Withers?'

He didn't, although he had heard the name.

Ffowlkes-Withers held out a welcoming hand and the Brigadier shook it.

'Pleasure to meet you, General.'

'You too, Brigadier, you too.'

The minister smiled. 'Good show. You'll do well to get on, since you'll be working closely together for the time being. Cigar?'

Ahh, this was along the lines of what the Brigadier had expected. He declined the proffered box, although Ffowlkes-Withers took one.

'I'll be your new liaison with the regulars,' Ffowlkes-Withers told him while attempting to light the cigar. 'Nasty business with old Billy Rutlidge.'

The Brigadier swallowed a smile. Nasty business indeed. Typical of the upper echelons, to understate a matter of national security like that.

'And a warning to us all,' added the minister. 'There have been ructions in the cabinet. Tobias Vaughn had influence at all levels.'

The Brigadier was immediately on the alert. 'Are we sure there's no further risk, sir?'

Ffowlkes-Withers bristled. 'Risk? Your report said Vaughn was dead.'

'He is, sir,' the Brigadier confirmed. 'But we don't know how potent his influence was.'

'Conquering the world from beyond the grave, eh?' Ffowlkes-Withers let loose a guffaw.

The Brigadier was frustrated to see the minister chuckling along.

'I think you can leave us to sort out the internal politics, Brigadier,' the minister told him. 'In the first instance, I need you to liaise with my secretary and set up a meeting with your central command at the UN, to introduce the general, here.'

'Face-to-face, sir?'

The minister appeared to consider a trip to Geneva or New York, momentarily, then seemed to think better of it. 'No, telephone will do – unless they've got that prototype videophone system working yet. Last time I heard there was a problem with the satellite receiver, or something.'

The Brigadier nodded knowingly, but he didn't need to go into that now. 'Yes, sir.'

'We need to show the public that we are responding.'

'Responding?'

'To the situation. Ffowlkes-Withers is proposing a leaner model for the British arm of UNIT going forward.'

The Brigadier was momentarily stunned. He ran the words through his head several times, checking that he'd heard correctly.

'But after what's just happened—'

'Because of that,' Ffowlkes-Withers confirmed. 'The public are on edge. The Government are licking their wounds. If we give UNIT prominence now, the public may assume more trouble is on the way and go into full-on panic mode.'

Again, the Brigadier took a moment to properly digest what he was hearing before responding.

'Damage limitation?'

'Spot on, man, spot on.'

'Then you're effectively making UNIT the problem. But we're there to *protect* the people, reassure them, not scare them.'

The minister held up a tan dossier. 'It's all in here. A system of intelligence reporting, with UNIT as a management resource, co-ordinating efforts, when necessary, but without the need for a standing army. The regulars can be sent in to do any actual work. Isn't that the gist of it, General?'

'On the nose, sir.'

The Brigadier's heart sank. *A management resource.* UNIT was only just off the ground and had scored a major victory protecting the planet. They should be being fêted, yet here he was having to defend his corner.

Ffowlkes-Withers continued. 'I appreciate your expertise in the field, Brigadier. You've an exemplary service history with the Home-Army Fifth Operational Corps. But I think we can be a little cleverer and more strategic in how we use that and how we treat UNIT. It is, after all, an *intelligence taskforce*, not an army.'

'Neither is it a call centre for passing on information to others, sir.' The Brigadier bristled despite his best efforts. 'This is a knee-jerk reaction. An unfair shifting of blame, refocusing attention away from...' His words died on his lips before he said something career-limiting.

'Away from what, Brigadier?' asked the minister, clearly aware of what the Brigadier had stopped himself from saying.

The Brigadier paused and sucked his teeth before continuing, more calmly, along a different tack.

'There should be time to reflect first, sirs. Surely the last invasion has shown that UNIT should be expanding, not shrinking. What about the move to Denham?'

The general cleared his throat. 'That'll be off the cards for a start.'

'But Central London is not a good base of operations. There's too much at risk, here, if we're targeted.'

'You've got the Hercules,' said the minister.

'For now,' added Ffowlkes-Withers. Another veiled threat.

The Brigadier knew this wasn't an argument he was equipped to win then and there. 'I need a more robust command structure, at least.'

'Your request to have Major Branwell transferred from Henlow Downs has been approved,' Ffowlkes-Withers told him.

A pyrrhic victory, he told himself. 'What about a scientific advisor?'

'Shame you couldn't keep hold of the fellow who helped you with Vaughn,' said the minister. 'He seemed just what you needed.'

'Yes, well, as I stated in my report—'

Ffowlkes-Withers cut him off. 'You've got a team of boffins, Lethbridge-Stewart, what more do you want?'

'Someone with a broader specialisation to head them up. As the minister inferred, recent events have shown—'

The Brigadier broke off as the intercom buzzed on the desk and the minister leaned forward to answer it.

'Yes?'

A garbled voice emerged. The minister clearly understood it, however.

'Thank you, Greaves.' He looked at his guests. 'I'm afraid we're out of time, gentlemen. My car's here.'

The minister locked the dossier away in a drawer and gathered a few things together.

'We'll pick this up again when you've set a date with

Geneva, Brigadier,' he said as he left.

As the door closed firmly behind the minister, the Brigadier looked across at General Ffowlkes-Withers.

'Major General Rutlidge – what happened to him wasn't UNIT's fault, sir.'

'That's as may be, Brigadier, but someone has to take the hit. That's politics for you. Better for Britain to aim it Europe's way than shoot ourselves in the foot, I think.'

It all comes down to politics at the end of the day. Politics and money. I just want UNIT to do the best job it can.

'I knew Rutlidge at Sandhurst,' he told the general, sadly. 'I'd have given anything to spare him that fate. But he was too far gone. Took matters into his own hands.'

Ffowlkes-Withers leaned forward and stubbed out his cigar. 'Then I ask you, would you do the same for me?'

The Brigadier eyed the general. 'I think you should ask yourself, sir, would I need to?'

The door opened behind them before Ffowlkes-Withers could answer. It was Greaves, the mole-like secretary, to see them out.

The Brigadier silently fumed in the cab back to Waterloo. Ffowlkes-Withers wouldn't make eye contact as they'd left the ministerial suite. A lazy salute and a mumbled, 'We'll speak again soon,' was all he'd received as the senior officer strode off.

The driver tipped his head back. 'Mind if I drop you on the roadside, guv? Then I can circle round and join the rank.'

'No, no, that's fine.' The Brigadier looked out the window. They were just crossing Waterloo Bridge. 'In fact, drop me at the end, here.'

'You sure, guv? It's on account.'

'I could do with the fresh air to clear a few cobwebs.'

The cab pulled over opposite the National Theatre and the Brigadier disembarked. The exercise would help calm him. He preferred not to arrive at HQ in a foul mood if he could help it. It did nothing for staff morale and was more likely to get him a bad reputation. Everyone worked hard enough as it was, and his woes didn't have to be those of the rank and file.

The hum of a crowded South Bank vied with the noise of

the heavy traffic. The July heat did nothing to improve anyone's temperament, but there was always a pleasant breeze this close to the river and that, at least, offered him some relief. However, by the time he'd reached St John's, he'd already noted several lingering glances from passers-by, not to mention a few muttered comments.

He should have expected this. The uniform, the UNIT logo, it was all much more in the public eye now. It was an unfortunate realisation, but he shouldn't do this again. He quickly hailed another cab to take him into the arches beneath Waterloo Station.

The Brigadier was pleased to note, however, that his unexpected dilemma had served its purpose. There was almost a spring in his step as he entered his surprisingly light and airy office.

Company Sergeant Major Heather Nicholls appeared as the Brigadier settled himself. She was a fine NCO, a real asset. Like any woman within the Armed Forces, she often had a tougher time of it than the men. She had learned, through necessity, to give as good as she got. The Brigadier had seen her deal with insubordination, and it was rare that the message wasn't hammered home first time. This was one of the key reasons Nicholls had been selected to join UNIT, and to help nurture its progressive agenda – with a small 'p'.

The Brigadier hoped Nicholls found UNIT a reasonably tolerant environment. He appreciated that he still had some work to do himself, adjusting to a more emancipated outlook. Of one thing he was certain, though: Nicholls tolerated no messing and took great pride in the efficient operation of HQ.

'The sentry said you'd returned, sir.'

'Indeed, Sergeant Major. And don't ask.'

They shared a smile. Nicholls had known where the Brigadier had spent the morning. He continued. 'I trust you've got some news to brighten my day?'

Nicholls grimaced. 'Shall I come back later, sir?'

That told the Brigadier all he needed to know for a start. 'No, no, spit it out. The day can hardly get any worse.'

As he listened to Nicholls' report, the Brigadier realised how far from the truth he'd been.

CHAPTER TWO

CAPTAIN JIMMY Turner stood in Tobias Vaughn's office on the sixth floor of the main IE building. It had been one of his less onerous postings, and with Isobel abroad on a photography job, there had been little for him to miss in London.

He gazed out over the Compound, the vast International Electromatics factory complex. Until recently it had been so much more than a factory and distribution centre. There was also the Community, where the workers resided. Row upon row of prefabricated chalets – little better than holiday camp accommodation. Regimented, ordered, and very, very bland.

But maybe there would be the chance to re-purpose the site for some nobler cause further down the line. UNIT was under strict instructions to monitor the site only, for now. IE London was being taken out. Prime London property was in high demand, of course. But as for the fate of the enormous factory site, that was awaiting a decision at Cabinet level.

Turner's musings were interrupted as his radio crackled into life.

'Greyhound Three, are you receiving, over?'

'Greyhound Three receiving. Is that you, Potter?'

'Sir. Message from Trap One. Can you call ops?'

'Wilco, out.' Still problems with the radio network then. He grabbed the telephone on Vaughn's desk and dialled HQ.

'UNIT HQ?'

'Savage, it's Captain Turner. Can you put me through to ops, please?'

'Connecting you now, sir.'

There was a click, and the call was answered by another voice. He recognised CSM Nicholls.

'Turner here. You wanted to speak to me?'

'Good to hear from you, Captain. Brig wants to know how things are your end.'

'Quiet. The workers are still here, but we've confined them to quarters for now. The factory and storage areas remain secure, as does the central office block.'

'No systems re-operating or half-converted labourers returned to life?'

Turner felt his jaw drop. 'What did you say?'

'Corporal Benton has encountered some problems at IE London.'

Benton. He's certainly got the knack.

Turner felt somewhat incongruous seated at Tobias Vaughn's desk, so when Lance Corporal Potter showed in Mr Chambers, the IE Works Foreman and Community residents' spokesman, Turner stood and walked around the desk to greet him.

Chambers was a man in late middle age. He had a firm but cold handshake. Turner had noticed that before. It matched the look in Chambers' eye. *Trade Union resolve*, Turner termed it. They'd come from very different walks of life, that much was obvious.

'Mr Chambers, thank you for coming over.' He looked at Potter, standing to one side, and dismissed him.

'I understand you're pulling out,' said Chambers. 'Does that mean I can instruct my fellow workers to return to their duties?'

Turner gave a tight grin. 'The situation has not changed. International Electromatics is no longer a trading company. There is no work to be done. I am needed back in London, but UNIT will remain in possession of the Compound and the residents will need to remain within the Community limits. I believe you are self-sufficient there?'

'For the time being, yes. It does feel oppressive, though, having armed guards on the gates.'

'All entry and exit points need to be secured, we told you that when we arrived. Have any of you made arrangements to move on yet, as requested?'

'None.'

Turner couldn't hide his disappointment. He'd have been much happier if the whole Compound area had been evacuated, but the Ministry had said no unless the residents decided to leave of their own volition. They felt the accommodation was sufficiently distinct from the factory areas.

'All right,' he said eventually. 'But I'm not sure you'll be able to remain here indefinitely.'

'We understand. We'll keep to the Community until informed otherwise.'

'Thank you, Mr Chambers. Lance Corporals Wright and Potter will be in charge of the UNIT squads remaining behind, with Wright taking lead. They can always contact me or Brigadier Lethbridge-Stewart if you have any pressing concerns.'

'Understood.'

There was an awkward pause.

'That's it,' said Turner. 'Unless you had anything else?'

Chambers gave an awkward smile and looked as if he was about to salute Turner. Instead, he simply turned and left.

Odd fellow, thought Turner. He grabbed the dossier from the desk and headed out himself.

Sergeant Walters had arrived at IE London with a relief squad not long before Captain Turner pulled up. Turner was immediately escorted inside. He was briefed as they walked, but no amount of forewarning could prepare him for what they'd found.

'Good grief.'

'Nasty, isn't it, sir?' Turner could hear the distaste in Walters' voice. The bodies had been piled up on the ground before them.

Turner hated this place. So much had happened here recently, yet it seemed the horrors were still far from over.

'We're sure they're all dead? Or deactivated, or whatever?'

'Yessir,' Walters confirmed. 'Benton and Tracy had dealt with them before we arrived. A couple had been blown to bits, the rest deactivated either before or shortly after they broke free. All we've done is drag the remains here so we can get 'em to the mortuary. And one casualty on our side, sir. Private O'Leary.'

Turner noted the UNIT uniform and realised he'd never have known the soldier's identity. His head was smashed to a pulp.

Tracy joined them. 'So much glass, metal, and plastic in some of them buggers, I'm wondering if we can hand them in at the Co-op and get tuppence back off our next purchase.'

Turner was far from amused. 'Thank you, Corporal. We'll let you know. I'm more concerned about whether or not these were the only ones. Have we checked the remaining crates?'

'Just finished, sir.' Tracy snapped to attention. 'No more of the... whatever they are... were found, sir.'

Turner looked again at the pile of six bodies, unsure if 'bodies' was the best term to use. They were a mishmash of human and cybernetic implants. Some barely had faces. They bore an aroma of antiseptic, mixed with the iron tang of blood. Mortuary stench.

'Good work, Corporal.'

Tracy began to speak, but the stench caught in his throat, and he had to turn away to cough.

'Let's step outside,' Turner said, to the evident relief of all.

Tracy closed the storeroom door behind them. 'What I was going to say was, that lot were all found roughly together, so we think the room must have been used for conversion.'

'As if we needed a reason to hate this place even more,' said Walters.

Turner gave a nod. 'Have you found any equipment yet to back up your theory?'

'Benton has gone to find a jemmy, sir. There are some sealed areas in the walls that we need to break into.'

'Careful that while you're trying to break in, you don't inadvertently allow something else to break out.'

'Sir,' snapped Tracy. Despite his glib tongue and roving eye, he was a good soldier. 'We'll maintain an armed escort at all times.'

'Then jump to it, Corporal.' Turner turned to Walters. 'What concerns me more is how or why these part conversions were activated.'

Walters gave a worried look. 'You mean like some sort of backup security protocol?'

'Everyone else that we know of, both here and at the compound, has been accounted for. The dead – where appropriate – are at the morgue. Everything is shut down here.'

'Could just be a survival instinct, sir. Something that kicks in on activation?'

Turner rubbed his chin. 'We need to check this whole place thoroughly for secondary and backup systems.'

'Sir?'

'Anything still in operation, no matter how innocuous, shut it down.'

'Yes, sir.' Walters snapped to attention and headed off at the double, barking orders as he went.

Benton wedged his jemmy into the thin gap between the wall slats. He found he didn't have to push too much before a mechanism pinged and the slats separated. They slid apart, revealing – as expected – some sort of conversion booth. There was a seat, rather like a commode. Beneath it was a kind of sluice channel, stained an unpleasant rusty brown. The top of the high-backed chair was more like the electric chair the Americans use to fry their hardened criminals. To either side were robotic arms. He could imagine well enough the cold embrace as those arms activated, stripping the flesh of the victim with their variety of surgical appendages, bringing in replacement parts from the nearby racks. Arms, legs, torsos – either complete versions or partial grafts. Armour that would slowly denature the flesh within, until it would need to be replaced wholesale. Nasty.

The light above the booth area was blue, but it wasn't working. Nothing in the booth was. Benton was thankful for that. No risk of accidental conversions of nosy parkers, or rookie UNIT personnel unaware of the dangers.

Benton became suddenly alert. He could sense someone there in the room with him. Someone stealthy. There shouldn't be a need for stealth among the UNIT personnel on-site. He clenched his fist and waited for the best moment to turn and challenge his unexpected visitor.

'Grief! Will you look at that,' hissed Captain Turner behind Benton's ear.

He let out an internal sigh. 'It's wrong, sir. All of it.'

'I know,' Turner said with a *hmmm*. 'Just be thankful it's us decommissioning it, Corporal, and not someone untrustworthy.'

'Captain Turner, sir,' burst Private English as he entered. He sounded mildly out of breath.

'Go ahead, English, what is it?'

'Sergeant Walters, sir. Up in Vaughn's office. Reckons he's found something.'

'Right. I'm on my way.'

Benton found himself alone again. Just him and the cubicle of horror he'd so easily broken into. He felt the weight of the jemmy still in his hands. How easy it would be to smash all the conversion equipment. But he had his orders. They all did. The boffins would want to check it over first, out at Wood Lane.

*

Turner could hear the shouting while he was still climbing the stairs. That was the downside to deactivating everything – no lifts. And Vaughn's office was a long way up. He wondered what Sergeant Walters had found to warrant such a ruckus.

'But Sarge—'

'Don't you "but Sarge" me. I'll have you back on desk duties quicker than you can say—'

Turner's arrival interrupted Walters tearing a strip off Private Hennessy. Only after Walters had paused mid-sentence did Turner register the mess in which they all now found themselves.

'I see you've been thorough, Private Hennessy.'

'Thorough? He's a bleedin' vandal, sir. What'll the boffins say? All the systems – ruined.'

It was true that the whole of Vaughn's office had been smashed up. If anything could be salvaged from that lot, it would only be small components at best.

'Sarge, you said to make sure nothing was still working,' protested Hennessy.

'That'll do, Private,' snapped Turner. 'Go and assist Corporal Benton on the ground floor.'

'Sir.' Hennessy snapped to attention and left on the double, his relief evident.

Turner's attention was caught by what looked like an annex room opposite. Stepping over the debris, he headed across to investigate. He found the twisted remains of some sort of structure. The components looked similar to those from the conversion chamber found by Benton.

'What on earth was this, I wonder?'

Walters had followed him. 'Can't blame Hennessy for that, Captain. I think that's what we heard Vaughn blow up over the Doctor's radio.'

Both men jumped back in surprise as a wall panel suddenly guillotined down from the right and sealed off the annex. The thud shook the whole room. Walters gave a nervous chuckle, probably thinking, as Turner was, how fortunate they'd been not to be standing beneath it.

Turner's foot collided with a metal control box that had been ripped out of the floor and discarded. He followed the trailing wires to where they disappeared beneath the raised floor.

'With the systems deactivated, it was presumably only a

matter of time before that happened.'

'This place. It's full of surprises,' grumbled Walters with a shudder.

Turner moved to the window and peered out through the vertical blinds at the Thames winding its way through London beneath them. Time he returned to HQ and reported in.

'I'll leave you to supervise the rest of the work here, Sergeant. Any problems, just yell. Waterloo's not far.'

'Sir. Perhaps you can get Hennessy to drive you back to HQ, sir, and find some suitably menial tasks for him?'

Turner couldn't resist a sly grin. 'Consider it done, Sergeant.'

True to his word, Captain Turner escorted Private Hennessy to the ops room upon arrival at HQ. Only CSM Nicholls and Lance Corporal Enders were present. Nicholls immediately assigned Hennessy to switchboard duty, to relieve Lance Corporal Savage.

'And you can mind that lip of yours while you're at it,' Nicholls barked at Hennessy's retreating back.

Hennessy stopped and turned around in surprise. 'I didn't—'

'I dare say. But I didn't get where I am without being able to detect under-breath mutterings, Private. I suggest you remember that in future.'

Looking stung, Hennessy continued on his way.

'I didn't expect you back so soon.' Nicholls added a swift, 'Captain,' remembering that Enders was also present. There had long been a comfortable respect and familiarity between her and Turner.

'We had some trouble with a few part-converted IE staff, but they'd been dealt with before—'

Nicholls interrupted Turner, staring at him pointedly. 'Maybe not here, sir. Perhaps on the way to the Brigadier's office?'

Turner glanced at Enders and found her also staring at him intently. He licked his lips, suddenly uncomfortable.

'As you wish,' he said, and left.

Nicholls followed. 'Sorry, Captain,' she said when they were clear of the ops room.

He stopped and turned to her. 'What's going on?'

Turner saw a hint of sadness in Nicholls' eyes. 'Lance Corporal Enders, sir. Her brother worked for IE. He's been missing for weeks.'

'Oh, good Lord. I see. Is it best posting her in the ops room, then?'

'If things heat up, I'll have her reassigned. Is that likely?'

'No, I don't think so. I was about to say that all the part conversions had been dealt with before I arrived. But the sight of it all... I can't shake the stench of antiseptic.'

'Sounds like you've had a gruesome day.'

Turner nodded. 'I can deal with corpses, but not when they look like butchers' leftovers. However, it should just be a simple clearance operation now.'

'Glad to hear it, Captain.'

Both Turner and Nicholls straightened at the sound of the Brigadier's voice in the corridor behind them.

'I was just coming to report in, sir,' Turner said quickly.

'Excellent.' The Brigadier turned to Nicholls. 'I've received confirmation that Major Branwell will be joining us from tomorrow. Can you make the necessary arrangements, please?'

'Yessir. Do you wish to show him around yourself?'

'I'll need to leave that for you, Sergeant Major.'

'Very good, sir.'

'Come along then, Captain. We have much to discuss.'

He turned on his heel and, with a raise of the eyebrows to Nicholls, Turner followed.

During the months prior to the invasion, Captain Turner had always felt very comfortable with the Brigadier. He'd looked on the CO as a mentor. And it had been reciprocated. The Brigadier wasn't old enough to be Turner's father, *per se*, but he was aware that the Brigadier looked upon him as something of a protégé. The familiarity and respect between the two was exemplified best by the Brigadier always referring to him as 'Jimmy', a freedom that only went one way, of course. The Brigadier reserved his use of the captain's rank for more formal occasions. Or when Turner happened to be in trouble.

Recently, Turner had been 'captain' a lot more – largely since he'd let the Doctor leave without the Brigadier's permission. Not that he'd known at the time that the Brigadier's permission was needed. And now Major Branwell had been assigned to UNIT, slotting between the Brigadier and Turner. There were other captains in UNIT, of course. Hawkins and Munro. Both currently posted elsewhere. Turner had, up to now, been UNIT's *de facto* 2-in-C. A hugely elevated position for a soldier of his age and experience. And he was very conscious of the burden that rested on his – but mainly the Brigadier's – shoulders because of the imposed command structure to date.

Unsure how he was going to be received, but desperate to do his best regardless, Turner followed the Brigadier into his office, closing the door behind him.

'Have a seat, Jimmy.'

Only then did Turner realise how much pent-up concern he'd brought in with him.

'How are you holding up?' There was genuine concern in the Brigadier's voice. 'Rough time at IE?'

'Gruesome,' Turner said with an embarrassed smile. 'But it's not that. I'm sorry, sir, I'm still...' He searched for the words as best he could. 'I know I messed up allowing the Doctor and his friends to leave—'

The Brigadier raised a dismissive hand. A far cry from how he'd been at the time. 'You're a damn fine soldier, Jimmy. Don't let one mistake overshadow all the good you've done. Everyone here at HQ respects you. Major Branwell will have some sizeable boots to fill when he steps in tomorrow.'

'And he'll have my full support, sir.'

The Brigadier smiled. 'I wouldn't have expected anything less. Now, what's been going on at the IE sites?'

The Brigadier leaned back in his chair, absorbing all the details as Turner explained what they'd found and experienced both out at the factory complex in Sussex and closer to home at IE London.

'Part-conversions, eh?' the Brigadier said, as Turner paused for breath.

'That's right, sir. Still largely human in appearance, but with some partially-applied cybernetics. I think in some instances the shock and trauma of their own state was enough to render them—'

'Harmless?'

'Inefficient. Easier to deal with.'

'Sounds to me like Benton and Tracy were putting those poor people out of their misery.'

'I think that's very much the case.'

The Brigadier shook his head, sadly. 'Imagine innocently going to work and then waking up to find yourself like that.'

'Which is why we need to be a little careful, sir. Lance Corporal Enders. You know about her brother?'

'You think he was converted?'

'No way of knowing at present. Nicholls is keeping an eye on the situation, to make sure she's not being compromised.'

'As a member of UNIT, I would hope she'd put her duty first.'

Turner realised he was potentially doing Enders a disservice. 'I don't think anyone is questioning her commitment, sir. Merely showing a compassionate awareness.'

The Brigadier grunted his acceptance. 'I've got a team of boffins itching to get at all the IE equipment. If you're certain everything is safe, I'll send them in.'

'Maybe best to start them off out at the factory complex, sir.'

'Ahh yes, Hennessy and his heavy-handedness.'

Turner had mentioned this in his report, feeling it was best to warn the Brigadier in advance.

'If Sergeant Walters was almost throttling him, goodness knows how some of our boffins will react.'

'Hate to see a grown man cry, eh?'

Turner gave a chuckle. The Brigadier continued.

'We'll tell them it's a jigsaw, Jimmy. Only with no picture to guide them. Keep 'em busy for months.'

'Any news on getting someone to head up the team, sir? They're all very good and that, but they do tend to get bogged down in their research.'

'No,' the Brigadier admitted. 'I've made the case as best I can for someone a little more… detached, someone with a broader perspective. I think if we're going to get anyone, we'll have to find them ourselves.'

'Maybe Major Branwell will know of someone.'

'Perhaps. I'd rather let him get the feel of what we do here, first. But time is rather of the essence.'

'No chance of Miss Travers coming back is there?'

The Brigadier smiled ruefully. 'She'd be ideal. But I doubt it. When you're being dazzled by bright lights and research grants in America, a concrete warren beneath Waterloo Station is hardly tempting.'

'What about Professor Watkins?'

The Brigadier balked. 'He's just as myopic as what we've already got, isn't he?'

Turner knew he was sticking his neck out a little here. He'd not cleared it with the professor, and with Isobel away on a shoot their limited time on the telephone had been used to discuss matters more immediate to them.

'I've spent a bit of time with him lately—'

'Yes, I'm sure you have,' said the Brigadier, with a glint in his eye.

Turner smiled and felt his cheeks redden. 'He's got a pretty broad scientific knowledge and an interest in more besides electronics.'

'Fair enough. At least he wasn't one of Vaughn's pawns.' The Brigadier paused momentarily as if taken with his own rhyme. 'See if the professor can come in for an interview tomorrow, would you?'

Turner nodded.

'And how is Miss Watkins? Still getting herself into trouble?'

'I'll find out later,' Turner replied. 'She's been off on another shoot these last three days. I'm due to collect her from the airport this evening.'

The Brigadier glanced over at the clock on his wall. 'In that case, Jimmy, I won't keep you any longer. We've all fallen in love at some point.' A slightly faraway look came over the Brigadier's eyes. 'Enjoy it if you can. Just remember, soldiering isn't the easiest profession in which to hold down a civilian relationship.'

CHAPTER THREE

THE BRIGADIER'S words were still echoing around Turner's head as he sat in his civvies on the Underground, heading out to Heathrow to collect Isobel. She was flying back from Greece, her first overseas job on her new contract. He was sure she'd have loads to tell him.

Maybe it would help take his mind off the day's events. Even though he hadn't been attacked by the part-converted human remains the sight of them – and Private O'Leary – piled up on the floor was an image that would stick with him for a long time to come.

She had plenty to tell him sure enough. After Isobel had flung her arms around his neck and then slotted her suitcase into his hand, Turner barely got a chance to speak again until they were emerging from Holland Park Underground Station.

'But that's enough about me. How's everything been with my dolly soldier?'

It took a second or so for Turner to acknowledge that the question was aimed at him.

'That's you, remember?' Isobel poked her tongue out playfully.

A few more seconds passed while he grinned at her, trying to formulate an answer. 'Fine,' was the best he could muster.

'Come on,' she said, hanging on his arm. 'There must be more than that?'

They crossed over the road, heading back to the house Isobel shared with her uncle; the house that was theirs as long as Anne Travers remained in America.

'I've just been working and missing you, that's all.'

'You're very sweet.'

'I know.'

'And modest. So, you're telling me there's nothing exciting going on with UNIT?'

At least one person looked their way. Turner lowered his head and dragged Isobel into a backstreet detour.

'Sorry, Jimmy,' she muttered. 'I was forgetting.'

'You can't do that,' he said, firmly yet not unkindly. 'Off duty, we shouldn't advertise our association with UNIT. As much as anything it's for our own safety – yours included.'

'I'm still getting used to it. None of my previous boyfriends have done anything as exciting as you. You saved the world!'

'It's not like that every day. Thankfully. Not sure I could cope.'

Isobel stopped and looked at him intently. 'Something's still troubling you, though. I can see it in your eyes. Tell me.'

He was suddenly self-conscious about what he might be giving away, but he couldn't shake the images of the cadavers piled high. 'I can't. I'm... not allowed.' He had to change the subject, break the thread. 'Look, shall we drop these things off and go out for dinner?'

'I've got a better idea,' she told him. 'I've got to unpack and get some washing on. How about a Chinese takeaway? My treat. We can pick one up from the high street on the way and have a cosy night in.' She paused. 'And a proper chat,' she added firmly.

He pulled her to him and kissed her softly on the lips. She cupped his face with her warm hands, and they kissed again, long and lingering.

'I'd like that,' he said.

Isobel unlocked the front door of number 18 and she and Turner almost tumbled inside, giggling away.

'Uncle Joseph?' she called. 'Woohoo.'

'Where do you want the case?' Turner asked. 'Upstairs?'

'Kitchen,' she replied. 'Most of it will go straight in the washing machine. Be a darling and grab some plates and cutlery while you're there.'

Isobel continued through into the living room with the bag of hot food.

There was a clatter and a cuss from the rear of the house.

Turner entered the living room just as Professor Watkins

emerged from his laboratory. He was, as usual, dressed in suit trousers and a waistcoat, with his shirt sleeves rolled up to the elbow. He beamed at Isobel and rushed to give her a big hug. He paused momentarily to clasp his thigh where he'd been shot before shaking Turner's hand.

'Captain. Good to see you, young fellow.' Watkins' somewhat unkempt hair seemed to move in sympathy with the handshake.

'Pleasure, sir. How's the leg doing?'

He ignored the question. 'And Isobel. How well you look after your trip, my dear.'

'Where's your stick?'

He tutted. 'You know I don't like to use it around the house.'

'You don't like to use it outside either. Honestly! If that wound is going to heal properly—'

But he turned away and Isobel appeared to realise that nagging him as soon as she got home may not be the best course of action.

'Sorry, Uncle.'

He changed the subject. 'I'm afraid there's little by way of food in the house.'

'We've brought a Chinese takeaway, sir.' Turner indicated the plastic carrier on the table. 'There's more than enough for three if you'd like to join us.'

Watkins nodded absent-mindedly and clasped his hands together. 'I had some fruit earlier, I think. Or maybe that was yesterday. I forget.' He glanced up at Turner – or rather *through* him. 'I do feel rather hungry now you come to mention it.'

'You don't look after yourself properly,' said Isobel.

'I'm all right,' Watkins grumbled.

Isobel started laying out the plates and miscellaneous cutlery. 'Did you hear back from any of your fellow nuts while I was away?'

Turner couldn't help but smile at Isobel's casually offensive chatter.

Watkins, however, gave no indication of having heard her. He dropped into an easy chair, seemingly lost in his own thoughts.

Steam and exotic aromas engulfed Turner as he removed the lids from the foil containers.

Isobel approached the back of her uncle's chair. 'Eh?

Nothing? Not even Cambridge?'

He shot a brief glance her way. 'They won't take my calls. Letters have been returned unanswered.'

'Oh, that's rotten.'

'That's the scientific community for you, Isobel. No one wants to touch me now.'

She looked at Turner. All he could do was shrug.

'But you haven't done anything wrong.'

'The curse of International Electromatics,' Watkins sneered. 'I've been tainted by association.'

'Look, Professor,' said Turner. 'Come and tuck into some of this. I have a proposition for you that may help.'

Both Watkins and Isobel looked at Turner with surprise.

'Oh, Jimmy, that's wonderful!' gushed Isobel through a mouthful of sweet and sour pork.

Next to her, Professor Watkins toyed with his egg-fried rice, seemingly considering the opportunity Turner had just placed before him. 'If you're sure, my boy,' he said eventually.

'Think of the opportunity, Uncle. The credibility it would bring you.'

'But, what of my private research?'

'All the boffins undertake their own side projects,' Turner said. 'It's an accepted compromise with an establishment like UNIT. Something to keep everyone occupied during any downtime.'

'Well, it's very tempting, I must say.' Watkins raised a forkful of tentatively balanced rice.

'Can you come for an interview with the Brigadier tomorrow?'

He nodded and they all stared as the contents of the fork toppled and fell. Watkins looked at his now empty fork with disappointment. 'I don't have anything else planned,' he admitted, sadly.

Isobel smiled at her uncle and passed him a spoon.

A while later, Turner and Isobel were cuddled up on the settee, some light music coming from the old horn gramophone in the background. Isobel's uncle had quickly made his excuses and left them to it after dinner. She suspected he'd be tinkering in his workshop until all hours. Like many an obsessive, he seemed to get by on very little sleep.

Turner was drawn by her eyes, as Isobel gazed deep into his. *I could so easily get lost in those*, he thought.

'Do you think he'll get the job?'

Turner hadn't expected the question. It rather broke the moment.

'It's not a foregone conclusion, I know that much. The Brigadier was a little sceptical when I suggested it.'

Isobel pulled a face. 'It's me, isn't it? Your Brigadier hates me after that business down the sewer.'

Turner squeezed her a little tighter. 'He doesn't hate you. And even if he did, that would have no bearing on your uncle's scientific abilities. If your uncle shows the Brig how brilliant he is, I'm sure he'll be fine.'

'I hope so.' She nuzzled in against his shoulder. 'I just want him to be happy again. He's all I've got left, really.'

'That's not strictly true,' said Turner, with mock umbrage.

Isobel gave him a cheeky smile. 'You're right. There's that mad old aunt near Swanage.'

'Oh, we've all got one of those.'

They laughed and leaned in for a kiss.

This is the tonic, he thought. *This is the escapism I need.*

Nicholls had nearly finished checking all the night duty staff were at their posts. Only the ops room to go. She was surprised to find Lance Corporal Enders still at her post.

'You should be off by now. Where's your relief? Is everything all right?'

'Sorry, Ma'am. Just filling in time before my next bus.'

'Surely the Tube would be quicker for you?'

Enders looked up. Not for the first time Nicholls saw the sadness in her eyes.

'I can see more people from the bus, Ma'am. On the streets. I like to keep a lookout. Just in case I spot Simon, you know. For mum and dad.'

Her missing brother.

Nicholls nodded. 'I understand. But if you don't get going soon it will be too dark to spot anyone. Go on.'

Enders stood and left with a smile of thanks.

As she did so, Private Lamb entered. He looked surprised when he saw Nicholls.

'And what time do you call this?'

'Sorry, Ma'am. I was running an errand for Corporal Potter.'

She raised her brows. 'From East Sussex? No wonder you're late for duty.'

Lamb pointed back down the corridor. 'No, he was just—'

Nicholls was not in the mood for this kind of nonsense and Lamb was well-known for such things. She was now late herself and poor Enders had been left on duty way past her shift end.

'That's enough of your lip, Private. You know very well Corporal Potter is at the IE Compound. If you're going to waste my time with excuses at least try to make them believable.'

'But—' he began.

Nicholls glared at him.

Lamb relented, looking stung. 'Sorry, Ma'am.' He took the position recently vacated by Enders.

'That's better.'

Now, perhaps, she could go home herself. She'd most likely spend a lot of the next day running around after the new major, so a good night's sleep was in order.

Turner looked at his watch. They were seated at the dining table again, nursing the remains of a pot of coffee. Loathe as he was to leave, it would take him a while to get home, and he still had to press his uniform for the following day. He didn't want to give Major Branwell any reason to criticise him on his first day with UNIT.

'I've got to go,' he said, easing his chair back.

Isobel smiled and shook her bobbed hair back into shape. 'I'm due at the agency first thing tomorrow anyway, to discuss the shoot. Hopefully, there'll be something else for me straight away.'

Turner pulled on his shoes. 'Maybe not so far away this time.' He regretted the words as soon as they were uttered.

'That's not up to me, though.' If she thought he was being overbearing, or clingy, she didn't show it.

'I know.' He left it at that. 'See you tomorrow, Professor,' he called.

There was another clatter from the laboratory, and Watkins appeared again. 'There's someone in the garden, watching me,' he said, his eyes looking mildly panicked.

Turner was suddenly on the alert.

'I'll get my camera,' said Isobel, disappearing upstairs.

'Stay here, Professor,' Turner told him. Then he crept through into the laboratory, clinging close to the wall.

It was still quite light outside. The back garden was an overgrown mess of bushes and trees. Whether the Travers' or the Watkins' lived there, Turner doubted any of them would have much time or inclination for gardening. He reached the open curtains and peered around the edge.

After a few minutes, it was clear that no one was there.

'Professor?' he called.

Discretely Watkins joined him.

'Where did you see the person?'

Watkins moved to the window and pointed to a tree at the rear of the garden, near the perimeter wall. Presumably a neighbouring garden was behind.

'Just there,' he said.

'What did they look like?'

'I'm not sure. I could just feel their eyes on me.' He gave an involuntary shudder.

'Whoever it is, they've gone now,' Turner confirmed.

Isobel bounded into the room. 'I couldn't see anyone,' she said, raising her camera. 'Shame, I've got to be a dab hand with the telephoto lens.' She looked at her uncle. 'Are you sure you didn't imagine it?'

Blunt as ever, Turner thought.

Watkins began to wander about and do some notional tidying. 'I... Perhaps...' he muttered. He seemed to come to a decision. 'An early night, that's what I need. Big day tomorrow.'

He grasped Turner by the hand and shook it vigorously twice.

'I'll have everything ready for you when you arrive at Waterloo,' Turner told him.

Nodding but not speaking another word, Watkins left the room. Turner and Isobel watched the silent garden for a few minutes more, then turned and left.

Turner descended the steps at the front of the house and readied himself for the walk back to Holland Park Underground Station. A flash of movement across the road drew his attention. He stood and stared in the last vestiges of the evening sunshine. Nothing. Maybe it had been a squirrel or a bird. Possibly even a cat. It was still a bit light for urban foxes, although hunger tended to make them bolder. But after what the professor had said earlier…

Turner was unwilling to leave the Watkins' house if they were being watched for any reason. But then why would anyone want to do that? Were they all just being a bit paranoid after recent events? Turner looked around once more, but there was nothing more to see than an ordinary suburban street.

He headed off, aware that he was alone but unable to shake the uncomfortable feeling that he was being watched all the while.

CHAPTER FOUR

AS THE car took him through the streets of London, Major Clifford Branwell considered the formal papers in the open briefcase before him. It was amazing, there was no other word for it. That such a thing even existed was a feat that could not be overestimated. And to think, Brigadier Lethbridge-Stewart was instrumental in it.

Branwell looked up briefly.

Astounding was probably a better word.

What have I agreed to?

Not that he had a lot of choice, of course. He was just a major, and if he squandered this opportunity… well, the odds were he'd never amount to much more than a major in charge of a missile command centre. And as important as his work at Henlow Downs Defence Base was, it paled compared to the opportunity he had been offered.

And, of course, although it was no promotion in rank, it was a promotion of position and, with it, came a healthy pay rise. Which, he considered with a grim smile, pleased his wife no end. He didn't really mind. After all, they had two children at secondary school, and a first-class education wasn't cheap. Besides, if it wasn't for Felicity, who knew where Branwell would be now? In his opinion, you could always judge a man by the quality of his wife.

Branwell shuffled the papers. Back to the beginning, he decided. Now he knew what he was walking into, it wouldn't hurt to know exactly what had led the Brigadier to approach the United Nations in the first place.

There was a stout rap at the Brigadier's office door.

'Enter,' he called.

As the door opened, the Brigadier immediately stepped out from behind his desk with a smile and extended his hand. 'Major Branwell. Welcome to UNIT.'

'Pleasure to see you again, sir.'

'Have a seat. Did you receive the briefing papers?'

Branwell indicated the case he carried. 'All here, sir. Fascinating reading.'

The Brigadier acknowledged Nicholls in the doorway. 'Thank you, Sergeant Major. Lay on some tea, would you?'

'Already in hand, sir,' Nicholls said, closing the door.

'Unfortunately, I don't have a great deal of time today, so I've asked Nicholls to show you around.'

'Thank you, sir. I've noticed a few women about the place already.'

The Brigadier gave a thoughtful smile. There were a few ways of responding to such a comment. 'We try to be forward-thinking here at UNIT, Major. Not to say "progressive". I trust this won't be an issue for you?'

'Not at all,' he replied. 'Happily married man, me. As long as it's not too much of a distraction for the rest of the men.'

It was clear to the Brigadier that the major was missing the subtlety.

'Well, you can see for yourself how much of a distraction it is when Nicholls shows you around.'

As if summoned by her name, Nicholls reappeared with a tray of tea and biscuits.

'Very efficient,' said Branwell with a smile.

'Anything else, sir?' Nicholls asked.

'No, thank you,' the Brigadier replied. 'I'll call once the major and I have finished.'

'Very good, sir.'

The Brigadier handed Branwell a mug of tea and placed the plate of biscuits on the desk between them.

'And so, Major, to business.'

There wasn't a main entrance into Waterloo HQ as such. There were a number of discrete staff entry points, plus the vehicular access. UNIT was keen not to draw unnecessary attention to itself with the usual trappings of signs, a welcome mat, a receptionist, and so forth. Turner had instructed Professor

Watkins to wait in a specific location under the arches, beneath Waterloo Station.

As Turner entered the ops room to check the CCTV monitors, he was pleased to see that Watkins was already outside. No walking stick. Isobel would be annoyed. He headed for the nearest entrance to collect him. It was the one used primarily by the civilian operatives – the typing pool and the NAAFI staff.

Turner emerged beyond the direct view of any passers-by, or the loiterers who often frequented the area. For someone wearing a suit and carrying a briefcase – perfectly typical in that part of London – Watkins was looking uncomfortably furtive.

Turner was reminded of Watkins' paranoia the previous evening. He paused, but from his vantage point, it was clear that no one was watching the professor. Turner called out a greeting to him and Watkins almost leaped out of his skin.

'My boy, you gave me a start,' he gasped.

Turner smiled but didn't apologise. He ushered Watkins through into the partially concealed entrance. 'How are you feeling?'

Watkins looked around at the concrete walls, floor, and ceiling and uttered a non-comital noise.

'Did you bring identification, as requested?'

He reached inside his jacket and produced his passport. 'Will this do?'

'Perfect.'

There was a chair outside the ops room on which Turner seated him. At a nod through the vision panel, Nicholls joined them.

'Professor, I need to leave you with the sergeant major here. She'll do the necessary checks and make you out a visitor pass. I'll go and see if the Brigadier is ready to see us.'

As he headed off, Turner could hear Nicholls attempting to make small talk with Watkins to little avail. The poor chap was understandably nervous. As was he himself, but for him it was the prospect of meeting Major Branwell for the first time.

Turner rapped at the Brigadier's office door and found he was immediately summoned inside. He stood to attention.

'Sirs, sorry to disturb you.'

'Not at all, Captain Turner. The major and I were pretty much done.'

Branwell stepped forward and shook Turner by the hand. 'Good to meet you, Captain. The Brigadier speaks very highly of you.'

'Likewise, sir. And the pleasure's all mine.' He turned to the Brigadier. 'Professor Watkins is here, sir. He's just being authorised.'

'Good,' said the Brigadier. 'Have Nicholls bring him here, then she can take Major Branwell to his office and show him around the rest of the Warren.'

Professor Watkins stood before the Brigadier, looking like he was about to be sentenced. The Brigadier appeared mildly amused. Turner had a chair just to the side of the Brigadier's desk and felt rather like a tennis umpire, his attention playing from one side of the desk to the other. He just needed someone to serve.

'Good to see you again, Professor,' said the Brigadier, breaking the silence. 'Don't look so worried. Do have a seat.'

Watkins sat, gingerly.

'Cup of tea?'

'No. Thank you,' Watkins replied. It was mumbled as if he was under duress.

'How have you been since the... Since we last met? How's the leg wound? Must be frustrating to have such a constant reminder.'

Watkins ignored the pleasantries and cut straight to the chase. 'You want me to work for you, Brigadier?'

'Well...' The Brigadier was somewhat taken aback. 'That's why we wanted to speak to you. See if you're a good fit for the team. And if you have the necessary scientific capabilities. I've seen your CV, of course.'

'Of course,' agreed Watkins.

'And Captain Turner here, speaks very highly of you.'

Turner gave a nod and a smile.

'Although,' the Brigadier continued, 'that really only counts as a character reference.'

'Would I be working here?'

'Yes, in the main. That would be our preference. Although we have several sites for various purposes. Would that be an issue for you?'

A shadow fell over Watkins' eyes. 'Concrete oppression. It reminds me too much of International Electromatics. I'm finding it difficult to relax here.'

The Brigadier made a note on the pad in front of him. 'Yes, well, as I said, there may be options. Do you have any questions about what we do here at UNIT, how we operate? I expect you gathered plenty on your previous encounter. Obviously, I can't tell you everything, but...'

Watkins pursed his lips. 'Like you say, Brigadier, I understand quite a bit already. I should make it clear at the outset that I don't wholeheartedly approve of militaristic methods. Will I be expected to salute, and kowtow to people like you? Go on route marches and so forth?'

Turner felt his stomach clench. This wasn't going well. Watkins appeared to be trying to interview the Brigadier, as if he thought the job was already in the bag.

'I'm sure we can dispense with the route marches, at least.' The Brigadier's words were spoken coldly and clinically.

However, Watkins seemed to miss the offence taken, and continued in the same vein, with a dismissive gesture. 'But on the other hand, it would be preferable to put my scientific skills towards something worthwhile. In the absence of a research grant. Or other opportunities. I'm waiting to hear back from some colleagues at Cambridge, you understand?'

The Brigadier smiled patiently. 'I understand. We endeavour to be *worthwhile* here at UNIT.'

'My main concern is to avoid working for another multi-national conglomerate. They have the money, that's for sure, but I don't trust... anymore. Too many places they can hide people away. Captain Turner indicated that I could continue with my own private research here, though.'

'As a side-line. Should the position become yours.'

Watkins beetled his brows. 'There's no one better, I can assure you.'

'Indeed.' The Brigadier sounded less than convinced. 'Have you any experience running a team?'

'Until I was incarcerated at IE, I always had research assistants to help.'

'Ahh yes, but this is slightly different. These will all be qualified specialists in their own fields, with you in more of a co-ordination role.'

Watkins nodded. 'It sounds a very stimulating environment. I trust your laboratories are equipped with all the latest technology?'

'Within reason. We're subject to budget limitations, of course. But we cannot do what we do without access to certain equipment.'

'And computers?'

'Captain Turner…?'

The moment of inclusion caught Turner by surprise. After all, the Brigadier knew full well how many computers they had.

'Enough for what we need, yes. With full data backup on all operational systems,' Turner confirmed.

Watkins nodded thoughtfully.

The Brigadier leaned back in his chair. 'Your main area of specialism is electronics, isn't it? Hence Vaughn's interest in you in the first place.'

This was met with a curt laugh from Watkins. 'Chemistry and physics, also. How else do you think I was able to induce emotional responses with my Cerebreton Mentor?'

'Ahh yes, your teaching machine, wasn't it?'

'That's how it started. Vaughn turned it into something heinous.'

The Brigadier glanced at Turner again, this time with concern. 'Are you telling us your machine—?'

'The Cerebreton Mentor.' Watkins reeled off the name as if it was a registered trademark.

'Yes. Are you telling us it was always designed to affect the emotions of the subject?'

'Quite so.' Watkins suddenly became very animated. 'Emotional responses are simply adjustments of the chemical balance in the brain, reacting, of course, to electrical stimuli—'

'Professor,' interrupted the Brigadier. 'Forgive me if I've missed something obvious, but why on earth would you want a teaching machine to stimulate an emotional response in the subject?'

'Any number of reasons. It would concentrate the mind, focus the attention. It could be used to contextualise a specific area of learning.'

Intentionally or otherwise, they had opened the floodgates and Watkins was off.

'As a society,' he continued, 'we are very reliant on the tradition of book learning. A narrow-minded philosophy, in my view. The human brain is an incredible organ, the mind within it a fascinating concept. There must be better ways of using the gifts natural selection has given us as a species. Imagine if a certain emotional response triggered iterative memories. How much easier would it be for everyone to recall information purely on a prescribed emotional stimulus?'

'So, a good cry before an exam might release information and help you do well?'

'That's a very basic way of looking at it, but—'

The Brigadier cleared his throat. 'Interesting. Food for thought, indeed. Is there anything else you wish to ask us or briefly tell us before we draw to a close?'

Watkins leaned forward suddenly. 'Yes. My hellish experiences at the hands of IE have shown me a new way forward. Consider this: wouldn't the world be a far better place if people like Vaughn could be controlled, through emotional stimulus? They'd never obtain dangerous positions of power and influence. And as for wars and disputes – ended.' He made a slicing gesture with his hand. 'No need for fighting ever again. Simply an adjustment to the emotional balance and all would be solved. Brigadier, my work could revolutionise the world. Make nations truly united. Now there's an initiative to present to your superiors in Geneva.'

The room was stunned into silence.

Captain Turner was the first to find his voice again. 'But surely, Professor, someone would need to have control over those emotional responses?'

'Of course.'

'Professor,' said the Brigadier. 'I wonder if you've quite thought this through? That person would then be a dictator.'

Watkins shook his jowly face. 'No, no. Someone decent, with strong moral values. And then with time, I could probably develop an automated system.'

'Putting the machine in absolute control.' The Brigadier spoke slowly, purposefully, making sure the meaning behind his words was crystal clear.

Watkins nodded vigorously. 'Mmm, yes, quite so. Totally impartial, incorruptible. *Perfect.*'

'Perfect. Yes.' The Brigadier sounded anything but

convinced. 'Anything you'd like to say or raise, Captain Turner?'

'Not right now, sir, no,' he replied. He'd not discussed the professor's work with him in quite that detail. If he had, Turner would never have even considered suggesting Watkins for the post.

The Brigadier stood, indicating that the interview was at an end. 'Well, Professor. That was most enlightening. We'll be in touch, I'm sure.'

Watkins took to his feet and stepped forward to shake the Brigadier's hand, but it was already being employed with the desk intercom.

'Send someone in would you?'

Corporal Tracy entered almost immediately.

The Brigadier looked sternly at Watkins. 'Just a reminder, Professor, as you leave. This interview and everything you've seen and heard today. All strictly off the record. Just like the previous business.'

'I know, I know,' he grumbled. 'Cloak and dagger.'

'It's necessary. To protect everyone. Thank you for your time. Corporal Tracy will show you out.'

Watkins nodded to the Brigadier, then across at Turner, before being ushered out.

The Brigadier seated himself again as the door closed. 'Good God.'

'How d'you think that went then, sir?' said Corporal Tracy as he escorted Watkins through the corridors.

'As well as can be expected when dealing with military types.'

'Where did Captain Turner bring you in, sir?'

'By some arches.'

'Civilian entrance. Right, we'll send you back out the same way, then you know where you are. Along here, please.' Tracy indicated a brick-lined corridor.

'Too kind.'

At the far end, Watkins reached for the push bar to open the door. Tracy held him back with a touch of the arm.

'Just a moment, sir. Procedure.' Tracy removed Watkins' visitor pass and searched the older man.

'Ridiculous,' Watkins grumbled. 'Are you lot that precious?'

'Procedure, sir.'

'Even if I wanted to steal a stapler or something, it's not like I had the chance. I've been escorted everywhere.'

'Staplers are fine, sir,' Tracy confirmed with a grin. 'It's other things we need to check for.'

The professor continued to mutter to himself as Tracy finished the job. Watkins gave a sort of bemused scowl when he was confirmed as clear and free to go.

'Where are you heading, sir?'

'Do you need to record that, too?'

Tracy decided not to pursue conversation with the prickly guest any further. He pushed on the bar and the door opened outwards.

'Thank you, Corporal,' Watkins said, looking genuinely relieved to be outside.

Tracy watched as the older man headed up the alleyway towards the sunlight of Waterloo Road. He glanced around to see if he was being observed, then he pulled the door to and activated the locking mechanism concealed behind one of the bricks at hip height. He returned to the ops room to confirm that Watkins had left the premises.

'I'm so sorry, sir. I had no idea.'

The Brigadier swivelled in his chair. 'Not to worry, Jimmy. But he's completely mad.'

'All I'd seen up to now was a blinkered, pernickety man but brilliant in his field. Yet here he was, dismissive of rank and authority, clearly driven by self-interest.'

'I had my suspicions before, but what we've just sat through confirmed it. Anyone who plans and develops any kind of machine to affect or manipulate emotions is on shaky ground as far as I'm concerned. Morally speaking. And despite what happened with Vaughn, he's still harping on about it. Professor Watkins could easily be classed as the sort of threat to mankind that UNIT has been set up to overcome.'

'What next, sir?'

'You're in a fortunate situation. I want you to keep an eye on Watkins. I can't see that he'll be able to do much with his plans if he remains in obscurity. Maybe you might talk to him about it if the opportunity arises. And lean on Miss Watkins as well. Between you both, you might make him see reason.

'I think his biggest problem is that he won't listen to

reason,' said Turner sadly.

'Jimmy, if the professor won't listen to reason, that's not just his biggest problem. It's the root of *all* his problems.'

Professor Watkins tugged at his sweaty collar as he headed towards Waterloo Road. The stressful buzzing in his head had lessened now that he was outside.

The interview had gone well as far as he was concerned. No point in standing on ceremony and hiding opinions from these people. He knew the young captain was pushing for him to get the position. His thoughts swelled and took flight at the prospect of continuing his research and developing his theories, with UN backing. Hopefully somewhere less oppressive.

He'd never set out to achieve fame and fortune or be the saviour of mankind. Perhaps a Nobel Prize, but who didn't covet such things? However, it seemed that now, at last, he could be on the road to achieving the ultimate prize.

So lost was he in his thoughts that it was only at the last minute that he detected the shuffling of footsteps behind him. Before he could turn, a body slammed into his back and a cloth was thrown over his mouth and nose. Watkins was held with a grip like iron. There was something in the cloth. It relaxed him, made him not want to struggle. He began to lose feeling in his legs and dropped to his knees.

Still looking ahead, where the arches joined Waterloo Road, he wondered why no one passing by was paying any attention to his predicament. Surely someone must have seen – especially those in the car parked across the entranceway. He noticed the car doors open, then something heavy landed on his head and he was lost to oblivion.

CHAPTER FIVE

MAJOR BRANWELL paused outside the NAAFI and looked both ways along the corridor.

'So, my office is...?'

'Through the double doors at the end, there, and around on the right,' said Nicholls.

'Ahh, yes, of course.'

'You'll get used to it, sir, soon enough. Usually takes a few days.'

They headed off again. By now, Nicholls had shown Branwell nearly all of the key areas she felt he needed to see on his first day. A whistle-stop tour, in the main.

'It's a bit of a warren down here, isn't it?'

'Unofficially, that's how HQ's known, sir.'

Branwell snorted. 'I might have guessed.' He paused. 'One moment, Sergeant Major.'

She followed his eyeline to the sign on the door where he'd stopped. The morgue. Fair enough. Nicholls slotted her pass into the access control box and input the code. They heard the clunk as the lock released. Inside the air was a frozen mist. There were several rows of trolleys, a shrouded corpse on each. The light was reverently low. She heard Branwell whistle a cloudy breath.

'Is it always this full?'

'It's mainly deceased IE staff. A lot of them had mechanical component parts. No one has yet made a decision about how they should be...'

'Disposed of?'

'Treated. We're holding them here until then.'

'I see.' He walked along the nearest row, peering at the name tags. Under ordinary circumstances, Nicholls might have thought he was being gruesome. But in this instance, she had a good idea where his interests lay. Vaughn and Packer.

'Last two bays, far end on the right,' she told him.

Branwell headed straight there. 'Thank you. Thought I should see the bastards in the flesh just once. After all the trouble they caused.'

She held back, leaving him to his moment of catharsis.

Branwell peeled back the first shroud and recoiled in shock. He reached across to the next bay and did the same. He checked the names on the bays.

'Everything all right, sir?'

He didn't answer, just began frantically pulling back the shrouds covering each bay.

'Major Branwell, please—' Nicholls moved to intercept him. He looked at her intently. 'Is this all of them? The corpses?'

What the hell was he on? 'Yes, sir. Isn't it enough?'

Again, Branwell didn't answer, he just turned and led her to Vaughn and Packer.

Where Vaughn and Packer should have been.

Where two dead UNIT soldiers lay instead.

'If you don't need me for anything else, sir, I should check in on Sergeant Walters and the others.'

The Brigadier gathered his papers and stood. 'Of course, Jimmy. I need to—'

The office door was knocked on and opened immediately.

The Brigadier looked surprised but not angered.

Nicholls was standing in the doorway, somewhat out of breath. Branwell hovered just behind her. He spoke.

'Sorry to barge in on you, sir, but we've made a rather alarming discovery.'

Nicholls stood to one side while the three senior officers took in the situation in the morgue.

'I don't recall Lester and Phipps being on the casualties list from IE, sir,' said Turner.

'They weren't,' Nicholls told him. 'They were assigned to morgue duties yesterday.'

The Brigadier looked appalled. 'What? Major, I need you to lead on this. I think you're going to get the run of this place very quickly.'

Branwell nodded. 'Sir.'

'Turn the whole of HQ over if you have to. I want those bodies found. I want to know who killed Lester and Phipps and why. Use everything we have at our disposal.'

'What about me, sir?' asked Turner.

'Proceed as planned. Return to IE London and check in on the squad at the Compound. Just in case… something is up.'

'Yes, sir. I'll leave immediately.' Turner headed for the door.

'Nicholls.' The Brigadier turned to her. 'The surveillance feed to the morgue. Is it recorded at all times or only by request?'

'At all times, sir, but not monitored.'

'That's understandable. Show Major Branwell the playback console. Probably a good place to start.' He turned to the major with a raised brow. 'Never a dull day.'

In the ops room, Nicholls was displaying footage on the bank of wall-mounted monitor screens. A small pile of time-coded tape reels sat on the desk. Major Branwell stood nearby, taking everything in.

'I'm fast rewinding back through today's footage,' she told him. 'No activity beyond us so far.'

They watched in silence. The lack of any activity was both reassuring and disturbing.

'I presume that unless the bodies need to be examined or passed on for cremation, no one ordinarily goes into the morgue,' said Branwell after a time.

'Yes, sir.'

The image broke to white noise. She changed the reel. More time passed without event.

'Which are the bays we looked at?'

'Bottom right-hand corner of the screen,' Nicholls pointed to the shrouded bays in question.

She loaded another reel. The screen came back to life.

'When are we now?'

'Early hours of this morning, back through to last night.'

Once again, the image broke to white noise. Nicholls jabbed the pause button.

'That reel felt a lot shorter than the last.'

She turned to Branwell. 'That's not the end of the reel, sir.'

'Keep playing and let's see what happens.'

The white noise passed after a minute or so to show two technicians setting out and tidying the mangled bodies of Private O'Leary and the part-conversions from IE London. Nicholls stopped the playback again.

'That's Phipps and Lester, sir.'

'Play the footage forward, then. Normal speed.'

They watched the gruesome tasks, noting the time code at the top of the screen. Phipps and Lester shrouded the final corpse, then the image cut to white noise. When the image stabilised again, the time code had moved on, and all activity in the morgue had ceased.

Nicholls paused the footage again. 'And that's the last time anyone was in the room until us today.'

'Someone's fiddled with the footage,' Branwell growled.

Nicholls removed the tape reel and examined the section they'd just played. 'Sorry, sir. Look. No cuts or splices.'

'Could someone have rewound the tape and recorded over that section?'

Nicholls shook her head. 'The equipment doesn't work that way. Only way to cover up footage is to physically remove it. Unless the camera itself was interfered with at source.'

Branwell gave a curse. 'Which would mean it was a planned operation, with insider assistance.'

A sudden idea made her start. 'Sir! The door is security-coded. The access log in the computer room will tell us who's opened it over the last twenty-four hours.'

'Excellent! Report to me as soon as you've retrieved the information. I need to check something with the Brigadier.'

Nicholls headed for the computer room.

The Brigadier offered Branwell a seat.

'Progress already?'

'Sir. Vaughn, and Packer. They were both... dead, weren't they?' Branwell's tone suggested he thought the idea was ridiculous but needed mentioning all the same.

'I checked them over myself. Both had been subjected to considerable modifications, but they were dead sure enough. There's the stench, apart from anything. Why, are you suggesting they got up and walked out by themselves, having killed Phipps and Lester?'

Credulity was important. He was careful not to make the

suggestion sound risible.

'There's interference on the CCTV footage, likely at source. Crucially, it's concealing what happened. I'm just considering the art of the possible.'

'I wonder if there's an outside influence at play. Someone who believes they can benefit from Vaughn somehow.'

Branwell shook his head. 'This is all well outside my field of experience.'

'And for many of us, Major. But it's the bread and butter of UNIT. How you apply yourself is most important. I don't expect anyone to come in, wave a magic wand and solve everything then and there.'

Branwell appeared somewhat relieved at this.

There was a knock at the door.

'Come.'

Nicholls entered, several pages of computer print-out in her hand.

'Anything?' asked Branwell.

She appeared disheartened. 'I've checked and re-checked. The computer records can't be falsified, but it doesn't make sense. Apart from us earlier today, there's only Phipps and Lester activating the morgue door yesterday evening and then nothing since the Brigadier's the day after Vaughn and Packer were brought in.'

'Not as straightforward as we might have hoped.' Branwell rubbed his chin thoughtfully. 'There's no other way out, is there? Floor, ceiling, all solid.'

'It's basically a concrete box,' said the Brigadier. 'Just the one door.'

'Unless whatever affected the camera feed also scuppered the security lock.'

'If that's the case, Major, whoever was behind it has the ability to open us up any time they choose. We can't have that. How long was the break in the footage?'

'About two minutes, sir,' Nicholls replied.

'Time enough for plenty to happen.'

'There is another alternative, sirs,' she continued. 'The security code is only required to get into the morgue, not out. The reader doesn't record exits.'

Branwell stood. 'Are you suggesting there was somebody already inside, who acted during those two minutes?'

'It's unlikely, sir, I'm sure.'

He glanced at the Brigadier and moved to the door. 'Before this gets beyond the bounds of common sense, let's leave the Brigadier to his work and review the camera feeds from the exit points.'

'Yes, sir. I've also got a list of all duty staff that day.' Nicholls indicated the papers she carried as she followed. 'And I've placed a permanent armed guard on the morgue.'

The door closed behind them, and silence fell on the Brigadier's office once again. He rubbed a finger along the bottom of his moustache, thoughtfully and eyed the telephone on his desk. Reaching a resolution, he grabbed the handset.

'Savage – sorry, Hennessy. Force of habit. Get me an outside line, please. International.'

He waited while the connection was made, knowing that Hennessy would be grumbling in the NAAFI later about being on switchboard duties and always being mistaken for one of the female staff.

'All done for you, sir. Ready to dial.'

'Thank you.'

The operator disappeared as the Brigadier began to dial the long number on the rolodex in front of him. As the line clicked, making the necessary transatlantic connections, he once again worked out what time it would be Stateside. With a final click, the call connected, and the distinctive American *brr brr* ring tone filled his ears. Just as he began to think it was a lost cause, the call was answered.

'UNIT lab?'

The Brigadier couldn't help the smile that spread across his face at hearing the voice. 'Hello, Anne,' he said.

'Alistair?'

'Hope I haven't called at an awkward time.'

'Busy, but not awkward. What can I do for you?'

He'd rehearsed this moment over and over in his head, yet when faced with the actuality of it, the words simply failed him. He paused, trying to decide where best to start.

'There's a problem, isn't there?' said Anne. She knew him well.

'A situation has arisen,' he admitted. 'To be blunt, I need you.'

'We've talked about this. Several times.' Anne almost sounded parental.

'Blast it, I wish these telephones were cordless. I could

really do with pacing up and down on a call like this. I need a scientific advisor here in London. We've got the boffins, but they're all specialists. I need someone with broader knowledge to lead them, focus their efforts. Whitehall are holding out on me. I interviewed Professor Watkins this morning, at Captain Turner's recommendation. The man's… well, frankly he's—'

'A banana short of a bunch?'

'That's about the size of it. I'm sorry, I know you worked with him at Cambridge.'

'How do you think I know.'

'I was hoping I might be able to tempt you back here – even for just a short while, to help cover?'

Anne made a distasteful sound.

'I know your passion these days is research, but is there anything I, or Her Majesty's Government, can do or say to make you consider a temporary posting here in London, instead of New York?'

'Does Bill know you're calling me?'

The Brigadier was surprised at how much this question caught him off guard. 'This is nothing to do with the Fifth. Just between ourselves.'

'Go on then, what's the problem?'

'International Electromatics. There's still some mess to clear up. I can explain more when you get here. If you're coming.' His voice raised hopefully at the end.

'One moment.'

There was some muffled chatter at the other end and a few indistinguishable noises. Then Anne came back on the line.

'Can Ted come too?'

Ted – Edward Travers from an alternative timeline. Anne's father and yet not Anne's father.

'You'd know better than me if that would cause problems. People here know him. Knew him, anyway. Professor Watkins, for example. Isn't he still living and working out of your old address?'

'Oh, of course. That's a pain. He'd know there was something odd about Ted.'

'It's your house – yours and Alun's, anyway. Just serve them notice.'

'Give me a day to think it over.'

'If you insist.'

There was a knock at the door.

'I've got to go. Duty calls.' He replaced the receiver before Anne could respond. 'Come.'

Lance Corporal Savage entered. 'Sir, there's a General Ffowlkes-Withers here to see you.'

'General Ffowlkes-Withers?' He quickly checked his open diary. Blank. 'I've nothing scheduled, Lance Corporal.'

'Thought I'd drop in on the off-chance, old boy, see what's going on.' Ffowlkes-Withers strode in past Savage. 'You don't mind, do you, Brigadier?'

The Brigadier knew that even if he did mind – and he did – it wouldn't make any difference.

'It's a pleasure to see you here at UNIT HQ, General. Savage…?'

'Sir?'

'Lay on some tea, would you?'

'Sir.'

Ffowlkes-Withers watched Savage leave with a lecherous turn. 'I need to get one like that for my office.'

The Brigadier decided to come straight to the point. 'General, is this an official visit?'

'It's not an official inspection, if that's what you mean. But I haven't been getting your daily reports.'

'My *what?*'

Ffowlkes-Withers fixed him with a stare. 'Daily reports. The goings on. What UNIT are currently investigating.'

'General, with the greatest respect you are simply our liaison with the regulars. You are not my commanding officer.'

'I am a senior officer in Her Majesty's Armed Forces.'

'With which UNIT liaises. I don't provide daily reports to UNIT Central Command in Geneva, and I have no intention of providing them to you. If you find that unsatisfactory, I suggest you raise the matter with Geneva.'

'It's on my list,' Ffowlkes-Withers said somewhat flippantly, and considering the conversation they had last time they met, the Brigadier didn't doubt it. Ffowlkes-Withers continued. 'But, Brigadier, don't you want me to find out more about what you do and how you operate?'

'I think that would be a splendid idea.'

'Then there should be no problem with me dropping in unannounced like this.'

Ordinarily, no. But how typical that the visit had fallen on the day that two dead bodies had gone missing. He had to keep that information from Ffowlkes-Withers, somehow.

So far, so good, thought the Brigadier a little later as they entered the ops room. Branwell and Nicholls were over the far side, eyes glued to the surveillance monitors. He'd try to keep Ffowlkes-Withers away from there if he could. No point in tempting fate.

'There's not much going on, is there.'

The Brigadier glanced archly at Ffowlkes-Withers but refused to be drawn by the obvious bait.

'Barely enough for a daily report, even if I was receiving them.'

He gave a curt smile. 'It's not wall-to-wall threats and invasions, sir, no. Otherwise, I imagine society as we know it would crumble under the pressure.'

Ffowlkes-Withers gave a hearty laugh. 'I'll remember that one for the Club.'

The Brigadier had shown Ffowlkes-Withers as much of HQ as he had been obliged to, but it had been a struggle to swallow his frustration at times, under the constant and ill-informed goading of the buffoon.

'We've got teams out in the field, sir. That's where most of the activity is at present.'

'So, your HQ basically acts as a liaison point, for information gathering and support.'

Was the man an idiot? 'It's the strategic centre of operations, sir. Like any HQ.'

'But it's the teams out and about who are doing the actual work.'

'With the current situation under investigation, sir, yes, but—'

Ffowlkes-Withers smiled at him. 'You see, your mode of operation and my ideas aren't too far distant from each other already.'

Several UNIT operatives turned to glance their way. The Brigadier was desperate to avoid any rumour or discontent. 'With respect, sir, I don't believe you're grasping the bigger picture.'

'We'll see, Brigadier, we'll see. Is that your new 2-in-C over there?'

Damn. 'Major Branwell, would you join us for a moment?' He leaned in towards Ffowlkes-Withers. 'His first day with us.'

Branwell stepped over to them and saluted.

'Welcome to UNIT, Major,' said Ffowlkes-Withers, as if it was within his gift.

'Thank you, sir.'

'How are you finding it so far?'

The Brigadier caught a sly glance from Branwell before he answered. Thankfully the issues at Whitehall had formed part of his welcoming brief that morning.

'It's a very stimulating environment, sir. There will be plenty of challenges ahead, I'm sure.'

'I've no doubt about that. Specially with those dollies in the typing pool, eh?' He guffawed and Branwell awkwardly joined in.

The Brigadier saw Nicholls very slightly shake her head.

Ffowlkes-Withers checked his watch. 'Anyway, I'm due back at Whitehall. Got an appointment with the minister shortly. Lay on transport for me, there's a good fellow.'

'Enders?' barked the Brigadier.

She obliged.

Seeing the minister, indeed. And feeding back his distorted view, no doubt.

Once Ffowlkes-Withers had left, the Brigadier was finally able to ask if there'd been any word from Captain Turner.

Lance Corporal Savage stepped forward with a note. 'Captain Turner has requested Sergeant Hart take a platoon to IE London, sir. Sergeant Walters is taking his platoon out to the Compound.'

'Good, that'll keep them all fresh. Ask him to report to me when he returns.'

'Sir.'

The Brigadier joined Branwell and Nicholls at the bank of monitor screens. 'Nicholls, if you should hear anyone spouting rumours about the future of UNIT after that visit, please be circumspect and quash them.'

'You can rely on me, sir.'

'Thankfully we managed to avoid drawing the general's attention to our little... predicament. Are we any closer to solving the riddle?'

'Possibly,' said Branwell.

Nicholls pointed at the monitor in question. 'None of the exit cameras show anyone leaving with any bodies. No one left HQ between the shift changeovers at 1900 hours yesterday and 0700 hours this morning.'

'In all honesty, I didn't expect them to. But thank you for checking all the same.'

Nicholls indicated a paused image on another monitor. 'This is the morgue at roughly the time the part-conversions began to reactivate at IE London early yesterday. Watch closely, sir.'

She played the image at normal speed.

Branwell smiled. 'Did you see it?'

The Brigadier eyed them both. 'Perhaps you could tell me what I'm supposed to be looking out for?'

Nicholls played the section again, this time pointing at the bottom right-hand corner of the screen.

A flicker, nothing more.

'Good grief! The slightest twitch in… is that their feet?'

'Yes,' said Branwell with a nod.

'That's an astounding spot, Nicholls. If you weren't looking for it, you'd never see it.'

'Major Branwell gets the credit, sir.'

'Fresh pair of eyes, that's all it is, I'm sure.'

'Keep it up, Major.'

'The movement only comes from those two bodies. Nothing from any of the others. And that's it for the whole time. No other movement until they're gone.'

'Activation,' said the Brigadier. 'Responding to a signal of some kind. And then, presumably, waiting for an opportunity.'

Branwell agreed. 'And when it happened, they must have been able to affect the surveillance camera signal to hide the fact.'

'But how could they have escaped from HQ without being seen by anyone?' said Nicholls. 'It doesn't make sense.'

The Brigadier glared at the frozen surveillance image. 'I'm afraid it does, Sergeant Major. Remember the manhole Corporal Benton found on his first day with us? There was an IE scanning device beneath it. They'll have got away through the sewers. Somehow, after everything, Vaughn and Packer are still alive. And now they're free.'

CHAPTER SIX

IT WASN'T like waking from sleep. The sensation was more akin to emerging from anaesthetic, where your body doesn't feel as if it belongs to you. Professor Watkins sat up with a start, dragging in deep breaths. His eyelids parted and his vision swam blearily for several moments as if searching for something definite on which to focus.

'Calm down, my dear fellow,' said a suave, reassuring voice just beyond his sight. 'It's all right. Take your time.'

Wooden panelling resolved itself before him. He quickly realised he wasn't seeing double or triple; the three rows of three circular screens embedded in the stepped wall were definitely all there. He had seen something like them before. No, not *like* them. Exactly them. Watkins turned his head from side to side. Double doors, wall, window. And outside the window? The sprawling factory compound of International Electromatics. He was in Tobias Vaughn's office. How the hell had he ended up back here?

A shudder of terror shot through him, accompanied by flashes of disconnected images from his abduction. He tried to move his arms and legs and was surprised to find he could. Watkins staggered to his feet, ignoring the sharp pain in his right thigh, and turned quickly to search out the owner of the voice. There was a figure seated at Vaughn's desk. Watkins' hand shot to his mouth to try to quell the fearful moan that instinctively emerged. It failed. He turned to one side and vomited, holding on to the back of the chair for support.

'I've had worse introductions,' the voice spoke again.

Watkins glanced again at the figure seated behind the desk. No, he refused to believe it. It had to be some side-effect of whatever had been used to drug him.

'You...' stuttered Watkins. 'You were killed.'

Tobias Vaughn smiled enigmatically and arched an eyebrow. 'Does the evidence of your eyes not tell you otherwise?'

'You're dead, Vaughn.'

'I can assure you I'm not.'

The professor began to stagger towards the desk. 'Dead, Vaughn. Dead, *dead!*'

Vaughn watched him approach, leaned back his head, and laughed.

Captain Turner was briefing Sergeant Walters in his office while the ops room located one of the corporals on-site at the Compound for an update. Eventually, a call came through to his desk telephone.

'Corporal Potter, Compound?'

Turner put the call on speaker for Walters' benefit. 'Are you secure, Corporal?'

'Yessir. We've set up one of the ground floor offices as a temporary site HQ.'

'Good chap. What's your sitrep?'

'No change from the daily reports, sir. All quiet and peaceful. Been a nice change for the lads, to be honest.'

'As long as no one's getting complacent.'

Potter cleared his throat awkwardly. 'Sentries on all entry and exit points to the Compound. Regular patrols of the grounds – all as instructed, sir.'

'Any hassle from the Community?'

There was a slight pause. 'You mean Mr Chambers, sir?'

'Yes. Have any of the IE staff started moving out yet?'

'No, sir. They keep themselves to themselves. Mr Chambers pops in from time to time, that's all.'

Turner was appalled. 'What the blazes for?'

'Said he had union paperwork to maintain.'

Turner suppressed a snarl. *Paperwork my... rear end.* 'He told me the Community were going to keep to themselves.'

'Can't do any harm, though, sir, can it?'

'Tell me he's at least escorted.'

'Well, he knows his way around, sir. He's worked here for years.'

'Not the point, Corporal,' he roared, before checking himself.

'Corporal Wright approved it all, sir.'

Turner took a moment to swallow his anger. 'Did he, indeed? It wasn't on any of the daily reports. You should have checked with HQ.'

'I assumed he had.'

'Assumption is the mother of all cockups, Potter. Don't let me catch you *assuming* again, understand?'

'No, sir, sorry, sir.'

'Next time have Chambers escorted to his office. Tell him to collect his paperwork and take it back to his chalet. Assist him if necessary.'

Walters gave a nod. 'I'll sort that as soon as we get there, sir.'

Potter sounded concerned. 'Is that someone else with you, sir?'

'Sergeant Walters. He'll be joining you with a platoon first thing tomorrow. We're stepping things up.'

'I don't believe there's a need, sir—'

'I didn't ask for your opinion, Potter. Maintain your current duties. I want you and Corporal Wright ready to hand over at 0800 hours tomorrow. Understood?'

There was a momentary pause, at the other end. Just enough for Turner to note, but not long enough to signal dissent.

'Yes, sir.'

Turner cut the call and leaned into his thumb and forefinger, thoughtfully.

'Sounds like they need a rocket up 'em, sir,' ventured Walters.

'Read 'em the riot act, Sergeant. Put Wright and Potter on a charge if you need to.'

'Yessir. One other thing, sir. I thought you wanted us down there tonight?'

Turner smiled. 'I do. Like you said, they need a rocket up 'em.'

Walters broke into a broad grin.

A hand reached out to an intercom terminal.

'Yes?' The voice came through the integrated speaker, with an electronic quality that made it sound oddly less than human. 'Chambers. Is Mr Vaughn there?'

'He's in conference. Not to be disturbed.'

'We've got trouble. UNIT will be here in greater numbers.'

'Are we still on silent running?'

'Yes, no emissions or external transmissions.'

'What about the work on the radio communications controls?'

'Should be finished today.'

'Should? It's taken you long enough.'

Chambers inwardly cursed. 'Will be. How close are we to the next phase?'

'That's what Mr Vaughn is... investigating now.'

'All right. What shall I do once I've completed my task?'

There was a thoughtful pause at the other end. 'We let UNIT get set up first, then we know precisely what we're dealing with. There's no reason they should know we're here. Remain on standby, just in case plans change.'

'As you say, Mr Packer.'

Professor Watkins was a scientist, a rationalist. A *pragmatist*. He'd never held with philosophy and the intangible. Hypotheses always had to be based on a firm scientific premise. His experimentation into the manipulation of human emotions, for example, had become possible only because his initial research had identified and isolated the relevant electro-chemical impulses which fed the necessary brain synapses.

He remembered being asked by the Dean years ago, at Cambridge, if he believed in the soul. It was a long-standing religion versus science challenge, often used to test how metaphysical or *broad-minded* the prevailing scientific thinking was. He told the Dean he would, undoubtedly, believe in the soul if someone could identify in empirical terms what the soul actually was.

Watkins was reminded of this now, as he stood staring into the face of a man he was assured had died – and by violent means. Something was different. It was Vaughn, but not quite as he had been before.

'We've got more visitors from UNIT, it seems. One has to admire their persistence. They won't be expecting us to be here, so we're under no threat if that's what you're thinking.'

Watkins shook his head. 'Your eyes—'

'What of them?'

They moved about, but they were dry, discoloured, lacking... life.

The discussion with the Dean seemed to haunt Watkins at that moment. It was as if he suddenly understood what the soul was. Because for Vaughn, it was no longer there.

'My god,' he hissed. 'What have you *become?*'

'Invincible. That's what.' Vaughn turned away and walked to the window.

Watkins watched him go. The movements slightly mechanical – lacking the fluidity and *zest* of humanity. He recalled how, not that long ago, he had been pressured into shooting Vaughn with a pistol at close range in that very office. The shock had been too much for him at the time.

'If your body is cybernetic. How can you feel? How can you function?'

'Your questions are meaningless, Professor. I feel as I always felt.' Vaughan didn't even do him the courtesy of looking his way.

'But how? How does the interface between the mechanical and the organic work? Machines can't have emotions.'

'My dear Watkins, you should know the answer to that already. Your research paved the way, after all.' This time Vaughn turned to face him. He unbuttoned his shirt front and pulled back one side to reveal a scorched but intact robotic chest plate.

Watkins felt a lump of bile rise in his throat as the plate opened.

Vaughn removed a small component on the end of a wire and held it up. 'They're all saved on micro-monolithic circuits.' He replaced the component and closed the chest plate. 'So much tidier and easier than relying on hormones and chemical stimuli, don't you think?' He spoke as if the terms were somehow distasteful.

Watkins had no answer.

Vaughn had turned back to gaze out through his panoramic office window once again.

'You'll be seen,' warned Watkins.

Vaughn turned and further raised his permanently raised right brow a little higher. 'I thought you'd have known by now. Vision is one way. There's a film between the inner and outer glazing. Industrial espionage has long been a threat.'

'They'll still know you're here eventually. I've seen the UNIT forces myself.'

'A handful of men only, led, if my information is correct, by a fool and a genius.'

'Why a genius?'

Vaughn looked hard at Watkins. 'Because he joined us.'

Watkins scoffed. 'But everything fell apart when your allies turned on you. Your plans were finished.'

Vaughn returned to his desk. 'Those plans, perhaps. But the work undertaken has paved the way for other opportunities, I'm pleased to say.'

An alert chimed. Vaughn pressed a button on his desk and information began to scroll across the wall screens. 'Interesting.'

Watkins eyed him, warily. 'You're receiving data?'

'From an unexpected source.' Vaughn smiled at Watkins. 'We've had a tap on the Ministry of Defence computers for some time now, thanks to Major General Rutlidge. I assumed that would have been found and disconnected, but it seems not. Fresh data is now being added by whoever is using Rutlidge's old office. And regarding UNIT, no less. These fools deserve all they get.'

'What do you want with me?' He couldn't keep the resignation from his tone.

'What I want with you is to rule the world. We already have everything in place. And it's all due to your research.'

'My research?' Watkins was aghast. 'You can't lay the blame at my feet!'

'Not the blame, Professor. The acclaim.'

'What are you going to do?'

'We, Professor. We are going to use your skills in emotional manipulation. With worldwide communication satellite coverage, we can broadcast signals that will reach everyone. Like the invaders planned with their hypnotic beam. Only ours won't paralyse, it will simply repress them – emotionally.'

'But that's monstrous!'

'You came to me with the idea in the first place.'

Watkins was appalled. He began to wander about, gesticulating as the words spewed from him.

'Yes, but that was part of my teaching machine… the concept… a theoretical way to simplify learning and increase brain capacity based on instinctive recall, *not* a method for mind control and—'

'Manipulation? How terribly prudish and parochial you are,

Professor. That's *precisely* what the machine was intended to do. You can hold on to your honourable protestations and false homilies all you want, but the evidence is plain for all to see. I'm offering you the only option for progressing that research.'

'Offering?'

Vaughn's face lit up with a broad smile. 'Quite so.'

Watkins scoffed. 'We've had these conversations before.'

'This will be a partnership. You, and I.'

'And if I refuse?'

'Come come, must we walk that walk again?'

Watkins' shoulders slumped. 'You just want to use me, like you wanted to use the—'

'Then be warned. Double-cross me as they did, and it will go the worst for you,' Vaughn interrupted, his voice hardened. 'But it needn't come to that.' He softened into charm again, in that curious non-sequitur way of his. 'We can be partners and share in the rewards of peace. Think of it, Professor. Making a better world for everyone. No violence. No hatred. No unrest. The start of a new order, a new Epoque. And anything and everything could be yours.'

Watkins didn't respond. He couldn't find the words. Because deep down, after everything that had happened, Vaughn had hit the spot. Watkins' imagination had been fired. Here was a legitimate opportunity. Maybe not to follow Vaughn's scheme blindly – he could deal with that in due course – but at least to progress, develop his theories, and have the finances and facilities to achieve *more*. With a shudder, Watkins realised that he must – he had to – agree.

Captain Turner entered the Brigadier's office.

'IE London is secure, sir. A concrete shell, little more. Sergeant Hart can run things there for now.'

'I thought Walters and Benton would get itchy feet after a while.'

'Do you want me to head down there, too?'

'No. For the moment I need you here, Jimmy. I'm getting some pressure from Whitehall.'

Turner nodded. 'I heard we'd had a surprise visit.'

'Yes, General Ffowlkes-Withers. Wants to turn us into a blessed call centre, have the regulars do all the leg work.'

'But surely, sir, we've only just started to prove our worth?'

'Scapegoats, Jimmy. Parts of the Government have been found wanting, so they search for anyone to blame other than themselves.'

'Surely Geneva would never allow it.'

'Doesn't mean we won't have a scrap on our hands. And if my focus is being pulled in that direction, I need to know there's an experienced hand holding the fort here.'

'But Major Branwell—'

'Is a fine officer and will be a great asset to UNIT, but this is only his first day.'

The telephone rang. The Brigadier scooped up the receiver with practised ease. He looked at Turner. 'It's for you. Miss Watkins.'

In all that had happened, he'd forgotten he was supposed to be going around to see Isobel that evening.

'Sorry, sir,' he said, as he took hold of the receiver. 'Captain Turner, hello?'

'Jimmy!' Isobel sounded worried.

'About tonight. Things have been a bit manic here.'

'It's not that. I've not seen my uncle all day. He's not come home and it's getting late. He never goes off like this.'

'Leave it with me. I'll call you when I finish later.'

Before Isobel could answer again, Turner somewhat sheepishly replaced the receiver on the cradle.

The Brigadier wore a knowing smile. 'Trouble at mill?'

'Professor Watkins hasn't been seen since we interviewed him this morning. And it's just occurred to me, he thought he was being watched when I was in their house yesterday evening.'

'You didn't see anyone?'

'No, when I looked it was all clear. Front and back.'

'Ordinarily, I wouldn't be too concerned. However, in light of the disappearances from our morgue…'

'Too much is happening almost under our noses,' said Turner with concern. 'This isn't right.'

'What we need is a good strong lead. Until then, Jimmy, I'm afraid there's not much we can do.'

Professor Watkins stirred in his seat. He was exhausted, hungry, and thirsty. He wasn't certain how long he'd slept, but it was now dark outside, so it had to be late in the evening. There was little light in Vaughn's office beyond a few lamps, all angled away from the panoramic window. Presumably, although the window allowed one-way vision, it didn't stop bright light from being seen from outside.

As his arm brushed the table next to him, Watkins discovered a tray with a jug of cold water, a pot of hot tea, and a ham salad. He didn't even ask where or how it had got there, he immediately quenched his thirst and satisfied his ravenous hunger. A saucer of custard creams just behind the pot of tea acted as a more than satisfying dessert.

'Better?' Vaughn's voice brought him crashing back to the moment. His food caught in his throat.

'Adequate,' he muttered. A thought struck him. 'Unless... You're not drugging me, are you?'

Vaughn spun in his desk chair to face Watkins. In the half-light, he appeared even more cadaverous.

'Professor. We're partners now, you and I. It's time to dispense with such duplicitous thoughts.'

Watkins eyed him warily. 'I know you too well.'

Vaughn inclined his head. 'The priority now is to keep you safe and well while we re-establish control of the Compound. You've a lot of work to do if we're to have control of the world within the next forty-eight hours.'

'Forty-eight hours?' Watkins hadn't expected such haste.

A door opened – not the main office door, he noted – and laboured footsteps entered. 'We're ready to go, Mr Vaughn.'

The voice was at once instantly recognisable and distinctly different. Watkins turned to look at the new arrival, recoiling from the stench. An animated corpse in every sense. The head was a sickly green colour beneath the uniform helmet. The black tongue lolled to one side, resting on a sagging bottom lip, all of which had settled firmly into position through rigor mortis. The eyes were, thankfully, closed. No other flesh was on display beneath the familiar black leather uniform, gloves, and boots.

Watkins realised he had no idea quite how much of Vaughn's henchman had been made cybernetic. However much it was, it was enough to reanimate him in the most terrifying way.

'Thank you, Packer,' said Vaughn.

Watkins couldn't help the yelp of shock he emitted upon seeing his old tormentor again, somehow not really alive, just *undead*.

'What about him?' The disgusting apparition raised an arm mechanically and gestured toward Watkins.

The voice. It was Packer's, but processed through a machine, not through vocal cords. He wasn't sure from where the voice was actually coming, nor did he intend to get close enough to find out.

'He'll be fine.'

Vaughn's smiling face began to swim, and Watkins wondered if he'd been right about the meal after all as oblivion reached out for him once again.

Tobias Vaughn looked down at Professor Watkins' unconscious form.

'Have him taken to the laboratory, Packer,' he said levelly.

'At once, Mr Vaughn,' came the eager reply.

The eagerness to please had not changed. But Vaughn was very much aware that his henchman had been left a shadow of his former self.

There was much about his own part-conversion of which he hadn't been totally aware until he received the re-boot signal. Vaughn now understood the connections between his organic components and his purely robotic parts, and how these could be controlled or affected.

His body contained a complete download of his consciousness. He need never die. As long as the circuits remained in operation, he *could* never die. It was this that allowed him to function as a person once again.

Vaughn found he could focus on the fluid that had replaced his blood, for example. He could – for want of a more accurate term – *communicate* with it as it went about its tasks. It was like being an external observer in his own body, understanding how everything operated. He had access to a constant influx of data, the like of which he'd never grasped before. And it was fascinating!

When he had first come to, in the UNIT morgue, Vaughn had lain enthralled for ages, observing within himself a readout of all his bodily functions and systems.

One thing he knew immediately was that his organic components had started to deteriorate before the system reboot had kicked in. And unlike his robotic and electronic parts, organic degradation was impossible to fix past a certain point.

Packer had passed that point, Vaughn knew. He'd had far longer than Vaughn in a decommissioned state. His organic parts barely functioned at all now. But Vaughn didn't know if Packer was aware of this or not. And to draw attention to it might induce considerable psychological defects.

Vaughn felt... what? Affection for Packer? Responsibility for him? He was someone who had never needed friends. People were there to be used and then cast aside when their value was spent. Despite this, Vaughn acknowledged that Packer was the closest he'd ever been to having a friend.

Having seen Packer blasted to death before him, Vaughn had realised how much he'd relied on the man, how much he needed him. Without Packer, he felt somehow less than complete.

That was why, despite the advanced decomposition, Vaughn had to have Packer with him now. There he was, struggling with Professor Watkins' stout frame. It made Vaughn feel relieved. This time everything would work out differently. Properly. *Successfully.*

CHAPTER SEVEN

CORPORAL BENTON knew the route from London to the IE Factory Compound well. He'd undertaken surveillance in the area before everything kicked off. However, it was more difficult to locate this time in the failing light. It hadn't really occurred to him how much attention the Compound had drawn to itself in full operation. Lights, activity – there was none of this anymore. Once they'd left the A21 it was just acres of dark, empty Sussex Weald. There were very few other vehicles on the road between Hurst Green and Burgh Hill, and nothing heading their way at all.

Chambers glanced in the rear-view mirror as the limo passed the UNIT convoy.

Packer turned his sickly green head to look at Vaughn, who sat in the back seat looking unconcerned.

Chambers noticed some distracting putrefaction behind Packer's ear. Surely the henchman's useful existence would be short-lived. Chambers had done much to keep Vaughn's interests alive. He was in prime position to replace Packer when the henchman became physically untenable. A satisfied smile played over his lips.

'Mr Vaughn?' Packer sounded nervous. 'Why don't we turn around and deal with the soldiers straight away?'

'You're hasty and impetuous,' Vaughn replied. 'If we do that before we're ready to enact our grand scheme, more troops will come and all we'll have done is draw attention to ourselves. Stealth is the way forward.'

'But we've got our inside man to use as cover,' Packer grated in response. 'UNIT will never suspect one of their own.'

'You have a vendetta lust, Packer. But you'll get your chance, don't worry.'

His passengers settled back into silence. Chambers was glad of the partition between them and him. He was sure the stench from the back seat would be atrocious.

Benton removed a hand from the steering wheel and pointed off to the left. 'It should be up here somewhere, Sarge. Place was lit up like a Christmas tree last time, of course.'

'When we get there,' said Walters, 'we'll ruffle a few feathers, set up camp somewhere warm and dry, then give the lads an early night. I'd rather tackle the place in the morning when we can see better, and we've all had a sleep.'

'Yessir.' Benton noted that Walters hadn't promised the sleep would be a good one. 'Should be plenty of sheltered places we can set up camp. Factory floors, outbuildings, wherever.'

'This looks promising.'

A UNIT sentry post appeared on their left up ahead. They'd found the Compound. Benton pulled up as Walters radioed the two troop carriers behind.

'What's this then? The relief wing finally arrived, has it?'

Benton recognised Corporal Wright's facetious Welsh tones before he'd even seen his grinning face.

'What d'you mean *finally arrived*? You weren't expecting us till the morning.'

'Believe me, fella, I wasn't expecting you at all!'

Walters was out of the Land Rover and instantly bearing down on Corporal Wright. 'You're a bloody disgrace, the lot of you. Didn't Corporal Potter tell you?'

'Tell me what, sir?' Wright spluttered, wide-eyed.

'Never mind.' Turner gestured for one of the privates to take over Wright's place at the sentry. 'Get in the vehicle, Corporal,' he told Wright. 'You can direct us around to the main factory area so we can set up camp. Then you can find Corporal Potter. Then, I'm putting you both on a charge.'

'A charge, Sarge? Whatever for?'

'Cos you're bloody useless, Wright, that's why.'

'I don't know what you've got to be so happy about,' Wright grumbled as he clambered into the front of the Land Rover next to Benton.

Benton wiped the smile from his face. He had little time for Wright, truth be told, but it was unfair to delight in the downfall of a colleague.

Walters squeezed in as well and slammed the door. 'Let's go.'

They moved slowly through the barrier and waited while the sentry post was reinstated before moving on. Wright began to direct Benton to the main building. The convoy followed.

'You might want your high beams on,' said Wright. 'It's pitch black out here now it is, especially since the place was shut down.'

'How have you been getting around?' asked Walters.

'By daylight, preferably,' Wright quipped. If he was hoping to lighten the tone, he failed. After a pause, he answered again. 'There's been a hefty amount of walking and nice bright torches.'

Benton snapped on his high beams. The land around them seemed to move suddenly. Benton slammed on the brakes. Behind them, the first troop carrier also squealed to a halt.

'What the—?'

'What is it, Corporal?' Walters sounded concerned.

Benton carried on staring out through the windscreen. 'I thought I saw something, Sarge. Movement.'

'I can't see anything,' said Walters, now gazing intently out to the side. 'Whatever it was must have scarpered off into the darkness.'

Wright shifted in his seat. 'Here, stop it, you two. You're scaring me half to death you are!'

'Any animals living on the grounds?' Benton asked. 'Cattle, I mean, or horses?'

'Not even a stray dog. Perhaps it was a trick of the light?'

'It's dark.'

'Trick of the dark, then!'

Benton didn't respond.

'Turn the beams off, then on again after a few seconds,' said Walters.

Benton did this several times, without results.

'Here, Sarge,' said Wright. 'We'll be attracting all sorts if he carries on flashing his lights like that we will.'

At a nod from Walters, they drove on.

It wasn't long before they reached the main building. It was a stylish approximation of the IE London office block, but set in acres of countryside, rather than on the bank of the Thames. Benton pulled up on the shingle by the front steps.

'Here we are then, Sarge,' said Wright, seemingly full of beans once again. 'The main administration block is that wing over there. This front block is top brass, and R&D. Shall I get the kettle on?'

One thing's for certain, thought Benton. *There's no keeping Gwyn's spirits down.*

Walters ignored Wright.

'We'll recce inside and check out the set-up,' he told Benton. 'It's late enough already so the lads can focus on their bivouacs.' Walters jumped down from the Land Rover. Only now did he turn to Wright. 'Where's your squad camped?'

'Factory canteen. Convenient facilities. Too hot under canvas, this weather.'

'Fine. Have one of your squad guide the platoon over there so they can get set up, then show me HQ. Benton...? Try to get Potter on the radio and then join us inside.'

'Sarge.'

Walters leaned into him conspiratorially. 'I'm not sure I entirely trust our escort just yet.'

Benton nodded and unclipped his radio.

The site HQ was all right, but it was also clearly someone else's workspace, and this did not please Walters in the slightest.

'It's a breach of security waiting to happen. You should have reported this whole set-up in your daily comms.'

'But, Sarge,' Wright protested. 'There was only the squad here. Light duties and monitoring, that's all. Seemed sensible to just squat in someone else's office.'

Walters seethed. 'Not if you were allowing them to continue using it.'

The Welshman's effrontery was almost admirable. He had a way of constantly appearing put-upon and aggrieved, often in the face of overwhelming evidence to the contrary.

Benton entered, distracting Walters from potentially

throttling Wright. 'Any luck locating Corporal Potter yet?'

'He's not responding, Sarge.'

Walters glared at Wright again, who simply shrugged. 'Perhaps he's dealing with one of the residents.'

'Chatting 'em up, more like. This is what happens when you treat a UNIT posting like a holiday. Benton, you remain here. As of now, this site HQ is codenamed Trap Four. Contact the Warren and let them know what's happening. In Potter's absence, Corporal Wright and I are going to look for Mr Chambers, the Community spokesman.'

'He's nothing to do with me, Sarge. Potter deals with the Community he does.'

'Don't give me that—'

'It's the truth! We split the site and responsibilities.'

'We know you gave Chambers permission to come here every day to do his union business – unescorted.'

Wright gave a splutter. 'That was Potter. I was here, wasn't I? Chambers just turned up one day, told me it was all approved.'

'That's your game, is it? Blame each other and hope you both get off. Shame nobody thought fit to mention any of this in the daily reports.'

'Thing is, Sarge, he's not here every day, and when he is it's never for long.'

Walters leaned in threateningly. 'You'd better hope Potter supports your story when we find him. Otherwise, I'll have those stripes off you.'

'Here, that's not fair. I'm not stupid you know. I worked hard to get where I am and I'm not going to let some two-bit Cockney screw me over with his bull shine.' He finished with a resounding nod, then quickly added, 'Sarge,' as an afterthought.

Two-bit Cockney, eh? Walters eyed Wright, then headed for the door. 'I'll assume by that you mean Potter.'

It was very late in the evening by the time Captain Turner returned to his digs. Neither he, the Brigadier, nor Major Branwell had been keen to leave HQ in case evidence suddenly emerged that might help resolve their immediate concerns. Benton had reported in from the Compound. It sounded like Walters was doing exactly what Turner had instructed. After that, the Brigadier had insisted that they all call it a night.

Turner's landlady, Miss Nugent, was still up, as usual. She was leaning against the sitting room doorframe waiting for him. In her dressing gown and slippers, she looked ready for bed. Turner knew it was likely she'd spent the whole day like that. Her tatty grey curls had long since given up the pretence of a purple rinse. He noted the somewhat faraway look in the eyes beneath her oversized glasses, and the misapplied lipstick coating her teeth.

'Good evening, Miss Nugent.'

'Late again, Captain.' Her husky voice a testament to her unapologetic forty-a-day habit. 'Work, or partying, I wonder?'

He gave a nervous chuckle. 'No time for partying in my job.'

She looked like she was about to continue the conversation, so Turner pressed ahead.

'And I've got an early start again tomorrow, so if you'll excuse me, good night.'

Miss Nugent mumbled something as she lit up, but Turner had long since learned not to draw these conversations out any longer than necessary.

His suite of rooms was on the first floor of the old Georgian townhouse. There were two other lodgers on the floors above him. Turner rarely saw them. The topmost was a single-room garret, occupied by a writer or journalist. He was pretty certain that the pin-striped civil servant living directly above him didn't in all ways match Miss Nugent's 'single professional males only' stipulation. Not if the nightly creaking footsteps were anything to go by.

There was a basement to the house as well, with its own external entrance. Turner would often see the face of a toothless old man pressed against the shadowy window there as he left in the mornings.

Isobel had come to visit once. Never again, she'd said. Aside from the basement tenant clearly attempting to peer up her minidress, Miss Nugent had given them both the third degree as they climbed the stairs. She cast aspersions on Isobel's character and repeatedly told Turner she kept a clean house in a respectable neighbourhood.

After a few choice words in retort, poor Isobel had stormed off. They'd agreed never to go back. They had the freedom of the house in St James' Gardens. And, after all, as their relationship progressed over time, they'd be starting to think about living together anyway. At least that's what Turner had in mind. He wasn't going to rush to suggest it, though, in case Isobel developed cold feet. They were fine as they were for now.

Turner let himself into his flat and flicked the deadlock catch behind him – another trick he had learned for keeping his landlady at bay. The sitting room was stuffy, having been shut up all day in the summer heat. He'd kept the heavy curtains closed to keep out a lot of the sunlight, but without any windows open for air movement the place just sat there and stewed.

Regardless of Miss Nugent's protestations about the *respectable neighbourhood* in which they lived, Turner wasn't going to leave windows open as a temptation to anyone while he was out. He wanted to throw them all open now and let the coolness of the night blow the day's stresses away. But he needed to make a telephone call first and he was ever conscious of confidentiality.

He dialled Isobel's number and waited. It had been too late to travel to St James' Gardens and see her in person. He knew she'd have an early start the next day, but hoped she wasn't yet asleep.

It rang on and on. Just as he was about to give up, someone picked up.

'Hello?' Isobel sounded nervous – no doubt due to the lateness of the hour.

'Darling, it's me.'

'Oh, hi!' Her slightly forced, slightly cheeky greeting always brought a smile to his face. 'Don't take this the wrong way, but—'

Turner anticipated her objection. 'Sorry, I know you've got an early start, but I've just got home.'

'No, no,' she corrected him. 'I was going to say I'd rather hoped you might be my uncle.'

That answered his question, but he continued regardless. 'Still no sign of him, then?'

'No sign, no word. Nothing. Jimmy, I'm really tired and I've got to be up at stupid o'clock to get to Bournemouth by train. Can you look out for Uncle Joseph while I'm away, there's a sweetie?'

'I'll try my best.'

'Well, I guess I can't ask for any more than that, can I?'

'No, because that would be greedy,' he teased. 'Try not to worry too much. Sweet dreams and a safe journey tomorrow.'

'Was there anything else?'

He paused for a moment. He was never too sure how much to say in moments like these. 'Nothing that can't wait until I see you again.'

'In a few days, then.' She blew him a kiss.

Turner reciprocated and replaced the receiver, allowing his grip to linger. He had half a mind to call the Brigadier at home. But no, they were better off waiting a full twenty-four hours before reporting Isobel's uncle, just in case. Vaughn, Packer and Professor Watkins all missing. There was no way they weren't linked, he was sure.

The Land Rover pulled up at the large double gates at the perimeter of the Community and Walters jumped out. This was the only illuminated area he'd seen so far. Streetlights lined the residential road beyond the gates. The fence line disappeared into the darkness on either side, beyond the reach of the sodium yellow wash.

'Shouldn't these gates be manned?'

Wright joined him. He had a sort of lolloping gait – another thing about him which Walters found intensely annoying.

'Potter?' the Welshman yelled.

Walters held out his hands in exasperation. 'So much for stealth, you idiot.'

Wright looked aggrieved – as usual when criticised. 'You wanted to find him. He's probably nipped off for a jimmy, that's all. These gates will be locked anyway.' Wright leaned on the gates, and they swung open, taking him by surprise. '*Coc y gath!*'

Walters silently mourned his fate as Wright wrestled with the gates. The man was an utter liability. 'Is this the only way in and out of the Community?' he asked.

Wright managed to bolt and lock the gates in place. 'This is the secure line, here. The Compound boundary. The other end of the residential area opens up to the rest of the world.

Like a normal village.'

There was little that was normal about the Community. They could see that from here. Rows and rows of prefabricated single-storey housing. Like a chalet park, maybe. Or a refugee camp.

'Thank you for your insightful observations, Corporal. So, people could be coming and going all the time?'

'Until they reach these gates, yes.'

'If they'd been locked, I'd be more inclined to agree with you.'

There was the sound of movement in the shadows.

'That you, Sarge?'

The voice took them both by surprise.

Corporal Potter crept from the shadows of the tree line. He looked haggard and drawn. He tried to salute Walters but ended up collapsing in a trembling mess on the ground.'

'Alec, you all right, fella? Where've you been?' burst Wright.

'Help me,' he pleaded, before falling unconscious.

Corporal Wright didn't say a word all the way back to the site HQ. There was a First Aid room on the ground floor and Potter was laid out on the bed there. Walters remained with him, sending Wright to wait in HQ until needed.

Walters wanted a word with Potter alone. He didn't have to wait long before Potter regained consciousness.

'Where am I?' Potter tried to sit up.

'It's all right, Corporal, take it easy. You collapsed.'

'I remember. Thank God you're here, Sarge.'

'What's been going on?'

'Corporal Wright. He decided he was in charge, see. And a right tyrant he's been, too.'

'*Corporal Wright?*' Walters couldn't keep the incredulity from his voice.

Potter nodded. 'I've done my best to protect the rest of the lads, but...' The words faded, leaving a very frightened-looking man behind.

'Look, I need to ask you some questions. Just be honest with me and I'll deal with the situation. Are you up to it?'

'Thanks, Sarge. Go ahead.'

'Firstly, why didn't you answer your radio when we were

trying to get hold of you?'

Potter reached under the blanket and removed his radio from his belt. 'Broken, Sarge. Wright said I had to take it for appearances.'

'Why were the Community gates unlocked?'

'That's my fault—'

'I know it's your fault, Potter. I'm not asking whose fault it is. I'm asking *why*.'

'Yes, sir. Sorry, sir. Nightly routine, you see. I pop through and do a quick patrol around the Community. It's helped foster good relations between us and them. Eased the fears and suspicions.'

'I see.'

'Credit where credit's due. It was Corporal Wright's idea. Anyway, I'd just done my patrol when I heard the vehicle approaching. Wright's done that before, been waiting for me. He's usually got something to beat me with.'

Walters placed a hand on his temple. 'I see.'

'In my haste, I must have forgotten to lock up.'

'Why didn't you report any of this to us back at the Warren?'

'How, Sarge? Wright controlled access to all the comms equipment.'

'How about the Community? Don't they have telephones? Couldn't you have asked that Chambers bloke for help?'

'Too risky. Him and Wright – thick as thieves.'

'I'm going to stop him coming in all the time.'

'Good luck. I suggested that a while back. Learned a hard lesson that day, believe me.'

There was a pause. Walters was feeling totally wrong-footed about so much. He really needed to speak with Captain Turner.

'Sarge? Have you got someone to cover my post yet? I don't want to give Wright any opportunities to accuse me of dereliction of duty.'

Walters gave a gentle smile and stood. 'I'm in charge now, Corporal. You leave Wright to me. Get some rest. We'll check in on you again in the morning.'

Potter was asleep before Walters left the room.

Benton was waiting for Walters outside the First Aid Room

and snapped off a salute. 'The platoon has set up camp successfully.'

They started walking back towards the site HQ.

'Anything else?' Walters asked.

'I've assigned cover to all the patrol points and sentry posts.'

This was what Walters had hoped for. 'Have the resident squad been rounded up?'

'Yes, Sarge. Good lads, all of them. Straight as a die.'

He was happy to take that judgment from Benton on trust. The problem – if indeed there was one – was with the orders and those giving them.

'None of them said anything about Corporal Wright being stern and overbearing?'

Benton stopped suddenly and scoffed. 'That wet fish? I wouldn't have the nerve to ask.'

Walters looked around. There was no one nearby. 'Between you and me, Benton, Corporal Potter is terrified of him.'

'Are we talking about the same person here? Gwynfor Wright. Wetter than a weekend in Wrexham. Everything's always somebody else's fault.'

Walters nodded. 'Potter said Wright put himself in charge here and he's been ruling with a rod of iron.'

Benton paused momentarily. 'Sorry, Sarge, but that's ridiculous.'

'Ordinarily, I'd agree with you. Potter is solidly built for a start – lifting him onto the bed was a real strain. Why he'd be intimidated by a long, thin streak of... Welshman is anyone's guess. Is Wright still in HQ?'

'He was when I came past. I checked for you there first.'

A wave of tiredness swept over Walters. He shook his head in resignation.

'It's late and we'll do better with a bit of shut-eye. You, me, and Wright, we'll head over to the Community tomorrow morning. We'll sort out the Chambers situation, then come back here and have it out. I'm gonna find out what exactly has been going on all this time.'

CHAPTER EIGHT

ISOBEL WATKINS hated early mornings. From the tinny warbling of her radio alarm clock to the tannin tang of the Teasmade. These modern devices were supposed to encourage her out of bed in a timely fashion. Instead, they simply made her angry.

One of the problems was that, no matter how much she prepared the previous evening, there was always loads to do when she got up. Some friends called her vain. A few of her exes, too. It was true that Isobel was particular about her appearance and liked to look her best. She didn't think of it as vanity. It was simply a standard of professional presentation she'd set herself.

Regardless, she was happy to drag herself out of bed, not just to switch off the inane chatter of the radio, but because she was doing a job she loved and finally getting decent money for her pains. If only there wasn't all the faffing and stress that went with it.

Maybe, she thought, *if Jimmy were here he could help. Or if we had a place together?* She smiled at her own coyness as she let her mind wander. She didn't want to risk frightening him off with such thoughts. He did rather tick all her beau boxes, though.

She hadn't heard any movement within the house during the night, but she knocked on her uncle's bedroom door just in case. No answer. And no sign of anyone having been in when she peered inside. She checked the laboratory as well, just in case. Same.

Isobel's shoulders slumped. She'd have to leave that problem with Jimmy for the next few days and concentrate on her work. She was just forcing half a slice of toast and marmalade into her mouth when she heard the doorbell. That would be the taxi she'd booked. It was an extravagance, but the agency was paying expenses, and she didn't fancy traipsing across London on the Underground with all her gear that early in the morning.

'Be right there,' she called.

She took a quick swig of coffee and dabbed her mouth on a tea towel before reapplying her lippy in the hallway mirror. Then she swiftly wrote where she was going, plus the date, on the wall in case her uncle returned home. Finally, she grabbed her holdall from the bottom of the stairs and opened the door.

'Can you take this for me while I grab my gear?'

She held out the bag, then dropped it as a cold, clammy hand took her by the neck.

Isobel desperately wanted to scream, but she couldn't catch her breath. As consciousness slowly left her, all she could think was *he's dead... he's dead... he's dead.*

Sergeant Walters turned over and groaned. The floor was hard and uncomfortable, but better than the chair in which he'd initially tried to sleep. Benton, across the other side of the room, was already sitting up and flexing.

The third occupant, Corporal Wright, snored resoundingly from his position, doubled over the desk, arms for a pillow. He bolted upright as the office door was flung open and Corporal Potter appeared with a hostess trolley.

'Tea up!' he bawled, like a comedy char.

'Thank you, Potter,' said Walters, standing. 'You feeling better?'

'Fit as the proverbial fiddle, Sarge.' He began to offload the trolley of breakfast items and refreshments onto a nearby cabinet. 'Get this lot down you, and you will too.'

Wright gave a long groan. 'Permission to die.'

'Granted,' muttered Benton, a little uncharitably.

'What's the matter?' Walters asked.

'Can't feel my arms. Back aches. Neck stiff. And I think...' Wright moved his lower jaw from side to side. 'Yes, I think my jaw isn't where it should be.'

'I think you'll find it's always been like that,' said Benton, stepping over to him. He grabbed him by the head and slowly manipulated it until Wright's neck clicked.

'Oh!' gasped Wright. 'That feels good!'

Benton then placed his left hand on Wright's lower back

and his right on Wright's upper chest and pushed on both. There was an unpleasant noise and another gasp from Wright that could pass for both pleasure and pain.

'You need to sort your posture out,' Benton told him, walking over to the makeshift breakfast bar.

'What about my arms?'

Benton's reply was lost behind a mouthful of toast, but Walters had a feeling it wasn't complimentary.

'I've eaten in the mess with the others,' said Potter, 'so I'll leave you three to it if that's all right, Sarge?'

Walters shook his head. 'Stay please, Corporal. I want you to start drawing up shift rotas. Include this HQ as well. I don't want anyone in the same place all the time.'

He checked for any reaction from Wright, but the corporal was still trying to get the life back into his arms and hands.

'Put yourself down for first shift in HQ. Once the three of us have eaten and freshened up, we're heading over to the Community to track down Mr Chambers.'

Wright looked over this time. 'Not that again, Sarge. Look, I told you last night, Potter here arranged it all. I never speak to the fellow. Why not take Potter and leave me here instead?'

Walters poured himself a strong black coffee and noticed Benton position himself very closely behind Wright. He drew a mouthful before responding.

'Put simply, because I don't trust you, Wright. That's why.'

'Oh-ho, that's charming, that is.'

'You want to hear less of my charm? Just follow orders. Now quit flexing your fingers like a pianist at a loose end and tidy yourself up. I want us moving in ten minutes.'

Chambers made much better time returning to the Compound. It was necessary if they were going to avoid problems re-entering and it was too much of a risk to wait until nightfall. This time Vaughn sat with him at the front, while Packer stayed in the back with their unconscious quarry. They had a plan, but with UNIT on-site in greater numbers, they were going to have to take particular care.

Next to Chambers, Vaughn sat with his fingers steepled before him enigmatically.

Benton assumed they'd drive around to the Community, but

Walters chose to walk – much to the dismay of Wright.

'You're determined to make me wear through this pair of boots before I finish here, aren't you?' he grumbled.

'Gives you a better grasp of the landscape, walking through it,' Walters told him.

'I've already got that. I've been here ages, remember?'

'Then shut up and enjoy the scenery,' snapped Benton, already fed up with the Welshman's griping.

Private Cowper was manning the gates when they arrived. He snapped to attention. 'Morning, Sarge.'

Walters acknowledged Cowper. 'Any sign of life through there yet?'

He shook his head. 'Don't suppose they've got much to get up for.'

Walters turned to Wright. 'Is there usually activity by now?'

Wright gave an exaggerated shrug. 'Search me, Sarge. I keep telling you, I don't know anything I don't. But no one's listening to me, are they?'

'Guard your lip, Corporal.'

Wright seemed to shrink back into himself.

Walters continued. 'I don't want to go in there and start knocking on doors if it's going to upset people, that's all.'

'I don't think we've got much choice,' said Benton.

Walters agreed. 'Open up, Private. Hopefully, we won't be too long.'

The three of them passed through the gates. Walters turned to Wright. 'Which way to Chambers' place?'

'I don't know where he lives.'

Walters handed Wright a slip of paper. 'I ripped this off a letter I found in his desk tray.'

'All right,' Wright said, after a while. 'This way, I think.'

Not entirely reassured, Benton looked at Walters and the two of them followed after Wright.

He led them a few rows along, into a cul-de-sac at the edge of the Community.

'Must be one of these.'

Walters double-checked his slip of paper. 'Looks like it.' He nodded at Benton, who stepped forward and knocked on the door in question. Benton watched the walls vibrate slightly under the repeated impact. The place didn't feel very solid.

No answer.

He bent over and lifted the letterbox flap. 'Mr Chambers?'

Still no answer. No sound of any sort.

He turned back to Walters and shook his head.

At a nod from Walters, the three of them proceeded to other abodes.

No answer from any of them. No sign of life at all.

'Maybe they've all moved away already,' Benton suggested. 'Looking for work?'

Walters looked sceptical. 'Captain Turner said they were all still here. It was a bone of contention.'

Benton indicated Wright. 'Even eagle-eyes here should have noticed if they'd all upped sticks and moved out since.'

'What do we do then, Sarge?' said Wright, pulling a face.

'We knock on every door we can. There must be someone here somewhere.'

Captain Turner awoke to a three-pronged attack. He sat up in bed to find the alarm clock ringing, the telephone ringing, and someone banging on his door. He must have been sleeping very soundly. In quick succession, he cancelled the alarm then ran into the living room and grabbed the telephone receiver.

'Hello?'

'Jimmy. At last. Anything wrong?' It was the Brigadier.

'Hold on a sec, sir, sorry,' Turner said, placing the receiver on the table while he ran to answer the door.

Miss Nugent was there, the usual dressing-gowned apparition, with fag ash accessories. 'Have you got any idea how long your alarm clock's been going off, and how long your telephone's been ringing off the hook?'

'I was asleep.'

'Don't get smart with me,' she yelled in his face. 'Decent folk that keep regular hours can't sleep with everything going off like that.'

Then, before Turner had had time to process the onslaught, Miss Nugent grabbed the door and shut it in her own face.

Somewhat bemused, he returned to the telephone. 'Sorry, sir. I believe I've overslept. I must have been more tired than I thought.'

'I'm just glad you're okay.'

Turner looked at his mantelpiece clock. Five past six. He'd overslept by a mere five minutes – not a disaster. But he knew what the Brigadier calling him at home implied.

'What's the alert, sir?'

'I'm going to come clean with the Ministry about Vaughn and Packer. I'm not sure we can manage this situation on our own.'

'I see, sir, yes.'

'I'd rather they heard it from me than anyone else.'

'I'll be at HQ as soon as I can.'

'That's not why I called. Is there any update on Professor Watkins?'

'No, sir. Late last night he still hadn't returned. Isobel was heading off early today. She's got a fashion shoot in Bournemouth. I can telephone the house, see if her uncle answers.'

'Call me straight back once you have. I'm at home myself.'

The call ended before he could respond. Doubtless, the Brig had a lot on his mind.

Turner immediately dialled Isobel's number. It rang and rang 'til it rang off. He dialled it again, just to be sure. Same.

He dialled a different number. The Brigadier answered on the second ring.

'No luck, sir, sorry. No answer at all.'

'Right. I'm sending Corporal Tracy for you. Check the Watkins' house. If I'm going before the minister, I want to be certain of everything we currently know – or don't.'

'I'll be as quick as I can.'

'Good luck, Jimmy, I'll see you at HQ.'

Turner prepared himself for the day with practised ease. He crept down the stairs as lightly as possible to avoid alerting Miss Nugent again.

Outside, the street was quiet save for a milkman nearing the end of his round and a postman in the middle of his. The old man in the basement was watching him, like a caged animal at the zoo, dulled by years of imprisonment.

A few minutes passed, then a UNIT Land Rover appeared at the far end of the street. Turner met it in the middle of the road and jumped in.

'Good morning, Corporal,' he said, sounding chirpier than he felt.

'Morning, sir,' Tracy returned. 'Where are we headed?'

Turner gave him the address. Tracy thought for a few moments, then nodded. Turner doubted there were many London taxi drivers who knew the streets as well as Tracy did.

Little more was said on the way. It was too early for small talk, and their mission, such as it was, was pretty straightforward. As they approached St James' Gardens, Tracy finally spoke again.

'Should I park somewhere discreet and out of sight, sir, or am I all right to pull up outside?'

'Outside,' Turner confirmed. 'We've nothing to hide and speed is of the essence.'

There was space to park immediately opposite and they saw instantly that lights were on inside – even though it was now daylight. Isobel could be scatty, so there was every chance she'd just forgotten to turn them off when she'd left. All the same, Turner proceeded with caution.

He stopped by the front door and looked around. There was little activity in the street. A few bowler-hatted gentlemen, with rolled umbrellas and briefcases, were heading off in the direction of the Underground. They made few concessions to what was sure to be another hot summer's day. He couldn't spot any unwelcome observers or surveillance operatives. Maybe he was being overly cautious – however, experience had taught him never to take things for granted.

Certain that he wasn't being watched, Turner reached out for the bell. As he did so, he spotted light around the edge of the front door. He pushed at the door and, sure enough, it opened to reveal a hallway with Isobel's familiar holdall just inside. She couldn't have left yet.

'Isobel?' he called. 'You still here? Professor...?'

He walked through the ground floor, switching lights off and becoming more concerned as he went. There was no sign that Professor Watkins had returned home at all. The remains of a slice of toast in the kitchen was normal, as was Isobel's photography gear – all packed up and ready to go on the dining room table. The only thing missing was Isobel herself.

Then Turner found the note scrawled on the wall in the hallway, with today's date. A chill ran down his spine. Front door left ajar, lights on, luggage and equipment still here – Isobel had been abducted.

He touched the words on the wall. *What have they done to*

you? Turner's heart was in his mouth. He knew panicking would do no good, but knowing and doing were entirely separate things. He took a few deep breaths, then grabbed the telephone.

'Savage? Captain Turner. Put me through to the Brigadier.'

There was a click and a pause.

'Lethbridge-Stewart.'

'Captain Turner here, sir.'

'Jimmy – is everything all right?'

Turner kept breathing steadily and heavily to quell his emotions. 'I'm at the Watkins' house now. Still no sign of the professor, but…' He stalled momentarily. 'All the evidence suggests that Isobel has been abducted.'

A pause. 'I see. You spoke to her late last night, didn't you?'

'Yes, sir. She said she was heading off early this morning. Her bags are still here and the front door was slightly ajar. She even left a message for her uncle in case he returned.'

'So, whoever took her did so as she was about to leave.'

'That's how I'm reading things, yes.'

'I'm very sorry, Jimmy.'

'Thank you, sir.'

'It seems likely that whoever has Isobel also has the professor, and will presumably use her to gain leverage over him.'

'That's what Vaughn did before.'

'Yes. I don't quite know how to put this over the telephone, but—'

Turner smiled at the Brigadier's awkwardness. 'You can rely on me to stay focused, sir. Bigger picture and all that.'

'Thank you. I'm going to update Geneva, then take all this to the Ministry.'

'I'd like to check with some of the neighbours before we return to HQ, sir. See if anyone saw or heard anything that could give us a lead.'

'Splendid. Anything will be better than what we have at the moment. Good luck.'

'You too, sir.'

Turner replaced the receiver and looked again at Isobel's scrawled message on the wall. This time, rather than opening a pit in his stomach, he felt galvanised into action. They had to get to the bottom of all this.

He strode to the front door and beckoned to Tracy to join him.

*

What a difference a few days makes, thought the Brigadier as he waited in the main reception at the Ministry of Defence. He didn't have a confirmed appointment and the minister was currently attending a briefing, so he had to wait to be collected by the mole-like secretary in the pin-stripe suit. *What was the fellow's name again? Greaves, that was it.*

No matter how plush the furniture, how good the coffee and how inspiring the surroundings, the Brigadier knew this interminable waiting around was time he could barely afford. Likewise, he knew it was a necessity. What was the phrase? A catch-22 situation, that was it. Damned if you do, damned if you don't.

Greaves finally appeared from a lift and scuttled over.

About time, the Brigadier thought. He tried to swallow his frustration – he'd curry no favour with the ministerial staff that way.

'Brigadier Lethbridge-Stewart.' Greaves didn't offer a hand to shake. 'The minister has a little time now before his next committee. I hope this is urgent.'

'I can assure you I wouldn't be here in person if it weren't.'

'Very well, follow me if you please.'

The Brigadier followed Greaves to the lifts and then up to the Ministerial floor in silence. He knew the meeting was likely to be difficult. Challenging questions would be asked – questions he wasn't yet able to answer. He paused to knock.

'Go straight in,' Greaves informed him. 'Five minutes maximum,' he continued. 'That's all the minister can spare.'

The Brigadier watched Greaves scuttle off to his own office. 'Let's hope that's sufficient,' he said quietly before entering.

'Lethbridge-Stewart,' said the minister, turning. He was standing before the bookcase, a tumbler of golden liquid in his hand. He raised it slightly. 'Quick constitutional before a Naval review committee. Damn things drag on for hours.'

It was clear that the minister wasn't offering the Brigadier a similar 'constitutional'.

'Good morning, Minister. Thank you for agreeing to see me at such short notice.'

'Come on then, what's so damned urgent?'

The Brigadier had played the situation out in his head

several times, but this was not yet how he'd imagined it. 'Tobias Vaughn, sir.'

He noticed the minister glaring. 'What of him?'

'He's gone missing, sir.'

'From where?'

'The morgue at UNIT HQ.'

The minister placed his now empty glass on a tray with others. 'How the hell did body snatchers get into your HQ? Or should we be questioning the loyalty of your staff?'

The Brigadier had anticipated that jibe at least and chose to ignore it. 'That's the tricky bit, sir. It wasn't body snatchers. It appears Vaughn wasn't as dead as we thought.'

'Wasn't as—?'

'He left by himself, as far as we can tell. Him and Packer. Their cybernetic bodies must have reactivated. We're not sure how.'

The minister stood agog.

An inner door opened, and Greaves' head appeared. 'Nearly time for your Naval committee, Minister.'

'It'll have to wait, Greaves. Something more urgent has arisen.'

Greaves gave a curt nod. 'I'll give them an hour's recess.' He vanished as discretely as he'd appeared.

The minister indicated his desk. 'Sit.'

They sat.

'When?' he asked.

'Two days ago. But it wasn't noticed until yesterday.'

'Wasn't noticed? Don't you have the area under surveillance?'

The Brigadier's shoulders dropped slightly. 'There was interference at the crucial moment, as far as we can tell. The footage from the time is missing.'

'I see.' The minister slumped back in his seat, miserably. 'Anything else?'

'Two other disappearances – likely abductions – both linked with the recent IE event. Professor Watkins, who worked for Vaughn – under duress – and his niece, Isobel. The latter just this very morning.'

The minister very calmly opened a drawer, reached in and removed a tan folder, which he held up before slapping it on the desk.

'Brigadier, Vaughn and Packer were dead. I have the reports here. *Your* reports.'

'Yes, sir. And I saw the corpses. As I said, the best guess we have is that their cybernetic bodies have somehow brought them back to life.'

The minister shook his head. 'This all sounds very fanciful.'

'As did the recent invasion. And any number of instances beforehand that I could mention.'

'All right, all right.' The minister held up his palm. 'Do I need to go straight to Number 10? Are we looking at another international emergency?'

'I hope not, sir. The problem is at the moment UNIT have got nothing to go on. We don't know what's happening, or where anyone is.'

'If this all blows up again—'

'I know, Minister. That's why I've come to you now. We may need to co-ordinate a response with the regular army and the civil authorities to understand the full extent of any potential threat.'

'Why didn't you raise this with General Ffowlkes-Withers yesterday? He was most displeased with the level of activity he witnessed. According to the report I received, he thought most of your staff were just wasting their time – and our money. He's escalating his plans.'

'Confound the man. He can't possibly justify such sweeping statements on the basis of one brief visit. He's got no idea how we operate and no right to—'

'Then show him. *Involve* him.'

That was all the Brigadier needed. 'With respect, sir—'

'With respect, *Brigadier*, I wasn't born yesterday. If you're playing a political manoeuvring game over matters of national security because you dislike your liaison with the Regulars, you're no good to me, the UK, or the UN. Situations like this can't be managed without full and immediate disclosure.'

'I know, sir. That's why I'm here now.'

'And with regard to General Ffowlkes-Withers, I'm inclined to sympathise with his views. We've supplied you with facilities, staff and the very best technology. At considerable expense to the Crown. If dead bodies can miraculously return to life and walk out of your HQ unseen by anyone, what the hell use are you?'

The Brigadier stood, incensed, but held his tongue.

The minister looked up at him but remained seated. 'Is that everything I need to know?'

'We have operatives out investigating and searching for leads. We've also increased our presence at the IE Factory compound, should Vaughn and Packer return there. IE London has been stripped bare.'

'Is it likely that they'd return to the scene of the crime? Wouldn't they try to vanish from sight and set up elsewhere?'

'We're just covering the known options. Anything further than that is beyond our reach at present.'

The minister looked away to his desk and grabbed paper and pen. 'I'll send memos to General Ffowlkes-Withers and also to the heads of the civil authorities, requesting that they give you assistance where possible.'

'Thank you, sir.'

'I'll also be contacting Geneva.'

Another veiled threat.

The minister continued to scribble away. 'Carry on as you are for now, Brigadier. Keep me informed daily through General Ffowlkes-Withers.'

'As you wish, Minister.'

The minister finally looked up at him again. 'I do. Now go and do your job and let me get on with mine.'

The Brigadier turned smartly and left. He hadn't thought he could leave the Ministry feeling any more angered and disheartened than he had two days before. How wrong he'd been.

CHAPTER NINE

TURNER AND Tracy reconvened after knocking at every door on the street. They'd left the Watkins house, which Turner had made sure was secure this time. They'd both made their way to separate ends of the street, then back along the other side until they met once again at the UNIT Land Rover.

Not every house was occupied, not every house answered the door and not everyone that answered had been polite. And despite the challenges and the abuse, they'd both returned with the same result: no one had seen or heard anything.

'Shame it wasn't around my manor,' said Tracy. 'People are nosy as hell where I live. Net curtain flickers, every man jack of them.'

'It was worth a try,' Turner admitted, 'but whoever took Isobel, it was clearly a professional job. They knew what they were doing. And that early in the morning you're unlikely to find many people up and about – least of all nosing about outside.'

'What next then, sir?'

'Back to the Warren, Corporal. As per the Brigadier's orders.'

Turner slid into the passenger seat and tried to fight the nausea gripping his stomach. He couldn't help feeling there was another very long day ahead.

Sylvie Lowe was wiping tables when the Brigadier entered the NAAFI. She could tell in an instant that things were not well with him. Years of experience meant she was well-practised at spotting signs of stress or concern. That was why she played a dual role at UNIT HQ. Officially she was the NAAFI manageress. Unofficially she was an understanding and confidential ear to anyone with troubles.

'Tea and something special coming right up, then you can tell me all about it.'

The Brigadier gave her what he clearly thought was a smile. If that was the best he could manage, there were real problems. Sylvie had developed a shorthand for these situations with the rest of the staff. She caught Kath's eye and winked.

'I think the bins need emptying,' said Kath.

'Good girl.' Sylvie watched her go, then poured a mug of strong, sweet tea and grabbed the remains of her homemade fruitcake. 'There you go,' she said, plonking them both before the Brigadier. 'Pure NAAFI gold, that.'

The Brigadier picked up the slab of fruitcake and appeared to savour the aroma. He frowned.

'Stop examining it and just eat it,' she continued. 'It will make you feel better. Major Branwell had some for elevenses and allegedly I'm now his favourite woman on the planet.'

'Fine praise indeed.'

'I'll be happy to reciprocate if he's able to take some of the stress off you and Captain Turner. I'm getting concerned at how often you burst in here like a fury.'

'I doubt Major Branwell could do anything about Whitehall.'

'I thought you were only answerable to Geneva?'

The Brigadier raised a brow. 'Geneva, New York... Whitehall, the chap who cleans the toilets at the MoD...' He took a large bite of the cake. He swallowed and spoke. 'I sometimes feel that my life is one of those games, you know the ones, where there's a blank square and you have to slide the pieces around to make a picture.'

She nodded. 'Haven't a clue what they're called.'

'Problem is, it feels like each of the pieces in my version of the game is someone I need to answer to. I'm not a soldier anymore. I'm a politician, an accountant, a seer, a whipping boy. This is excellent cake, by the way, and the best cup of tea I've had today.'

She nudged him fondly with her elbow. 'I bet it's the only cup of tea you've had today.'

'Rumbled,' he said, before his face broke out into a broad grin.

'It'll get better,' Sylvie told him.

'You can't know that.'

'We're still new. UNIT is still bedding in. We may have

delivered a national service over that IE business, but everyone – the general public, the Government, even the UN – they're still working out who we are and how they relate to us. When it all settles down, the boot will be on the other foot, and you'll be the one asking the questions.'

He nodded. 'Perhaps.'

'And that'll be one pound thirty, by the way,' she deadpanned. 'Including consultancy fee and cake.'

The Brigadier looked momentarily stunned, but Sylvie couldn't hold a straight face for long.

'Mrs Lowe, you're a villain.'

'The worst,' she agreed. 'That's why you keep me here.'

They were interrupted at this point. Lance Corporal Enders entered. She looked upset and headed straight for the corner.

'Everything all right, Corporal?' asked the Brigadier.

She looked up, as if she hadn't really noticed he was there. 'Yes, sir, sorry, sir. I just need a few minutes. Sergeant Major Nicholls said it was all right, sir.'

'Indeed it is, Enders. And if a few minutes aren't enough, take a few more. I can recommend Mrs Lowe's fruitcake.'

'Which you've just had the last of,' Sylvie hissed.

'Ahh.'

Enders smiled through her tears. 'I shared a slice earlier, sir. It's been the talk of HQ all morning.'

Sylvie grinned and felt her cheeks redden.

The Brigadier looked at her and she nodded.

'Round two coming up.'

'Thank you,' he said quietly, as he passed her to leave.

'All part of the service, Brigadier.'

She popped back behind the counter and grabbed two mugs of tea this time, then she slipped into the seat next to Enders.

'Drink this,' Sylvie said. 'It'll help. Always does.'

'Thanks, Sylvie.' Another teary smile.

'Now, what's brought all this on?'

'Oh, it's nothing, really.'

Sylvie had heard the story a million times before, from all sorts of servicemen and women. And it was never 'nothing really'.

'Of course, love. That's why you've hidden away in the NAAFI for a bit to sort yourself out.'

'It's just all this IE stuff. Mum and Dad haven't been the

same since, and I still miss him, you know.'

'Your brother?'

Enders nodded. 'I thought it was all done with, but we've had to send a platoon back out to the Compound. Brings it all back to me. I just wish we knew what had happened to him, that's all.'

'Can Nicholls not put you on different duties?'

'I don't want to let anyone down.'

Bless her. 'You won't, I'm sure. But if it's upsetting you this much—'

'It's not normally this bad. I ran out of smokes this morning, and I'm flat broke, so that hasn't helped.'

Sylvie jumped up. 'Why didn't you say!' She popped back behind the counter and fished in her coat pocket.

Kath poked her head out of the kitchen. 'Can we come back yet?'

Sylvie nodded and whispered, 'Although I might need you for something else.'

Kath rolled her eyes.

When Sylvie returned to Enders, she slipped the remains of her packet of Embassy into the girl's hand.

'On me. Do me good to go without, I'm sure.'

'Sylvie, I can't—'

'You bloody well can, and you will. Go on. Have one to calm your nerves now before you go back. Kath'll go with you, won't you, Kath?'

Kath peered over the top of the cake stand. 'Me? I'm gasping! Come on, Jules.'

Enders gave Sylvie a quick hug as she passed by. 'Thanks. I owe you.'

Sylvie smiled and watched the two girls head off, happy in the knowledge of a job well done.

Professor Watkins had awoken in what he recalled was Gregory's main research laboratory. Instinctively he knew he'd had a very long and very refreshing sleep. But had it come about through him being drugged, or just plain exhausted? He had a vague recollection of feeling let down, but only in the way that one does after a particularly vivid dream.

He was lying on a camp bed under a rough blanket. More memories returned. Gregory would often sleep in his lab, working long hours to try to get to grips with – or simply to understand – whatever challenge Vaughn had set him. Much good it had done in the end, by all accounts. People promoted above their abilities were always found out. That's why Watkins knew he'd be all right – he'd always been far more able and intelligent than he'd ever been given credit for. By anyone.

He was relieved to note he hadn't been undressed in his somnambulant state. He rose and stretched, then rubbed at his leg. No doubt Isobel would be displeased that he didn't have his stick with him.

He splashed his face with cold water, before grabbing the pot of coffee from the side. A momentary pause to sniff the caffeine-rich aroma. *Oooh, the joy.* He could already feel doors opening inside his brain in response to the stimulus. His fingers twiddled in anticipation of a good day's work ahead.

A door behind him opened. He hadn't even bothered to check if the room was locked or not. His focus had been on the important things. A foul stench gradually reached him, even masking the coffee beneath his nose.

'Hello, Packer.'

'How's the leg doing, Professor? Sorry I shot you.'

It was the least sincere apology Watkins had ever heard – and he'd taught undergraduates. He gave a derisive snort. He had no fear of Packer anymore, only disgust. He took another sip of coffee, then spoke.

'What do you want?'

Packer sounded irritated. 'Aren't you going to look at me?'

Watkins clenched his jaw and shook his head. 'I find you... off-putting.'

'Harsh, Professor. I had a mother, you know. Someone who loved me unconditionally.'

'Would she now, a robotic cadaver?'

'Just get on with your work.'

'Careful. I'm Vaughn's partner now, and you're only staff. You should moderate your tone.'

'Partner or not, I'm still here to make sure you crack on. There's a computer terminal for all your calculations and profile modelling. It feeds direct into the mainframe database. UNIT haven't managed to shut everything down.'

'All very efficient, I'm sure.'

'Mr Vaughn wants a prototype based on your previous

model ready for testing later today. Understand?'

'Does he, indeed. And what about what I want?'

'What do you want, Professor?'

'I want you to go away and leave me to my work.'

A pause. 'All right. But I'll be coming back soon to check on your progress.'

The door closed and Watkins stood a moment with his eyes closed, appreciating the silence and waiting for the stench of decomposition to fade. This was his time, his opportunity, his *moment*. He would make the world a better place, make people *better*.

He had to start small, though. Test the hypothesis and extract from that how to develop his theories further – follow the scientific method. What was it that thug Packer had said? A prototype later that day? No problem. And the IE mainframe database to explore – now that would be interesting.

The design and specification for the Cerebreton Mentor was indelibly imprinted on Watkins' brain. Even the changes Gregory had forced him to make to turn the thing into a weapon. Adapting the design to allow it to feed into the local communications system should be child's play. This wasn't so much a scientific project for him as a love affair. He was enraptured by his own theories.

Grabbing components left, right, and centre, while the computer terminal booted up, he started work.

'NAAFI break, sir?' asked Tracy as he and Turner entered UNIT HQ from the vehicle depot.

Turner nodded. 'Yes, go on. I could do with a cuppa myself, but I should let the Brigadier know what's going on first.'

They went their separate ways.

At the Brigadier's office, Major Branwell was there looking extremely put-upon. The Brigadier was on the telephone. He indicated for Turner to sit.

'No, I appreciate that, Nicholls. I'd just rather we limited her exposure – for her own benefit.'

The Brigadier listened to the reply. 'I see. Not everyone is suited to switchboard duties, of course.'

He listened again, this time showing signs of irritation. 'With Savage? Yes. Just do as you see fit. Thank you.'

He put the telephone down and hissed a long breath.

'Have we all had quite the morning then?' Turner looked with concern between Branwell and the Brigadier, who gave a nod.

'Major Branwell here, has been on the phone with Geneva. Officer-level induction.'

Branwell scowled. 'It was exhausting. Mostly politics. I'm supposed to be a soldier.'

The Brigadier nodded. 'There's an unfortunate confluence of both when you're a senior officer in UNIT, Major. There are always wider implications to consider. I may have neglected to forewarn you about that when I offered you the post.'

Branwell seemed to take this good-humouredly. 'I'm sure I'll come to terms with it eventually, sir. I think I'd take my morning over yours with the minister any day.'

'Not good then, sir?' Turner asked.

'It was never going to go well. The Ministry has already decided to make us fall guys for the Government's embarrassment. There was only one way they were going to receive the news that Public Enemy Number One, previously deceased, had returned to life and was at large somewhere as yet unknown. Let's face it, it's too far-fetched even for the Sunday papers.'

'And yet,' said Branwell, 'here we are.'

Turner shrugged. 'That's UNIT for you.'

The Brigadier's telephone rang. He immediately scooped up the receiver.

'Lethbridge-Stewart.' His face darkened. 'General Ffowlkes-Withers. To what do I owe this—?'

Turner looked at Branwell. They were both concerned. They offered to rise and leave but the Brigadier indicated for them to remain.

'Not at all, General. I wasn't aware you were expecting a call from me.' Another pause to listen. 'Yes, I saw the minister this morning, briefly. I see. No, that wasn't my intention at all. Sir—'

More listening. 'Yes, I will. No, you wouldn't have, sir. He's been occupied with Major Branwell all morning.'

The Brigadier's brow grew heavier, and his tone grew firmer. 'General Ffowlkes-Withers, as I've stated previously, you may be my superior within the British Armed Forces, but you are *not* my commanding officer. No matter what the minister may claim. I will report *to* you when there is anything to report. I had hoped to have heard from the minister's liaison with the civil authorities by now. We're going to need their assistance to widen the net.'

The Brigadier's jaw dropped. 'You did *what*? But we're not resourced to manage that. I see. Yes. I understand, sir.'

He replaced the handset. 'The general stood down the civil authorities. He says this is a UNIT internal security matter and must remain so.'

Turner felt just as flabbergasted as the Brigadier looked. 'But…'

'It's all part of Ffowlkes-Withers's plan. They're setting us up to fail. The situation is playing directly into his hands.'

'Can't Geneva help?' asked Branwell.

'You should be able to answer that yourself, after this morning, Major.'

Branwell nodded. 'It'll take time, won't it?'

'Precisely. And time is a luxury we may not have. Captain Turner, I need you to lead on the IE business for now.'

'Sir.'

'I think my time is going to be taken up holding off Ffowlkes-Withers and playing at politics. Major Branwell, you understand, I'm sure. It's only your second day and I need a more experienced hand to rely on out in the field.'

'Of course, sir. As long as the captain isn't a bit too close to it all, what with Miss Watkins being involved.'

'Well, Captain Turner. Will you be led by your head or your heart?'

'I know my duty, sir. UNIT first, always.'

'There you are, Major.'

'Sir.'

Turner glanced at Branwell, but he didn't look convinced.

Isobel sat at the window seat on her train, her forearms resting on the table as she watched the scenery whizz by. A wash of summer greens, broken by occasional bursts of concrete grey as they sped through another commuter town. The rest of the carriage was empty. She didn't recall it being empty when she boarded. She didn't recall boarding. But she knew she had to be on the train in order to get to her gig.

She placed a hand on her camera bag. She always kept it on

the seat next to her when travelling. It wasn't there. Maybe she'd popped it in the overhead racking? It had been a very early start for her, after all. She tried to think back. There was something about leaving the house…

The light outside suddenly changed. Moonlight reflected on the sea as she travelled along the coast. *Long journey*, she mused. Isobel felt suddenly exhausted, as if… Had she done the gig? She must have. She was on her way back to London. It was late. Very late. Jimmy would be waiting for her. At the door. Outside the door. Like this morning.

There was now someone seated opposite. She suddenly felt self-conscious. Was the rest of the carriage still empty? Isobel looked at the figure seated across the table from her. He hadn't been there before. But he had been outside her front door that morning. And he'd been the most terrifying thing she imagined she'd ever see. And he was there, now, again, with her on a train. Alone. Coming closer, and closer, his deathly green face set in a rictus grin of corruption.

Packer.

Hands grasped her arms as the face leaned in close. Isobel turned her head to the side and screamed.

She awoke. She was sitting in a chair in a room somewhere.

Packer was there with her, cold hands clasping her forearms, his face leaning in close and the stench of decomposition almost strangling the air.

Isobel turned her head to the side and screamed again.

Blackness engulfed her.

CHAPTER TEN

PROFESSOR WATKINS stepped back to admire his handiwork. The Cerebreton Mentor, Mk III. It had a linear beam transmitter which could be set to deliver either a narrow focus or a wide wash. This was overridden if the jack plug was in use, to prevent burn-out.

'Excellent work, Professor.'

He turned in surprise at Vaughn's voice. 'I didn't hear you come in.'

Vaughn gave no answer. He simply stared at the machine.

Watkins' grabbed it, protectively. 'How long have you been there?'

'Long enough to appreciate a genius at work.'

Sycophant, Watkins thought, although he wouldn't deny the label.

Vaughn continued. 'Amazing how quickly you constructed this. You seemed to take forever to build the others.'

'I was working under duress, unwillingly. It's easy to find ways to drag these things out. But this is the mark three and you know what they say, practice makes perfect.'

'Perfect,' echoed Vaughn, he approached and gently took the Cerebreton Mentor from Watkins' grasp, holding it up for examination as if it were a holy relic.

'Not yet,' Watkins warned. 'It needs calibrating.'

Vaughn looked directly at Watkins for the first time. Watkins noticed something around the edges of his eyes. And the smell. The stench of death.

'You need a test subject?'

'Ideally, yes. For an accurate calibration.'

Vaughn handed the machine back and turned to leave. 'I'll

have someone brought to you shortly.'

Watkins had a sudden thought. 'Vaughn...?'

'Professor...?'

'Did you drug me last night?'

'You were exhausted, Professor. I think the excitement of the day had been too much for you. Do you feel as if you were drugged?'

Watkins ran his tongue around the inside of his mouth. Despite the coffee, there was still a faint taste of something else.

'I'm... I'm not sure. But we can't work effectively together if I can't trust you.'

'Well, quite. We're partners, after all. Why not take another break now? You've earned it.'

The door closed behind Vaughn.

Watkins placed the machine on the lab bench and wiped his sweaty palms on his borrowed lab coat. He reached for the coffee pot but, having second thoughts, headed for the door instead. Locked.

There was another door opposite. He tried that too. The same.

He wandered back over to the coffee pot, his head asking questions he couldn't answer.

Private Hennessy poked his head into the ops room. 'Sergeant Major? You're wanted at the security reception.'

Nicholls left her post and headed out into the corridor.

'Any clues as to what's awaiting me, Hennessy? I'm not that keen on surprises.'

'UNIT scientist from New York, apparently. She has a pass and says the Brigadier's expecting her. Ordinarily, she'd have just walked straight in, but under the temporary additional security measures—'

'Yes, yes, yes,' spat Nicholls, gesturing him away with a flick of her hand. 'I drafted those measures. You don't need to quote them to me.'

'Sorry, ma'am.'

Nicholls followed Hennessy, feeling relieved. She'd posted Lance Corporal Enders to the new security desk as a way of giving her a responsible position without exposing her to operational updates from the field.

'Sergeant Major Nicholls?' the lady, dressed smartly in

civilian clothes, held out one hand to shake, whilst displaying her UNIT pass with the other. 'Dr Anne Travers. Good to meet you at last. The Brigadier speaks very highly of you.' Dr Travers looked from Nicholls to Enders and gave an approving nod. 'And it's particularly good to see a strong female contingent running things here in London.'

'Thank you, *Dr* Travers. You're here to see the Brigadier?'

'Stepping in as temporary scientific advisor. He's expecting me – except he's not. We last spoke yesterday, UK time, and I said I'd think about his offer and call him back today. I figured it was easier to assume I'd accept, so I went straight to the airport. Thought I might surprise him.'

'She's clean, ma'am,' confirmed Enders, placing the security wand back on the desk. 'And the luggage.'

'I should think so, too.' Dr Travers gave Nicholls a look and stepped aside to reveal a large suitcase. 'Anywhere I can store this for now?'

'Hennessy?' Nicholls snapped.

'Ma'am.' Hennessy jumped to attention and took the suitcase.

'Now, Dr Travers,' said Nicholls, leading her away from the security reception. 'If you'd like to follow me, I'll show you to the Brigadier's office.'

'Anne, please,' said Dr Travers once they were out of earshot of the others. 'I don't like reducing everyone to a title or a rank.'

Nicholls pulled a face. 'I'm not really supposed to be that informal, as an NCO.'

Anne smiled. 'All right. Just between us, then. Any other time you can call me what you want.'

Nicholls smiled.

'And what can I call you, off the record?'

'Heather.'

'Pleasure to be working with you, Heather.'

'About the Brigadier—'

'He's an old friend.'

'I should warn you, he's been at Whitehall this morning, so—'

'So, my appearance here is no doubt just the tonic he needs,' Anne finished.

Nicholls indicated the Brigadier's office door, at the far end of the corridor and hoped Anne was right.

*

Benton, Walters, and Wright gathered once again on the main approach road through the Community.

'All those chalets, and not one of them occupied,' said Wright, puffing out his cheeks. 'My feet are killing me.'

Benton shared a look with Walters, who eyed Wright sceptically.

'What's our next move then, Sarge?' asked Benton.

'Back to site HQ and report to Captain Turner. Then…' He shook his head and sighed. 'I'm still struggling to understand what's been going on here. Nothing makes sense.' He looked at Wright again. 'Least of all you and Potter.'

He turned and trudged off towards the gates. Benton and Wright followed just behind.

As the Compound perimeter drew closer, Benton looked for the sentry, but there was no sign of Cowper.

'Probably gone for a jimmy,' said Wright.

'Not that again,' grumbled Walters. 'You're obsessed.'

Cowper hadn't gone anywhere. As they approached, Benton spotted him lying on the grassy verge.

'On your feet, soldier!' he barked.

Cowper didn't move.

'Private Cowper!'

Still nothing. Benton jogged the remainder of the distance to the gates. They were unlocked and very slightly open. Benton could see from this distance that Cowper wasn't asleep. The angle of his head – a broken neck.

'Oh, bloody hell man,' muttered Wright.

'Lock the gates,' ordered Walters, looking around for potential threats.

Benton checked the body. There was no sign of any other injury. He did, however, spot tyre marks on the tarmac. He was sure they hadn't been there when they'd entered the Community earlier.

'Sarge,' he said, indicating the light soiling of tyre tread. Having seen it here, they could now see further evidence of it. The trail began the other side of the gates and travelled through, heading off around to the right. That was the most direct route back to the factory and main office building.

'Coming in or going out, I wonder?'

'Definitely coming in,' Benton confirmed. 'The road through

may be single lane, but the driver is favouring the left-hand side, see?'

Walters produced his radio. 'Greyhound Ten to Trap Four. Do you read me, over?'

There was a brief pause, then Potter's voice replied.

'Reading you loud and clear, Greyhound Ten. This is Trap Four. Go ahead, over.'

'Sentry position West Five found compromised. Sentry attacked and deceased, over.'

'Acknowledged, Greyhound Ten. I will issue a stretcher party, over.'

The response sounded oddly cold and business-like to Benton.

Walters continued. 'And sentry cover, over.'

There was a slight pause. 'Acknowledged. Is that everything, over?'

'No. There's evidence here of recent vehicular incursion. Anything reported by patrols, over?'

'Negative, over.'

'Check in with all surveillance patrols and sentries and then report back to me, over.'

'Acknowledged. Over.'

'We'll wait here and liaise with the stretcher party. Update me with their ETA. Out.'

'Sarge?' added Potter.

Walters raised the radio again. 'Greyhound Ten receiving, over.'

'Mr Chambers is here to see you, over.'

Walters' brow furrowed. 'Acknowledged, Trap Four. When had you intended to report this to me, over?'

'I figured you'd be back by now, over.'

'Tell him to stay there, I'll join you shortly. Out.' Walters turned to Benton and Wright. 'Maybe Mr Chambers can tell us where everyone from the Community has gone.'

Benton shook his head. 'This feels wrong, Sarge.'

'I know.'

'What's Potter up to back there?'

'Until we can get Chambers out of there, Trap Four is effectively compromised. Try radioing the stretcher party.'

Benton unclipped his radio. 'Greyhound Thirteen to stretcher party, come in, over?'

Static.

He spoke again, very precisely. 'Greyhound One Three to stretcher party, come in. *Over.*'

Still nothing.

'Try Potter,' said Walters.

'Greyhound Thirteen to Trap Four. Come in, over?'

Static again.

'Greyhound One Three to Trap Four. Come in. *Over.*'

Nothing.

Wright and Walters tried also, both with the same results. They couldn't raise anyone.

'You were right, Benton. Something is definitely wrong. Wright, you remain here and guard the gates.'

'What? After what happened to Cowper?'

'No argument. Keep your wits about you. Join me back at Trap Four once the relief has arrived.'

Wright looked like he'd been handed a death sentence. '*If* it arrives.'

Walters turned to Benton. 'We need to get hold of Captain Turner, give him a sitrep. One of those Community chalets must have a telephone connection – you can see the overhead wires. Get word back to the Warren, then join me at Trap Four.'

'Is it wise for us all to split up, Sarge?'

'Probably not, but there's a lot to do and only us to do it right now.'

'But if Trap Four *has* been compromised...'

'We'll just have to keep our wits about us.'

Walters set off and Benton turned to Wright, who was struggling to unlock the gates for him. How were they both UNIT corporals? Wright seemed such a liability, physically and mentally.

It was precisely then that Benton realised. It was so easy to blame Wright, to mock him and highlight his shortcomings. Too easy, in fact. Benton had his own imperfections – arguably every soldier did. He had deficiencies of which he was starkly aware. They made him feel vulnerable at times. He wondered how he'd be feeling if the tables were turned, and the finger of suspicion was pointed at him instead.

Right now, he had the ear of Sergeant Walters – they'd worked together several times since he'd joined UNIT. It was like being 'in' with the cool kids at school. That made it easy to victimise those on the outside. To bully them. And that's what he and Walters had been doing to Wright.

Like his initial reaction when Walters reported what Potter had said. It was ridiculous to think that Wright had strong-armed everyone into doing what he wanted. Somehow Walters had been won over, dismissing Wright's continual protestations of innocence.

Benton watched him now, as he wrestled cack-handedly with the lock and the gates. Only a master confidence trickster could engineer a façade so expertly. And Benton knew – everyone in UNIT knew – Corporal Gwyn Wright was, at heart, a decent bloke. They had been manipulated. Benton felt ashamed.

'Here, Gwyn,' he called. 'Let me help.'

Wright gave him a goggle-eyed look. 'Thanks, John.'

Benton smiled at him. 'Sorry about... all the *stuff*. Just be the best you can – that's all I do, that's all UNIT can expect from us.'

'I will – I do. It may not be much, but it's something.'

Benton slipped through and, telling Wright he wouldn't be long, he headed off to find the nearest chalet with a telephone line.

Benton hadn't stopped to think when he, Walters, and Wright were knocking on all the doors, but the Community was actually a pretty unnerving place. Essentially a ghost town – seemingly abandoned mid-activity. Behind the net curtains through some of the front room windows, he could see shadowy tableaux of ordinary life. But without pets, without people.

The silence bothered him. And he'd made the mistake of glancing behind at one point. It's an unfortunate truth that once you've glanced behind, the temptation to continue doing so at regular intervals is irresistible. He'd long since lost sight of Wright at the gates, as he wound his way through to the far left of the estate. That appeared to be where all the overhead wires were connected.

Common courtesy made him knock at the chalet door when he'd chosen his target, even though he knew there was no one in. He tried the door. Locked, but there was some give under pressure. A firm shoulder barge and he was soon inside.

'Hello?' he called, desperate not to appear to be breaking

and entering unduly. There was no response. The chalet didn't smell like a home, didn't smell *lived in*. But superficially it appeared that way. *Another concern for another time*, he thought.

He found the telephone in a corner and lifted the receiver. Nothing. He checked the connection. It was all good. He tried the receiver again. Still nothing.

That was when he heard the creak of the floorboards behind him.

Too heavy to be an animal.

Someone was there.

He tensed and replaced the telephone receiver as naturally as he could, balling his fist as he did so. He spun on the spot, crouching low as he moved in case whoever was behind him threw a punch.

It was a savvy move. An arm swung above his head. The figure – a man – was wearing the navy-blue overalls of an IE factory worker. Benton rose, smacking his fist into the exposed flank of his assailant. With a cry of pain, he cradled his fist. Was the guy wearing body armour? He felt like solid metal.

Before Benton had time to think further, a punch caught him right on the jaw, sending him staggering back against the telephone table and the rear window. Benton righted himself as quickly as he could and shoulder-barged the aggressor.

His shoulder met an equally solid barrier and jarred painfully. The man took a single step back, but that was the assailant's only concession.

The next thing Benton knew, he was picked up by the collar and waistband and hurled through the front window.

Dazed, Benton tried to get to his feet outside, but another blow sent him to oblivion.

CHAPTER ELEVEN

ISOBEL BLINKED back into consciousness. She hadn't dreamed this time – at least if she had she couldn't remember. She was alone, which was a huge relief. The recall of Packer was almost as terrifying as the real thing. He'd tormented her and Zoe plenty during their previous encounter. She knew from Jimmy that he'd died – and, perhaps shamefully, she'd found some pleasure in that.

Yet she'd seen him, up and about, not dead and buried. He'd been waiting for her outside her front door. The sense memory of his touch gave her the creeps. She'd lost consciousness. He may not be dead, but he sure as hell looked it.

Anyway, she thought, *at least he's not here now.*

Isobel had plenty of other problems without bemoaning the lack of a walking cadaver. She'd missed her agency gig, so she'd have some explaining to do there – although abduction should prove to be a pretty persuasive excuse. And where was she? There was a window with the blinds drawn. She took a look between the slats.

Isobel had been half-expecting what she saw. The view was slightly different but similar enough to last time for her to recognise it immediately. She was back at the IE Compound in the country. Only this time she didn't have anyone to talk to and no one to help her escape. If only there was some way of contacting Jimmy.

Isobel checked all around the room for anything to help her escape, eventually coming to the door. She'd assumed she was locked up in there and that was that. She joked to herself as she reached out to try the handle. *Wouldn't it be typical if I could have just walked out all along?*

It was locked.

*

Despite what he'd told Potter, Walters didn't head for the main IE building immediately. He had a niggling feeling that he'd been taken for a ride and that Corporal Wright was a clueless victim in all this. He hoped he'd be proved wrong, but not knowing what he was walking into he wanted some backup.

Three privates were on duty at the nearest security patrol checkpoint.

'Lovegood, Morris, I want you both with me.'

'Sarge.'

'Jeakins, if your radio works, get some backup. If not, you'll just have to manage on your own for now.'

'Sarge.'

Lovegood and Morris set off with Walters.

'Pardon me, Sarge, but what are we gonna do?'

'We may need to take back control of the site HQ.'

Walters, Lovegood, and Morris paused at a distance from the main IE building, housing their site HQ. Walters drew his pistol. The two privates brandished their rifles, looking for all the world like their lives depended on them. Maybe they did. They'd find out when they entered.

'Ready when you are, Sarge,' whispered Morris.

'Doesn't look like there's much going on,' said Lovegood.

Walters nodded. 'You two flank me. Only fire on my order. Let's move.'

The three of them marched across the open ground to the building's entrance, up the steps, and inside. It was a short walk through the reception area and along the corridor to the left. Trap Four was situated in an office on their right as they approached.

Without knocking, Walters grabbed the door handle and entered.

A suited figure he'd never seen before rose from behind a desk and offered his hand in greeting.

'Sergeant Walters, I presume. Welcome.'

There was no sign of Potter. Walters cautiously stepped forward to challenge the man. There was a flash of movement in his peripheral vision. Walters turned. He'd somehow missed the two overalled figures standing to either side as he'd entered.

They reached out and grabbed Morris and Lovegood, swiftly breaking the soldiers' necks with a deft movement and a sickly sound. The bodies dropped to the floor with a clatter.

Walters was surrounded. He'd walked right into a trap. He turned back to the man behind the desk, who smiled at him genially. Walters glared and trained his gun on the man.

'Where's Corporal Potter?' he demanded. 'What have you done with him?'

'My name is Chambers.'

Walters had already figured this to be the case.

Chambers continued. 'We wish you no harm.'

Walters indicated the two dead privates.

'True,' Chambers continued. 'But it's only you we want. Why not have a seat and be civilised?'

Walters wasn't going to fall for any charm. 'I'll ask again, where's Potter?'

'Out and about following instructions, I shouldn't wonder.' This was a different voice. It continued. 'You see, I knew we'd have a challenge with the sergeant, here.'

The new figure entered from another doorway. Walters had never met him, but he knew the man immediately. Tobias Vaughn.

Walters backed away to the side, trying to keep the rest of the room in his sights. 'What's going on here? You're dead.'

'Am I?' Vaughn looked mildly amused as he crossed to join Chambers.

'I've seen you in the morgue.'

Vaughn raised a finger. 'A temporary arrangement, nothing more.'

'What are you doing here?'

Vaughn shared a look with Chambers. 'Finally, an intelligent question.'

Walters split his gaze between those behind the desk and the men who'd killed Lovegood and Morris. They looked like IE factory workers, the sort of people he'd expected to meet in the Community. There was something solid and brutal about them – more than met the eye. They'd dispatched Lovegood and Morris with supreme ease, so maybe he wasn't far from the truth. He wondered if they'd also done for Potter, too.

They were joined by another new voice. Processed, electronic, yet with underlying human tones. 'Shall we kill him, Mr Vaughn?'

'Oh no,' Vaughn replied. 'The good sergeant is far more use to us alive.'

Walters' attention was drawn by a putrid stench, causing him to cough and retch. He soon discovered why.

Packer wasn't quite the man he used to be. *If he really is alive,* Walters thought, *he must be in excruciating pain.* Patches of skin around his eyes and ears, and down his neck, were decomposing. Sticky ooze was dripping from his lolling black tongue onto his uniform front and glistening unhealthily.

The cadaverous apparition was too much for Walters. He could look at such things in the morgue, but that was different. Seeing them up and moving about in some appalling mockery of life was another matter – one against the laws of nature. One even his service with UNIT couldn't make him countenance.

Walters swiftly brought his pistol to bear on the approaching Packer.

'Keep back,' he yelled. 'What the hell's going on here?'

Packer didn't respond, but Vaughn gave a hearty laugh.

'My dear sergeant. All of us here, apart from you, can live forever.'

Walters was swinging his focus from Vaughn to Packer, trying to keep a grasp on his sanity and figure out his next move.

'That?' he said, disgusted. 'That's not living, it's—'

Everything went black.

'Come on, come on...'

Wright muttered to himself under his breath as he paced back and forth before the gates, wondering where the stretcher party had got to. It was bad enough being left on his own, let alone with a dead comrade lying nearby. He periodically glanced through the metal-barred gates to see if Benton was returning. That would at least be a comfort – particularly as he seemed to have finally convinced the others that he wasn't the bad guy after all.

The day had already stretched into the afternoon. He'd missed lunch, not to mention his morning tea break. A glance at his watch told him he was well on the way to missing his afternoon tea break as well.

I'm likely to waste away at this rate.

He raised an arm as if assessing whether or not it had withered since he'd dressed.

There was a crash of breaking glass in the distance. He spun, bringing his rifle to bear and watching through the gates, but there was no sign of a target. No sign of any movement at all.

Probably Benton breaking and entering to use the telephone.

Convinced by his own logic, Wright relaxed a little. It wouldn't be long before Benton returned.

He was surprised, then, when he turned back to the Compound to find Corporal Potter approaching.

'Hey, Potter,' he called, glad to finally have some time to talk to him alone. 'What the hell's going on around here then? Why were you trying to stitch me up with the sarge, and where's the stretcher party for poor Cowper, here?'

Potter smiled. 'Why the rush to recover a dead body? It's not like he's going to get up again. Unless you believe in ghosts, Gwyn?'

Wright wasn't in the mood for frivolity, for a change. 'It's not about me, it's about respect for the deceased. Just a young lad, too. So unfair.'

'He knew what he was getting into when he signed up for UNIT.'

'Did he? Do any of us, really?' He paused and thought. 'Apart from me, that is. I'd had a bit of previous, you see.'

Potter nodded. 'I know. It's all around the barrack room. Can't keep secrets for long in the army, *Driver Evans*.'

'That's not my name or my rank, butty. Not anymore anyway.'

That was all he needed. His change of identity had been something of an open secret, but backbiting was rife and if he didn't quash such things then barrack room chatter might get out of control.

Potter seemed unmoved by Wright's spirited response. 'Where's Walters and Benton?'

'The *sarge* was going to meet up with you. If you're here, who's there with that Chambers?'

'Don't let that worry you.' He raised his rifle. 'Drop the gun.'

Wright dropped his rifle.

Potter continued. 'It would be easier if you came with me quietly.'

Wright had been anticipating treachery at some point. He found he was more hurt than surprised by it all.

'Why, Alec? Why would you betray UNIT like this?'

Potter gave an angry snarl. 'Don't try appealing to my better nature. Just move.'

Wright eyed Potter, running through options in his head very quickly. He had to get away, that was a given. The Community was a no go. He'd never get through the gates and under cover in time before Potter shot him. He had to get past his erstwhile colleague and hide in the Compound. He didn't enjoy the more physical side of soldiering, it was true, but needs must at times of desperation. He stepped towards Potter, raising his hands in surrender.

'All right,' he said. 'I'm—' He suddenly glanced over in surprise to where Cowper lay. 'What the—?'

Potter fell for it, looking over at the unmoving corpse to see what Wright had spotted.

Wright smacked Potter's rifle aside with his left hand and shoved him squarely in the chest with his right before running hell for leather for the undergrowth on the other side of the roadway. He only hoped he'd done enough to get to cover before risking a bullet in his back.

Corporal Potter was solidly built, but Wright's unexpected move totally unbalanced him. He floundered for some seconds, by which time his quarry was nowhere to be seen.

Frustrated by his own gullibility more than Wright's actions, he looked around, searching for tell-tale movements in the bushes and shrubs. The beige UNIT uniform was not great camouflage, as a rule. There was nothing. He didn't fancy playing cat and mouse through the IE grounds. He had a good idea where Wright would be heading, anyway.

He set off, along the road, back to the main building.

Corporal Wright peered out from behind a bush. He'd wait until Potter was out of sight, then creep through the gates and join Benton in the Community. Just then Wright spotted an IE worker approaching the gates, Benton thrown over his shoulder like a rag doll.

Dead too?

Potter quickly returned to the gates and let the worker through. There were hasty words between the two. Wright saw Potter pat Benton fondly on the cheek, but there was no sign of life from the corporal.

Potter took Benton from the IE operative, hoisting him over his own shoulder with ease. The IE operative then remained on sentry duty at the gates.

The IE lot were taking over again. But where the rest of the Community had gone remained a mystery.

Wright knew he must trail Potter. If only to confirm whether

Benton was still alive and could be rescued.

He clenched his jaw in frustration. How many more of the UNIT force had been turned into IE agents? It must have happened long before Walters arrived with his relief platoon. He could have kicked himself. Surely he should have noticed?

Remaining hidden as best he could in the undergrowth, Wright crept after Potter.

Wright hadn't been trailing Potter for long when another of the men in overalls approached. It seemed to be the standard dress for IE operatives. The man was clearly patrolling the area, doing UNIT's job. He hoped that more of his colleagues hadn't met the same fate as Cowper.

Potter handed Benton over to the man, presenting Wright with a dilemma. Who to follow? Thankfully, the point became moot. Potter and the IE operative headed off together.

Relieved of his cumbersome load, Potter would periodically stop, turn a full three hundred and sixty degrees and call out.

'I know where you are, Wright. I know you're out there. There's no escape. But carry on, you're only walking into a trap.'

The first time this happened, Wright froze, panicking that he'd made an incautious noise. But Potter simply turned in his circle, never attempting to stop and make eye contact, and then continued on his way.

When it happened again, and Potter delivered the same words with the same actions, Wright was reassured that he was still safe. Potter was trying broad-stroke tactics to unnerve him and force him to reveal himself.

Wright continued to trail Potter and the IE operative almost all the way to the main building, as far as he could remain concealed. Potter repeated his announcement once more, on the shingle forecourt, then he followed the IE operative and the still-unconscious Benton inside.

Wright stayed crouched in the bushes and considered his next move. If he approached the main building now, he'd almost certainly be spotted and taken. He checked his watch. 1600 hours. His stomach grumbled as a reminder that he'd eaten nothing since breakfast. If he was going to wait for the cover of darkness, that was still about six hours away. He couldn't remain where he was for six hours. He wasn't sure he could remain there for six minutes – his legs were already starting to cramp.

The factory canteen – that's where he needed to be. He could check on his colleagues there and also get a bit of grub. Hopefully. If any of the platoon were there, then maybe they could work out a plan to storm the main building. He nodded approval, as if giving himself moral support, then set off again.

'We're agreed, then?' said the Brigadier. 'I'll remain as active as I can, but if I'm not around don't wait for me. You're both empowered to take the decisions you need in order to get the job done.'

Turner saluted, as did Branwell.

'When Sergeant Walters reports in from the Compound, I'll take a judgment on heading down there also.'

'What if he doesn't?'

The Brigadier looked at Branwell. 'A judgment call will need to be made, regardless.

They were interrupted by a knock at the door.

'Busy,' called the Brigadier.

The door opened anyway.

'Not too busy to see me, I hope?'

They all turned to see the owner of the voice and Anne Bishop stepped into the room.

The Brigadier looked thrilled. 'Anne!' He rushed around from behind his desk to welcome her. 'I was expecting a call from you today. But this is far, far better.'

She smiled indulgently at the Brigadier. 'I figured it was quicker to fly over here and think on the way, Alistair, rather than add more delay. Has the situation changed?'

'Not in a positive way, no.' He turned and gestured to Turner and Branwell. 'Captain Turner, you know, of course.'

'Good to see you again, Mrs Bishop.'

'Dr Travers will do,' she said, 'after all I am here in a professional capacity.'

'And this is my new 2-in-C, Major Branwell, late of the RAF at Henlow Downs. His work was invaluable in fending off the invasion.'

'Pleasure to meet you, ma'am,' said Branwell.

'Thank you,' Anne said, 'but I'm not the Queen.'

Branwell looked momentarily flustered.

'Anne will be our scientific advisor—'

'Temporary.'

The Brigadier continued. '...For now, Major. You'll find she's a little unorthodox at times. Doesn't always like the military style.'

'Rather like Dr Flynn, then,' said Branwell wryly.

The Brigadier raised a brow at Branwell before turning back to Anne. 'Our temporary MO. The two of you will no doubt get on like a house on fire.'

'No doubt. Could we, perhaps, continue this over some strong coffee? I slept on the flight but not well and I could do with a pick-me-up.'

The Brigadier was about to say something, then appeared to have a change of heart. 'I have some... *clerical* issues to which I must attend. Can I suggest Captain Turner and Major Branwell show you around, starting at the NAAFI? The captain is leading on the Vaughn business, so he'll require your input.'

Anne smiled. 'Certainly, Alistair. I'm all yours, gentlemen.'

'I'll join you in the NAAFI,' said Branwell. 'I need to make a call first.'

'Come on, Dr Travers,' said Turner. 'I'll introduce you to Sylvie. After the Brigadier, she's probably the most important person in UNIT HQ.'

'NAAFI manager?'

Turner grinned and led her from the room. 'You got it.'

Benton came to lying on a padded surface. He tried to open his eyes, but the splitting headache he'd been left with prevented him from seeing anything. He tried to speak but his mouth and throat were parched. Whoever had knocked him out had done a very thorough job. All he could do was hold his head and groan.

There were voices nearby. Cold hands slid behind his back and propped him forward. A mug or glass was placed into his hand, and he instinctively drank from it. Water. Clean, fresh, cold. He sipped at first, allowing the liquid to soak into his dry mouth and throat. When he could, he began to swallow and very quickly drained the vessel.

It was taken from him, refilled, and given back. He downed this second lot immediately.

'More,' he managed to say.

He was given a third lot, which he downed immediately again.

The hand was removed from his back. Without the support, Benton collapsed again. He drifted in and out of consciousness. Occasionally he heard voices.

'Who is he?'

...

'Concussed.'

...

'Our fellow did too good a job on him, it seems.'

...

'Any likelihood of permanent damage?'

...

'He's no good to me unconscious.'

...

'I can't calibrate with a brain-damaged subject.'

Benton had no idea for how long he slept, but when he finally awoke properly and was able to open his eyes without flashes and pain, he found himself in a laboratory or technical workshop.

He was lying on a padded bench seat against the wall. There were three figures staring down at him. He recognised them all, but he couldn't quite believe what he was seeing. Tobias Vaughn, looking very unhealthy. Packer, looking like he should be six feet under. And Professor Watkins. UNIT had gone to great efforts not very long ago, to rescue the latter from the clutches of the other two. And here they all were, as large as life and twice as ugly. He sat up, slowly.

'Take it easy, Corporal,' said Vaughn.

Packer adopted an aggressive stance. 'And no sudden movements.'

Benton looked up at him. His voice sounded like it was being played in over a speaker, like a talking doll.

He put a hand to his mouth and nose, involuntarily. *That smell.*

'How's your head?' The question appeared to be from Watkins.

'It feels about as good as Packer's looks,' Benton mumbled through his hand.

Vaughn turned and started to cross the room away from them. 'You can begin, Professor. If he's *compos mentis* enough to crack jokes he should be able to withstand a little, shall we say, *tête à tête*, with the machine. Begin.'

CHAPTER TWELVE

'ANY FRIEND of Captain Turner's is a friend of mine,' said Sylvie, as she passed Anne a mug and a plate.

'Thanks, and it's a pleasure to meet you.'

Anne hoped the strong, sweet coffee and slice of chocolate cake would help perk her up. If not, she was sure she could keep trying. The NAAFI was pleasant enough and Sylvie Lowe was instantly likeable. She had an air about her – not quite matronly, more like an aunt that you could happily confide in.

She took a table and Turner followed. 'You're well-liked around here, Jimmy.'

He shrugged and smiled. 'I just do the best I can, that's all.'

Anne grinned into her coffee at his modesty. The aroma was good. She was already perking up just smelling it.

'How does our HQ compare to New York?'

'A lot less glass. A lot less shouting. A lot less posturing. Probably a lot more work goes on here as a consequence.'

'Would you like to be based here?'

Anne took a large mouthful of hot coffee and allowed it to slowly drain down her throat. 'You weren't wrong about this place,' she replied, 'but I'm not sure I'm ready to adopt the life of a mole just yet.'

Turner grinned. 'It does feel a bit that way at first, but you kind of get used to it after a while.'

The doors opened and Branwell joined them. His frustration shone like a beacon.

'I've got an old friend in the police,' he told them. 'Just made some enquiries about them maybe trying to help us out.'

'But General Ffowlkes-Withers said—'

'Yes, he did. I thought this might be a backdoor route. But

it seems Ffowlkes-Withers has done a thorough job. No assistance to be given to UNIT. No exceptions.'

'Tell me everything,' said Anne, leaning forward on her elbows. 'Assume I know nothing.'

Turner and Branwell looked at each other and nodded.

'Well,' said Turner. 'It all started when Benton got attacked.'

Anne laughed. 'I think I've heard that one before. The Brigadier reckons he has a "knack".'

Benton had been bound hand and foot and seated on a wooden chair in the middle of the room. Once there, Packer had secured him with a rope. That had been an ordeal for Benton in itself. He wondered what the hell was keeping Packer going. Something to do with Vaughn, no doubt.

Despite the sensory assault, Benton's head had cleared. Maybe there was something in the water he'd been given to drink.

'What is that thing?'

Watkins was tweaking and adjusting a Heath Robinson affair, affixed to a piece of wood about the size of a Haynes car manual, as far as Benton could see.

No response.

'Professor Watkins?'

Watkins looked up, his eyes wide in shock. 'You know me?'

'Yes, sir. I was part of the platoon that rescued you from Gregory in the car.'

Watkins looked away again, hurriedly. 'I'm sorry, I don't recall you.' He then fixed Vaughn with a glare. 'Did you know this?'

Vaughn gave an enigmatic shrug. 'It doesn't matter, surely? It might even be an advantage. Familiarity brings an emotional link of sorts, depending on the corporal's view of you – which may also have changed in the last minute or so.' He smiled, then grew suddenly intent. 'Use it, Professor. Use that link. Use the machine.'

Benton wasn't sure precisely what happened next. He felt a fuzzing, buzzing in his head – but not like the headache he'd recently lost. His whole body began to tremble as if he was no longer in control of himself.

He was vaguely aware of Watkins adjusting the machine he held. Slowly the trembling and the buzzing lessened. Instead,

Benton found he was gripped with sudden and strangely powerful feelings, seemingly on a whim.

He was disgusted by everyone else in the room, sickened. They were the epitome of everything hateful and loathsome about humanity.

No. No, they weren't. They were beautiful. The most serene and perfect beings he's ever laid eyes on. Benton was madly in love with them, all of them.

Yet just as suddenly he wasn't. The room, the people, everything all around him was utterly terrifying. He had to get away. But he couldn't. He couldn't move. They were going to kill him. There, Then. Horribly. His stomach churned. He turned his head to the side and vomited. It did no good. Unable to resist, Benton threw his head back and screamed in abject terror.

And yet – why was he staring at the ceiling? Why the hell was he stuck here when there was work to do? How had he got himself into this situation? Why wasn't the Brigadier here, taking command? Why wasn't the Compound flooded with UNIT troops? Why was it always down to *him* to get things sorted? He raged and swore and gnashed his teeth.

Benton tried to stand, only to find he was bent nearly double, and unable to walk. He had to free himself from his bonds. He flung himself backward onto the floor with as much force as he could muster. The wooden chair shattered beneath him. He felt his back jolt and a number of splinters in his thighs, but he still wasn't free. His hands were behind his back and his wrists and ankles were still bound. He began to thrash around, trying to loosen the bonds. Then he could get at whoever had done this to him...

...Only to find he didn't want to. He was happy as he was. Glad for the bonds. Relieved by the back pain and splinters, and content within himself. All was right with the world. It was a beautiful place. The figures around him – Watkins, Vaughn, Packer – they were beautiful souls, wonderful human beings. Utter perfection.

And then... he felt the trembling return to his body, the fuzzing and buzzing in his head once again.

'What... the... hell... is... happening... to... me?' he managed to hiss. And then blackness once again.

*

'Fascinating!' gushed Vaughn. 'Will he be under our control when he wakes?'

Watkins shook his head. 'I've had to release him, allow his brain to equalise, otherwise there might be permanent damage. The readings I took should enable me to calibrate the machine accurately.'

'How long?' snapped Vaughn, eagerly.

'An hour or so. These delicate adjustments can't be hurried.'

'Use the computer. I want everything recorded.'

Packer nudged the unconscious Corporal Benton with his boot. 'What do you want done with this?'

'Lock him up. He may be of further use to us at some point. And have some dinner brought up for the Professor.'

Watkins looked over at the departing Packer, dragging Benton behind him.

Vaughn appeared at his side. 'Come, Professor, let's not worry about peripheries. Concentrate on the job in hand.'

'What shall we do next, once it's calibrated?'

'You need to be immune to the effects yourself. How did UNIT avoid the invaders control signal?'

'A neuristor, worn at the back of the neck. Should be simple enough to replicate.'

'Good.' Vaughn stepped back and smiled. 'And then, we shall give your wonderful machine a live test.'

'On whom?'

'Wait and see, Professor. Wait and see.'

Turner drove what had become for him a familiar route, back to Isobel's house in St James' Gardens. Of course, it had only been the Watkins' abode temporarily, while Anne was away. Now she was back she was keen to take look at the old place once again.

But that wasn't specifically why she was in the passenger seat. Anne had already checked in at a local hotel in Waterloo. Not the most salubrious establishment, but certainly not the worst the area had to offer, and within easy walking distance of the Warren.

No, their journey had another purpose. Anne had listened patiently while Turner, and occasionally Branwell, had brought her up to speed on the Vaughn situation. It hadn't taken all that long. They didn't know very much, and that was the main problem.

Turner was keen to extrapolate possibilities from what they knew and try to create leads that way. Branwell was against guesswork and was focusing instead on interrogating the security systems at HQ. Anne could see both sides but was inclined to sit with Turner. If UNIT weren't going to get support from the civil authorities, they had to take the initiative. If that meant stumbling once or twice then so be it.

That led to where they were now, approaching St James' Gardens. Anne reasoned that there might be clues Turner had missed in the house when he discovered that Isobel had been abducted. It was the most recent event, and that would be where the scent was warmest.

'Present circumstances excepted, of course,' said Anne as they drove. 'But is everything going well between you and Isobel?'

'Yes. Thank you, it is. She's quite a spark.'

'I don't know her very well. We've only really met in passing.'

Turner said nothing in response to this, as he concentrated on the road.

She continued. 'You're not the first to have met someone in the course of duty, as I'm sure you know.'

'Yes, you and Major Bishop, for a start.'

'Indeed. And it's not always easy. Relationships look different to outsiders.'

'The Brigadier knows I'm primarily a UNIT man.'

'It's not always the Brigadier you have to convince.'

Turner gave a light chuckle. 'I think Major Branwell is a little sceptical. But he's only just joined us, and I can understand him not wanting to accept everything at face value.'

'That's very magnanimous of you, Jimmy. I didn't tell you this, of course, but it's your judgment he's concerned about. I suspect he's also a little frustrated being assigned to HQ duties while you're off out in the field.'

'I'll watch my back. Thanks.'

With that, they pulled onto the side street and parked up almost precisely where Tracy had parked earlier that day.

They were out of the Land Rover and crossing the road when Turner spoke again. 'You have a key, I presume?'

'No. Well, I do, but it's at my home in Edinburgh. I don't usually carry it around with me on my travels, and a trip to London wasn't on the cards…'

Turner stopped between two parked cars. 'But I don't have

one either. Isobel and I haven't been going out all that long.'

Anne glared at him. 'Credit me with a little common sense, please. I don't have a key, but I know where one is. Always have a back-up. I wouldn't have dragged you out here otherwise.'

'Sorry,' he said, sheepishly.

'Now, avert your gaze, please.'

He did. Looking around to check they weren't being obviously watched, Anne moved the heavy plant pot, lifted the loose flagstone, removed the key, and then replaced everything as before.

'All done,' she said, slipping the key into the lock and gently turning it.

'Where did you find that?'

'Now, now, Captain Turner,' she said with jovial haughtiness. 'I'm not about to reveal such secrets to you. Think of poor Isobel's reputation. Can't have you letting yourself in at all hours.'

He rolled his eyes. 'I'm hardly the Milk Tray man.'

Anne smiled at him teasingly. 'And that, my dear James, is precisely the point!'

They went inside.

Anne did her best to conceal her surprise and displeasure at what she found inside her family home. They had never been a particularly tidy family, but somehow one's own disorder was always less conspicuous than someone else's. And as for the state of the wall in the hallway...

Turner showed her Isobel's discarded overnight bag and camera equipment, and the message she'd left scribbled above the telephone table – including why it was there.

'You can't lose a wall, indeed,' Anne scoffed. She noticed the pained expression on Turner's face and immediately regretted her tone. He really must be very fond of Isobel. 'Sorry,' she said. 'Was there anything else of note?'

'Half-eaten toast in the kitchen. To be honest, the place is still pretty much as I found it.'

'Let's keep it that way for now. I presume the professor worked in what was my father's old laboratory?'

'The basement? No, Watkins prefers to be above ground, so he's using the room at the back.'

It was a mess. Of course it was a mess. She shouldn't have

expected anything less. It was the workspace of a fussy old genius. Behind the door, however, was a kind of admin area. Anne saw ink stamps, paper, envelopes, a chequebook, and a pile of letters. The letters were all addressed to Professor Watkins. To one side was a sheet of A4 with a long list of names. She recognised them all. A mix of eminent individuals in the scientific community, along with research organisations UK-wide, within the public and private sectors. All of the lines had ticks against them. Some of the names had been neatly struck through.

Anne looked again at the pile of letters. It was private correspondence, and she knew she was being nosy, really, but they were also investigating two disappearances. She told herself she couldn't afford to leave any stone unturned. She picked up the letters and began to flick through them.

It was clear almost immediately that the names that had been struck through on the list were those from whom Watkins had received a response. He'd written to everybody asking for work, research opportunities, or lecturing vacancies. The responses he'd received made for uncomfortable reading. Anne knew when someone was being fobbed off, either with excuses or false hope for the future. Hell, she'd had to do the same herself from time to time. No one wanted Watkins.

But what had caused him to become blacklisted? He'd been slightly odd when he'd taught her at Cambridge, but frankly, that was par for the course in the scientific community. Obsessives, eccentrics, come one, come all.

Could it be his connection with Vaughn and International Electromatics? All the letters post-dated the invasion and word would surely have spread that he'd been working on research projects for IE. But it was too soon for a shift of this magnitude. Scientific research advanced at pace, but community attitudes tended to lag for a while unless there were immediate financial pressures. And the tone of some of the responses Watkins had received suggested to Anne that more was at play.

She recalled her comments to the Brigadier when they'd spoken about him interviewing for UNIT. She realised it wasn't Watkins or who he had most recently been working for. It was his research, his myopic focus on emotional manipulation. He'd worked himself into a corner and now he couldn't get out because he was simply too dangerous to employ.

And what does a dedicated research scientist do when no one else will employ them? They take the only door that opens to them.

'Any luck?' Turner's words dragged Anne from her thoughts.

'Not for Isobel, but I've got a few thoughts about the professor. Are you sure he was abducted?'

'He's not been seen since he left the Warren. He never returned here. We know he's missing. It's an extrapolation, I agree, but I don't think it's too far-fetched to believe that he's been abducted,' Turner finished on a shrug.

'I'd lay any money on him working for Vaughn again, and willingly, too.'

'After last time? That doesn't make sense.'

'You're being rational. He's not. He wants to keep doing what he loves.' She held up the sheet of paper containing the names. 'This list tells us no one else will employ him to do that.'

'But Vaughn will.'

'Probably easier to sell your soul to the devil when you've worked for him once already.'

'Then why abduct Isobel, if not to hold her to ransom?'

It was Anne's turn to shrug. 'Extra leverage, maybe? Some people like to hold all the cards.'

'All right, but it still doesn't tell us where they are, or where they've taken Isobel.'

'You say IE London has been totally decommissioned?'

'It's a concrete shell now, nothing more.'

'And we don't know of any other bolt-hole IE created during the height of their operations?'

'Not that we ever found out about. And we had them under observation for quite some time before it all kicked off.'

Anne held her palms out open. 'Then there's only one place they can be.'

Turner shook his head. 'But we've got a full assault platoon there. And we've had a squad there the whole time. How could they still be operating without us knowing?'

Wright finally made it to the factory canteen. There was no obvious movement inside, but another of the overalled IE operatives was patrolling around the exterior.

As with the main building, there was no cover approaching

the canteen entrance. *Typical*, he thought, but then also, *why should there be?* No one should need that level of stealth in order to obtain a pie and chips for lunch. Wright watched the patrol, timing the route so he knew precisely how long he would have while the operative was out of sight.

All or nothing. There was no going back once he started. Only halfway across the approach did Wright even consider that the canteen entrance door might be locked. A wash of panic swept over him. He came to a halt before the door and pulled. It wouldn't open. Frantically he tried again. Still, it wouldn't budge. The IE operative was due to appear again any second. Then Wright saw the 'push' sign. The door swung inwards easily, without a sound. He nearly wept with relief as he collapsed on the cold floor inside, hidden from view.

He was alone. Ensuring he couldn't be seen by the patrol, he gingerly crept about. Kit and equipment were all there, but of the soldiers, there was no sign.

Wright was gripped by sudden hunger and thirst. Apart from the occasional lapse, panic and adrenaline had largely covered for the fact that he hadn't eaten or drunk anything since breakfast. Faced with the opportunity to rectify that, Wright indulged himself freely.

Having eaten and slaked his thirst, fatigue reared its head. He found his cot, tucked away in the corner where he'd set it up. *Just a quick nap*, he told himself, *to help the energy levels.*

Branwell glared at the CCTV monitors, as if by force of will alone he could browbeat the footage into revealing the secrets he sought. He'd been through it all several times already.

Nicholls watched him, wondering if she could – or should – offer to help in any way.

'Who's that?'

The words took her by surprise. She almost scuttled to join him. 'Private Lamb, sir. He's on nights this week.' She checked the time and date on the screen. 'That'll be him arriving for his shift.'

'Not him, *him*.' Branwell pointed to the top right hand of the screen where there was little more than a dark fuzzy blur at present. 'Watch.'

Branwell ran the footage back a few seconds, then played it through again. If you didn't know someone was there, you'd be forgiven for not noticing it – which must have been what had happened so far because Nicholls was certain the footage had been reviewed at least twice already.

A hooded figure followed Lamb through into HQ. He, or she, was almost perfectly camouflaged into the grainy background, betrayed only by a half-glimpsed nose and chin.

'Interesting. Hennessy?'

'Ma'am?'

'Check access control records. I want to know who entered HQ immediately after Private Lamb two nights ago.'

'No one did, Ma'am.'

'What are you, psychic?' barked Branwell.

'No, sir, but I've already checked the data myself today. Twice. Private Lamb was the last of the night rota staff to arrive for duty that day.'

Branwell looked at his watch, then at Nicholls. 'We'll see what he's got to say for himself when he arrives later.'

CHAPTER THIRTEEN

VAUGHN THREW open the laboratory door and strode in. Watkins staggered in surprise, nearly dropping the neuristor he'd been adapting. Up to now, Vaughn had been distinctive by his stealth. In fact, everyone operating within the main IE building had, out of necessity, to hide from UNIT. What had changed, he wondered.

'Are we ready for a live test yet?' Vaughn demanded.

'I believe so. Here,' Watkins handed Vaughn a neuristor.

He brushed it aside. 'I don't need that.'

Watkins gave him a sceptical look. 'There's no telling how the Cerebreton Mentor might affect you.'

'I'm immune. You don't think I'd have tried to take over the world and still be susceptible to such chicanery, do you? Grant me that much common sense, at least.'

As he fitted his own neuristor to the back of his neck, Watkins recalled being offered an audio rejection implant a while ago. Like the offer of a cybernetic body, he'd declined.

Night had fallen outside.

'Come,' said Vaughn, with a flourish. 'Let's get your... what do you call it? Cerebreton Mentor?' He smiled, broadly, clearly relishing the moment. 'Let's get it connected up to the internal public address system and test it.'

Watkins felt a twinge of excitement himself. This would be a major moment for him and a true ratification of his work.

Isobel was thoroughly bored. She'd sat, wandered around, laid down on the hard floor, laid down on the desk, slept, dozed, cried. By this point, she was virtually catatonic. She was, then, quite surprised when a sudden feeling of elation gripped her.

She'd not felt this happy for some time. She found herself calling out her positivity, giving voice to how happy she felt.

One of Vaughn's goons unlocked her door. He didn't look any more or less happy than usual. Isobel was glad it wasn't Packer visiting again. Wordlessly, she was guided from the room and led away. No force was used, but she found she was unable to resist. It was as if the extreme emotional state took away her free will and left her susceptible.

She heard a loud cheer from somewhere. It made her happy to know that other people were also happy.

Wright awoke with a start, certain he'd heard a loud, distant cheer. Whatever it was, there was nothing now except the darkness. Several hours must have passed. He cursed himself, but then remembered that the cover of darkness was what he'd been waiting for in order to sneak into the main building. He felt refreshed after a meal and a sleep – perfect for a desperate rescue attempt against the odds to try to save the day. He still didn't relish it, though.

As his eyes gradually adjusted to the darkness of the canteen, he began creeping about slowly, making his way to the entrance without colliding with anything noisy. The patrolling IE operative was using a torch, so he could take his cue from that. Again, he watched them pass a few times, timing the route to check for consistency. Then, he pulled the door open and slipped out, tearing across the ground to his previous hiding place several hundred yards away.

The loud cheer was also heard by Vaughn and Watkins in the main communications room. It had come from the direction of the factory gymnasium.

'You hear that, Professor?'

'I need visible proof!' snapped Watkins.

Vaughn smiled. He seemed remarkably unconcerned for someone who, only minutes before, had been so demonstrably keen. 'You shall have proof, Professor. It's being brought here now.'

'One of your UNIT prisoners?'

There was a knock at the door.

'Oh no, Professor. I've brought you someone far better than that. Enter.'

The door opened and one of Vaughn's factory workers escorted a figure into the room. A girl. The expression on her face showed that she was very happy and suggestive – but not in a recreational drug-induced way.

Watkins was embarrassed that it took him several seconds to register that the girl was Isobel! He hadn't expected her to be there, so he hadn't been looking out for her. He silently mouthed her name and turned to Vaughn.

'You've not harmed her?'

'Why ever should I? Her current state is solely down to you.'

Watkins scoffed. 'After last time—'

'Last time was different. We've already established that. She was… my insurance. I don't need insurance this time. Do I?'

The question sounded like an afterthought. Watkins chose to ignore it. 'Then what's Isobel doing here?'

'Surely, she's safer here, with us. I thought you might like to have her close, being family. It stops anyone else using her to get at you.'

Watkins licked his dry lips. Isobel's presence made him feel unaccountably nervous. 'Yes, I suppose that makes good sense.'

Vaughn stepped closer. 'And besides, is she not a suitable test subject?'

'I don't really think so.'

'Because she's your niece? A little too close to home, is it?'

Watkins struggled to find his words. 'Not at all. I just…'

'You'll need to curb these scruples, Professor. No matter where your niece is, when the signal – your signal – is boosted nationwide, she'll fall under instantly, the same as everyone.'

'Yes, but…'

'Or were you planning on protecting her, somehow?'

'I… err…'

'Because I'm afraid she's too close to the UNIT organisation to be allowed to remain at large when we move into the next phase.'

'Yes, I appreciate that. It's a shame, really. I don't like to stand in the way of youthful dalliance. Maybe she's better off under the influence.'

'I think so,' said Vaughn, levelly. 'I have a suspicion that she wouldn't approve of your actions.'

As if inspired by his own words, he leaned forward and

adjusted the dial on the Cerebreton Mentor to *disgust.*

Isobel had never felt so powerless before. So violated. She was aware and yet seemingly lacking in control over her emotions and over herself. It wasn't mind control, because she could think. But she couldn't *act* on those thoughts. Her feelings were all over the place and bore no connection to her situation. The frequency and randomness with which they changed suggested they were under the control of others. As a consequence, she was left with a sense of disparity. Her feelings and her thoughts were at odds and in the confusion her body barely responded to either.

There was Uncle Joseph with Tobias Vaughn. They were fiddling with some sort of nutty lash-up. Her uncle looked surprised to see her. For her part, she suspected he'd be here. That's why she'd been abducted. What she hadn't expected to encounter was him being here so willingly. Something had changed within him. It must have.

Vaughn was supposed to be dead. In fact, he looked dead, but nowhere near as dead as Packer. And there was the background stench already. Decomposition, corruption, decay. What were these IE zombies up to?

Isobel stopped feeling disgusted as quickly as she had started, just as the feelings of joy had come and gone earlier. Yet in her thoughts, she was still disgusted. Disgusted and angry. Only she couldn't manifest that because her brain was telling her she was surprised instead.

Presumably, she looked surprised because Vaughn acknowledged it and her uncle looked smug. Her uncle, with whom she'd been living. Who she regarded as a surrogate parent. In whom she'd always had the utmost trust. Isobel stood there, feeling like nothing more than a shop window dummy under their gaze.

'Private Lamb!'

Guilt flashed over his face as Nicholls barked his name. 'Sorry, Ma'am, I'm not late again, am I?'

'Not at all. Follow me.'

She led him into the ops room, where Major Branwell was waiting. Lamb looked even more confused.

'Private Lamb?'

'Sir.'

'Two days ago, Lamb. Who followed you into HQ when you arrived for duty?'

'No one did, sir.'

Branwell indicated the hazy image frozen on the CCTV monitor. 'Then who was that?'

'Corporal Potter, sir.'

'Corporal Potter?' Nicholls was aghast. 'But he's been at the Compound.'

'He was outside HQ when I arrived. Said he'd forgotten something important and asked me to help. If you recall, Ma'am, I did mention it because it made me late for duty.'

Branwell turned and glared at Nicholls. 'Well, Sergeant Major?'

She held her own. 'I remember. But as far as I knew, Potter was at the Compound, so I dismissed the story as a poor excuse.'

Branwell seemed to accept this. 'What did Potter have you do, Lamb?'

'He said Captain Turner had asked him to bring up a data conversion device from the old IE factory. It needed to be placed in the computer room.'

'So that's what you did?'

'Yes, sir. Is there a problem, sir?'

'That remains to be seen.'

There were no lights visible around the Compound, and Wright found himself emboldened by this. He quickly found his way back to the main IE building. There were hints of lights on inside, around the edges of window blinds. He crept across the shingle forecourt, not wanting to raise the alarm through careless footfall.

As the shingle crunched quietly beneath his feet, a floodlight snapped on, capturing Wright in its heartless glare. He found himself grasped by many strong hands, with no hope of escape, and led off towards the main building.

'Thanks,' he muttered. 'I was heading here anyway.'

He was led through the ground floor to a set of back stairs. A few comments on the way went unanswered, so he stayed quiet and noted possible escape options instead. The stairs led up and down. His group went down. They descended two floors to a basement level, lit by dim sodium-orange bulbs swinging back and forth at a high level.

One of the operatives approached a nearby door and unlocked it. Immediately a figure in a khaki uniform inside charged him. The operative didn't budge, simply absorbed the attack, grabbed the uniformed assailant by the shoulder, and threw him back. There was a clatter as the figure collided with whatever else was inside.

Wright was thrown into the cell also. He looked up from the flagstone floor to find Sergeant Walters and a battered and bruised Benton staring down at him from either side.

'You're both alive!' he said, with genuine relief. 'Bloody hell, butties, we've got problems.'

Anne had anticipated stopping off at her hotel after the St James' Gardens trip if only to freshen up. Instead, the adrenaline rush – or possibly Captain Turner's adrenaline rush – was carrying her through successfully. They returned to HQ and headed straight for the ops room.

'Lamb, is Sergeant Major Nicholls still here?'

Nicholls appeared from behind the open door. 'You should know by now, sir, I don't go home. I gave up a life outside of UNIT months ago.'

Anne liked Heather a little more each time she saw her.

Turner didn't openly acknowledge the sarcasm. 'Any update?'

'Yes. And no. Tried to get a heli flyover, but it was already too dark. It's prepped to try again at first light. But Major Branwell has discovered something, courtesy of Private Lamb, here.' Heather turned to Anne. 'He asked if you would join him in the computer room as soon as you returned.'

'I'll show you the way,' said Turner, marching off.

They found Branwell examining a small box on the side of one of the big reel-to-reel analogue units in the computer room. It was about the size of a Sellotape dispenser and was humming gently. A red lead from the base of the box was jacked into an input socket on the computer.

Before Branwell could even acknowledge their presence, Anne rushed over and began scrutinising the device. Branwell filled them in, and Turner returned the gesture.

'We can be thankful, then, for Lamb's honesty and your keen vision, sir.'

'It's a shame Nicholls didn't pick up on it at the time.'

'True,' Turner nodded. 'But her actions were perfectly understandable.'

'This is of IE manufacture,' said Anne. She had the lid off the box and was examining the exposed parts. 'I'm trying to work out if it's safe to remove.'

'Do you know what it's doing?' asked Branwell.

'Monitoring, converting to digital, and broadcasting, as far as I can tell.'

'That's a lot for one small box,' said Turner, somewhat wryly.

'Trouble is...' Anne reached into her handbag and produced a screwdriver. 'If I pop this off and deactivate it, they'll know we've found them out.'

'They?'

She looked at both men, squarely. 'International Electromatics.'

'Was this what compromised our systems and allowed Vaughn and Packer to escape?' Branwell asked the question with a tone that suggested he already knew the answer.

'I'd say it emitted the signal that reactivated their bodies, too.'

'I see.'

'And if I leave it connected it will continue to interfere with our systems, compromise our data, and all sorts.' Anne paused while an idea formed in her head. 'Unless... Could one of you boys find me a length of copper wire?'

Branwell spotted a reel of it in the corner of the room. 'How much do you need?'

'About twelve inches. Just enough to create a feedback loop.'

'A what?' asked Turner as Branwell snipped off the requested length.

Anne took the wire and connected one end of it to a circuit at the top of the box, looping the other end around underneath and connecting it just beyond the input wire. She then removed the jack from the computer unit. The parasitic box continued to function. 'There. It's feeding on – reporting on – its own activities now, not ours.'

Turner licked his dry lips. 'Won't they notice?'

'Eventually. It depends if they have someone constantly monitoring the data feed at their end.'

He looked at Branwell. 'Next problem – Corporal Potter.'

Back in the ops room, Nicholls was trying to raise Trap Four on a tapped line. After what seemed like an age, the call was answered.

'Sergeant Walters?'

'Corporal Potter, Ma'am. The sergeant is over at the Community. Mr Chambers invited him for a drink, I believe, after they sorted out the access issues earlier.'

Turner's expression told Anne how much he believed this. 'What about Corporal Benton, or Corporal Wright?'

'They've gone too, sir. All very friendly.'

'You must feel left out.'

'Not really my scene, sir,' Potter replied. 'Besides, someone's got to stay on duty.'

Anne mouthed, 'Spin him a yarn.'

Turner frowned then nodded. 'I received your daily report. Still quiet there, then?'

'Nothing happening at all, sir,' came the workmanlike reply. 'Only the patrols going around.'

'All right. Well, we're following up on some other leads, so things might change. There's an unconfirmed rumour that Vaughn and Packer are staying at a hotel in Rhyl. Makes sense for them to try to hide away in full sight, somewhere public and remote. We're liaising with the civil authorities, but we might need to pull everyone out and send them there instead.'

'Yes, sir.'

Turner looked at Anne, who looked at Nicholls. The three of them nodded their agreement. They'd heard enough.

'Thank you, Trap Four. Trap One out.' Turner replaced the handset. 'You're sure that line was tapped at their end, Savage?'

'Yes, sir,' Corporal Savage nodded. 'There was a distinctive click.'

'That was careless,' said Anne.

Turner looked concerned. 'And I know full well that Walters wouldn't have gone off socialising, not after the briefing I gave him. Benton neither for that matter.'

'What's our next move, sir?' asked Nicholls.

'I need to head down to the Compound. Potter has been compromised. Vaughn must be there. And if he's there, Professor Watkins and Isobel surely will be too.'

Chambers nodded at Potter in the Compound HQ and replaced the telephone handset.

'Did you get that, Mr Vaughn?'

'Yes. I hear it's very nice in Rhyl at this time of the year. A transparent deception, nothing more. Make ready to receive further UNIT operatives. They will make excellent recruits.'

'And Potter?'

The UNIT corporal sat gazing across, waiting for instructions.

'They'll know he's been compromised. Post him somewhere inconspicuous until we can use him again.'

Potter silently stood and made his way from the main building, his instructions received.

Anne was seated to one side. She watched as the Brigadier looked up from his desk at Turner and Branwell before him.

'Blast this whole business. No wonder we've been getting nowhere with IE in control at both ends.'

There were nods all around.

'None of which is going to make my report any easier.' He gave a frustrated sigh and shuffled some papers.

'Sir,' said Branwell, looking uncomfortable. 'I know it's extreme, and I'm not suggesting we do so without trying to get our lads out first, but if it's a lost cause couldn't we get the RAF to flatten the site?'

Anne exhaled a lengthy breath. New boy, looking to prove himself – dangerous ideas.

The Brigadier reached into a drawer and drew out a thin manilla file. Wordlessly he passed it over to Branwell who opened it and scanned the few pages within.

He snorted. 'More politics.'

Anne grabbed the file. Inside were several government memos regarding lobbying from Human Rights organisations to protect the IE workers, and some vague interest from foreign multinational conglomerates who might take up the site. The IE Factory Compound was an asset and the instructions were clear: it was not to be damaged.

'So, you see,' said the Brigadier at last. 'Even if we wanted to, bombing the site is out of the question.' He turned to Captain Turner. 'Do we think we've lost the whole platoon?'

'At the moment, sir, there's nothing to confirm we have, but at the same time—'

'Nothing to say we haven't. Yes, I see.'

'I think it's best I get there, soon as, and in strength.'

The Brigadier puffed out his cheeks. 'I'll need to requisition more men from the regulars, which means…'

'General Ffowlkes-Withers.'

'Yes.' He glanced at the clock. 'It's too late to get a decision tonight.'

'This could be urgent, sir.'

'I know, Jimmy, but there's only a squad available. If you head down there now and run into trouble, that's not going to have helped anyone.'

'Besides,' said Anne, 'I'm going to need some sleep first.'

'You?' Major Branwell's expression suggested he'd spoken hastily, but honestly.

Anne stood. 'You have a problem with that?'

'Are you field trained?'

'Miss Travers is perfectly capable, Major. If you have any concerns, I suggest you direct them to me.'

Branwell looked from Anne to Turner and then to the Brigadier. 'Sorry, sir. This mission could be vital. I want us to send the best people, without risk of compromise.'

'Your opinion is noted, Major, but I've made my decision. Carry on, Miss Travers.'

'We don't know what we're dealing with yet. If Watkins is collaborating willingly, it'll be with something along the lines of his most recent research – emotional responses and manipulation. I'll need to assess the situation if we're going to require countermeasures.'

'Having said *that*,' offered the Brigadier, 'if anyone reports in overnight and gives us a better picture of the situation, we'll reconsider.'

Branwell looked unconvinced.

Turner looked disappointed.

'We'll get Isobel out okay, Jimmy, don't worry,' the Brigadier added with a smile. 'Now, since we're all supposed to be off duty, I suggest we retire for a good night's rest. I suspect we'll have a challenging few days ahead.'

Watkins stared at the door as it closed behind Isobel. He was not happy about this development. Vaughn, meanwhile, was obsessed with the Cerebreton Mentor, stroking its contours reverently.

'If the range is dictated by the transmitter, surely this very machine could be used to, erm, *improve* everyone in the world?'

Watkins pursed his lips and shook his head. 'With a machine this size the effect would be spread too thinly. I am concerned that it is almost at its limits here in the factory complex.'

As if timed to perfection, the Cerebreton Mentor chose that moment to fizz, spark and die in a cloud of smoke.

Vaughn's eyes flashed with anger. 'While it remains inoperative, we are vulnerable. Remember that.'

Watkins began to fuss over the burnt-out components. 'It can be fixed.'

'We must at least cover the whole Compound.'

'I know.'

'And for worldwide coverage…?'

'A much bigger model is required, that's all. Or more likely a sequence of bigger models, working in sympathy.'

Vaughn almost chuckled. 'How very apt. You have everything you need?'

'I believe so.'

'Then proceed with all speed, my dear fellow. We'll grant our test subjects a little respite. Meanwhile, I'll see what our data feeds are telling us about UNIT's movements.'

In equal measure exhilarated, exhausted, and bothered by Isobel's proximity, Watkins allowed himself to be led back to the laboratory.

CHAPTER FOURTEEN

'**Hey!**' **Walters** banged on the door. 'When are you going to let us out of here?'

Wright was tending to Benton's wounds as best he could with the three handkerchiefs they had between them, plus the remains of a jug of water. It was clear that Benton had not only received a thorough going-over, probably by a group of thugs, but his head had also been messed with. Every now and then he'd give an odd nervous reaction to no particular stimulus.

That was before the odd feelings had begun for them all.

First had been joy, then disgust. The emotional responses seemed to prevent Walters from being able to think clearly or take any action. Afterward came a kind of cooling off or come-down period of inactivity as his brain reset itself. Then the physical exhaustion kicked in. Muscles and joints ached like the morning after a rigorous route march.

Wright seemed to be suffering the most, being physically the weakest of the three. Benton's brain seemed to be taking a little longer to reset. Walters felt it was unfair to draw any conclusions from that.

His foot nudged a tray on the floor. Food and drink must have arrived while they were under the influence.

'Come and get yourselves some grub, boys. Should help you feel better.'

'What the hell's going on, Sarge?' For once, Wright's nervousness was totally in context.

'I dunno, Wright, I—' Walters paused as he gingerly squatted by the tray. Underneath an overturned mug there were three small, round electronic devices. They had a self-adhesive pad on one side. He'd seen something like them not too long ago. They helped protect the wearer against the invader's control signal.

Wright squatted opposite. 'Here, what the bloody hell is this?'

Walters thought about the strange feelings they'd all experienced. He made a very quick decision. 'Take one. Stick it at the back of your neck like this.'

He showed Wright.

'What's it do?'

'Protect us, hopefully,' said Benton, applying his.

Succumbing to peer pressure, Wright affixed his own. 'Come on then,' he said. 'Can I get Radio Luxembourg on this like?'

'If I've assumed correctly, they should counteract whatever that psychic influence was.'

Benton frowned. 'And they were on the refreshment tray?'

Walters nodded. 'Someone is trying to help us.'

Tobias Vaughn stared at the data readouts on his wall screens. He scowled and looked at Packer. Packer's degraded state made it impossible to read his expression until he spoke.

'It's just the same thing on loop. What does it mean?'

Vaughn deactivated the screens. 'It means that our little incursion has been rumbled, Packer.'

'What do we do now? UNIT will be moving against us. But how soon?' He sounded nervous. As a kind of token gesture, his hand rose towards his mouth, although he was long past being able to chew his fingernails.

'Don't worry. The professor's machine will be operational again before they arrive. We'll have the whole Compound covered.'

'You're sure?'

Vaughn gave one of his enigmatic smiles. They'd danced this dance often before. 'I am. But you might see how he's progressing, just to be certain.'

'He's not easy to threaten anymore. You've given him a confidence he never used to have.'

'Then use your initiative, man.'

Packer turned and left.

Vaughn approached his panoramic window and gazed out at the first glimmers of sunrise. A natural phenomenon, repeating itself daily. Regular, ordered, consistent. Just how he liked things to be. But day and night was just a concept to him now. He hadn't slept since his reawakening. He hadn't needed to. That had not been the case before his... death. His brain had still required sleep and dreams even after his body had been converted. This had begun to trouble him.

He looked at his hands. Was it a trick of the low light, or were they now truly tinted green? He caught the remains of his reflection in the window. A sickly, diseased pallor gazed back at him. What would his brain be like inside? The part of him he treasured most. The part he refused to give up. The source of his individuality.

He still remembered. He still felt. He continued to register such sensations. But that in itself was a worry. Registering was different from experiencing, wasn't it? One was pure data, the other, *life*.

His internal readouts had told him much since his revival. There was a micro-monolithic motherboard in his chest. It had backed up his brain patterns. Theoretically, it could be installed into any cybernetic host body. Vaughn had been searching for a way to conquer and control all of mankind, but instead, he'd stumbled across a method of immortality. He need never die.

It troubled him, all the same. Was he in control of himself anymore? Could he imagine, could he create? He'd planned – but that could be simple data extrapolation. Was he still capable of original thought? Trapped within an environment of pure data, could he ever tell?

He looked out again at the sun creeping up over the distant hills. He tried to appreciate it for its own natural beauty, rather than summarising its empirical aspects as pure data. A new day. Would it be his day, at last?

Vaughn felt a tear run down his cheek at the majesty of the moment. He reached up and brushed it aside. Not a tear. This was dark and stank of corruption. The evidence was clear, the end result a foregone conclusion. Packer had already shown him the way. His organic parts were rotting. Likely it was his liquifying brain that had started to dribble from his eye.

Vaughn sank to his knees and welcomed the new day with a moan of despair.

The depolariser had settled Benton, allowing him to drift into a much-needed sleep. Wright had also slept like a log – albeit a noisy one. But Walters could only snooze fitfully. The room was too stuffy. He couldn't get comfortable on the floor. He couldn't get comfortable on the chair either. He told himself it was ridiculous – after all, he'd slept in far worse conditions out on manoeuvres. But the more he thought about this, the more difficult he found it to settle, and after a while he became resigned to the fact that he wasn't going to sleep at all.

He studied the door. It looked like an ordinary wood-panelled affair. But there had been something odd about the noise it made when Wright had joined them. And there was definitely something odd about it when he'd tried shoulder-barging it. Metal-plated, most likely, and sealed by magnetics.

The only window was high up on the opposite wall. They weren't getting out that way. Walters had raised Wright on his shoulders. The Welshman had reported that the window was dirty, had no opener and looked out at ground level – as best he could tell in the dark. Even if they could break it, they had nothing to break it with and only Wright was anywhere near thin enough to escape that way – providing he wasn't mortally lacerated in the process. Wright wasn't keen, and the situation wasn't yet desperate enough for them to need to take such a risk.

'I wonder if we'll get breakfast,' mulled Wright, after yawning and stretching.

His whole demeanour suggested he'd had a very refreshing sleep, thank you very much. This did nothing to improve Walters' mood.

'Don't bank on it.'

As if to prove him wrong, there was the sound of heavy bolts shooting open and the door swung ponderously inwards. A large, impassive figure in IE factory overalls was standing there holding a tray of refreshments.

'Don't try anything,' he said, before stepping inside. As he handed Wright the tray, Benton launched forward from his seated position, trying to shoulder barge the figure about the stomach and take him down. The man stood firm and there was a *thunk* as Benton's shoulder impacted on something solid.

Benton slid to the floor, clutching himself. 'I've done it again,' he groaned. 'Why is everyone around here solid?'

'I told you not to try anything.' The IE operative sounded

more annoyed than anything. 'I'm going to get you out of here if I can.'

The three UNIT operatives looked at him, each one aghast. Was Walters dreaming? 'You what?'

The man looked from one to the other to the other. 'Are you wearing the neuristors?'

'You bet,' said Wright. 'You on our side, then, butt?'

The man didn't respond directly. 'Check the breakfast tray, it's the best I could manage.'

Underneath the platter cover was Walters' pistol. He took it at once.

'Difficult to get two rifles on a tray that size, so you'll have to make do.'

'Thanks,' said Walters with a nod. 'We need to get out of here and somewhere we can contact our HQ.'

'What about the platoon?' asked Benton.

'You can't help them right now,' said the man. 'Follow me.'

They did.

'How are you getting on, Professor?'

Packer. Watkins loathed that voice, loathed the man. Even more so now he was little more than an automated corpse. He continued concentrating on his calculations, refusing to look at his erstwhile tormenter.

'I want to see my niece.'

'You already have.'

'I want to see her without influence. I want to talk to her. In private.'

'I'm not sure Mr Vaughn would approve.'

'Damn Vaughn,' Watkins burst, slapping his hand on the bench in anger and turning to face Packer for the first time. 'We're supposed to be partners.'

'How's the machine coming along?'

Watkins indicated the computer screen and papers before him, as if addressing an imbecile. 'I'm working on the revised calculations now. I can't design and build it until I know how powerful it needs to be. Broadcast bandwidth, power input, vibration dampening, that sort of thing.'

Packer sucked his teeth. 'Mr Vaughn won't be happy.'

Watkins ignored the implied threat and continued with his work.

Packer continued. 'What if I was to bring your niece up to see you, like you asked?'

Watkins patiently placed his pencil on the page. 'Then I imagine my work would come to an abrupt halt, at least until we'd spoken. I should have thought even you might realise that.'

Packer came closer and spoke more quietly. 'What if I was to hurt her?'

Again, Watkins didn't give Packer the satisfaction of looking at him. 'I wondered when we'd get to that.'

'I could.'

'I don't doubt it. And I don't doubt you'd enjoy it. But is Vaughn prepared to risk the consequences over his guaranteed success – that is if I'm allowed to continue at my own pace, properly and without intimidation?'

Packer pulled a face. 'Get on with it, then.' He turned and marched out.

Anne entered the Brigadier's office nursing a mug of coffee.

'Good morning,' he said. 'How did you sleep?'

She pulled a face and slumped into a chair. 'I don't like this situation. I don't like any of it, which is one of the reasons why I'm dead set on getting it sorted.'

He could see Anne had a lot on her mind. He let her continue.

'We've got someone who specialises in meddling with people's brains – no matter what the professor might plead to the contrary. Using his notes at the house, I could probably create a counterwave. But I'm not sure we have the time. And I certainly don't have his skill. So, it would be crude, possibly even damaging. We'd be making a battleground of people's brains.' She paused briefly. 'I'm not sure my conscience would let me carry that burden.'

'Are you saying bullets are the only answer?'

'God forbid that I should *ever* say that, Alistair.'

As they were alone and speaking informally, he didn't mind her familiarity. In some ways, he found it comforting.

'No, what we need is some way to block or repel Watkins' signals before they can have an effect.'

'What about those neuristor things the Doctor came up with? We've still got a load of them kicking around. Could they be of any use?'

'Potentially. But they were keyed to the invaders control

signal. This may be different.'

The Brigadier had some in his desk drawer. He grabbed them and dropped them on the desk, fitting one into place at the back of his neck. They'd do the HQ staff at least. *Better to be safe than sorry.*

Anne took one and popped it in place. 'I'll let you know if it works – or not, as the case may be.'

'So that's our position, is it?'

'I don't think I can tell until I've been there, and I know what's going on. Are we going in mob-handed?'

The telephone started to ring.

'Hopefully, this is the call I've been waiting for with General Ffowlkes-Withers to discuss that very subject.' He raised the receiver. 'Lethbridge-Stewart?'

'Your call is ready to connect, sir.'

'Thank you.' There was a click followed by a brief dial tone, then the call was answered.

'Good morning, Brigadier,' said Ffowlkes-Withers. 'I'm afraid if you're expecting a response to your security measures, the Telex is still sitting in my in-tray.'

'Not at all, General. I need to request more men to move in on the old IE Factory Compound.'

'It's abandoned, isn't it?'

'Apart from the Community, where the ex-employees live.'

'Not going in against civilians, are you? Bad form, that.'

Somewhat predictably, Ffowlkes-Withers was going to make this difficult.

'We're not sure what we're going in against, sir. We've lost contact with the platoon on-site, hence the need for further action.'

'Surely a reconnaissance squad is all you need? You should be able to resource that.'

'We've already sent a chopper over the area. They couldn't see any activity at all. The place seemed abandoned.'

'Brigadier, I don't know what sort of agreement you had with Rutlidge, but I'm going to require actual proof before I authorise the use of Her Majesty's forces, funds and resources on what could turn out to be a prank.'

The Brigadier nearly exploded. 'A prank? General Ffowlkes-Withers, UNIT does not engage in pranks. If my men have gone missing then something serious is happening –

probably involving Tobias Vaughn.'

'Supposition.'

'Surely the British Government wouldn't want to take the risk of further embarrassment?'

There was a rustle at the other end. The voice changed. 'Brigadier, are you threatening us?'

The Brigadier raised his brows. 'Apologies, Minister. I wasn't aware you were there.'

'Immaterial, Lethbridge-Stewart. Answer the question.'

'I'm not threatening anyone, Minister. I'm simply concerned about the situation and trying to take the action I see fit to avoid a serious incident.'

'I'm not sure I approve of your methods, but get General Ffowlkes-Withers the proof he needs, and we'll consider your request. But we are not going to entertain a mere whim.'

With that, the call was ended. The Brigadier looked at Anne. It was clear she had heard both sides of the conversation. He found his annoyance reflected by worry.

'If I didn't know better, I'd say they have their own agenda.'

The Brigadier scowled. 'If you didn't know better...'

'How secure is your role, Alistair?'

'You can't possibly think—'

'I'm afraid I do. They show you up to be incompetent. General Ffowlkes-Withers steps in, both he and the minister become national heroes—'

'And the Government heals its wounds.'

'Politics, Brigadier. And you thought heading up the Fifth was fun.'

'This is a whole other ball game.' He picked up the telephone again. 'Savage... Oh, Enders, you're back there. Yes, yes, I appreciate that, Corporal. Thank you. Have Captain Turner report to my office immediately, please.'

As he replaced the handset, Anne spoke.

'You have a problem with Corporal Enders? Or shouldn't I ask?'

'Trying to protect her, that's all. Damn girl is just too dedicated. Her brother worked for IE. He went missing when it all kicked off last month. Not been seen since. It all gets a bit much for her from time to time.'

'That's your trouble, Alistair,' she said. 'You inspire too much loyalty. I'm also a case in point.'

He smiled. 'And it is thoroughly appreciated, I can assure you.'

There was a knock at the door and Captain Turner entered. 'You wanted me, sir? Is everything sorted?'

The Brigadier indicated that Turner should sit.

He looked between the Brigadier and Anne. 'I take it that's a *no*, then.'

'I'll explain on the way,' Anne told him.

Turner frowned.

'Stealth surveillance is the order of the day, Captain,' said the Brigadier. 'We need to provide General Ffowlkes-Withers with insurmountable evidence before we get our additional resources.' Remembrances of Isobel Watkins' blurry sewer photos came to mind.

'I see.' Turner tried to hide his disappointment. 'Do we take the squad?'

'No. Take Corporal Tracy. I'll hold the squad back here. They can be your immediate back-up if we need it.'

Turner looked at Anne. 'And you're happy to come on this mission?'

She nodded. 'I think I have to. This isn't just about men with big guns.'

'Take care, both of you. I want you each back here in one piece.'

Turner stood and came to attention. 'Thank you, sir. We will.'

'And Captain Turner, if you happen to find Vaughn make sure he's dead this time.'

Isobel awoke back in her cell. She was seated, lying forward across the desk. Her head felt clear, but her body ached – particularly the muscles and joints. Not as a result of her position, more like because they'd been exercising heavily, or straining.

She tried to remember what had happened. There were flashes, vague sensations, but nothing really tangible except a strong image of her uncle. Her uncle and Tobias Vaughn, together in a room. Working together. She began to tremble. Whatever had come over her uncle to want to work with the man who had only recently imprisoned him and tried to take over the world?

There was a tray of refreshments on the desk. The sight of this brought home to Isobel just how hungry and thirsty she was. As she tore at the bread, she noticed something pulling on her skin at the back of her neck. A small device had been affixed there. She didn't need to look at it to tell what it was. The memory was all too recent, all too clear. A depolariser. She wondered how it had got there. Was it part of what had happened to her?

Or maybe her head was clear because of the depolariser. Maybe someone was trying to help her.

She continued with her food and water and thoughtfully felt the sturdiness of the refreshment tray.

Anne slept for most of the journey to the Compound. They only had one option for gaining entry, and that was via the Community. Turner knew that still left them with a perimeter fence to negotiate, but he and Tracy both agreed that it offered them the best chance of remaining undiscovered for the longest period. They'd leave the unmarked staff car near the main road and trek through the Community on foot. Turner hoped it wouldn't be too disappointing for Anne when she woke.

If it was, there was no time for argument. She was still asleep when they arrived. Tracy had a knack for being able to park discretely. There were those within UNIT who put this ability down to certain nefarious activities for which he was known – correctly or otherwise. Turner suspected they were just jealous. Tracy was an able and capable member of UNIT, with a solid skillset. He had a roving eye and a cheeky demeanour, which occasionally required keeping in check, but there were plenty of others out there who were much worse in that respect.

Turner woke Anne as gently as he could.

'Did I snore?' was all she said.

'Not really,' he lied with a smile. 'Do you feel up to moving?'

She looked around, blinking.

Tracy was smoking by the front of the car.

'Where are we?'

Turner explained. Anne didn't mind. She'd come dressed for stealth and activity anyway.

Outside, the three of them agreed where the car keys would be hidden. That way, if any of them needed to escape, or return to HQ, they could.

'Are we going to split up and meet at the other end of the village?'

'The Community,' Turner corrected.

'You know what I mean,' Anne snapped.

There was sense in her suggestion. They didn't know what surveillance methods might be operating. If three UNIT operatives moved through the Community together, would it draw more attention than each of them individually?

Turner agreed. 'Tracy, you go first. I'll count to fifty and follow. Then Anne. We'll meet along the perimeter fence at the far end of the Community.'

'Do we need to call out "coming, ready or not!" when we reach fifty?' said Anne, but her expression was only vaguely glib.

Turner reached fifty and gave her a nod. 'See you there.'

CHAPTER FIFTEEN

Tracy welcomed the opportunity to put his stealth training into operation. So often recently he'd been simply a driver, or on surveillance or escort duties. This was a rare chance at some proper field work, so he was going to take full advantage.

He surveyed all the lampposts as far as he could see. No mounted cameras. No telegraph poles either. It very quickly became apparent that all the residences were unoccupied. Unoccupied, but not vacant. Too many signs of recent life.

Tracy resigned himself to the fact that there was little point in him pretending to try not to be seen. There was no one to see him anyway, no one looking out for any kind of activity. The place was a ghost town.

Turner had quickly come to the same conclusion, as he zig-zagged his way through the side streets on the right-hand side, off the central spine road.

He reached the far end of the Community without issue. There was a short stretch of wasteland before the perimeter fence. He could see the double gates and the narrowing road leading up to and away from them. There was no patrol manning the gates.

Tracy appeared. They signalled to each other to meet at the gates. Just as the two soldiers met, Anne appeared.

'When shall we three meet again?' she quipped.

'No sign of life?' asked Turner.

'Nothing. I watched you two acting like commandos, then I just walked straight down through the middle, bold as brass. What now?'

Turner hissed for them to be quiet, and they squatted down.

'What is it?'

Turner pointed through the fence. 'There's a body through there. Looks like a UNIT uniform.'

'Yes, sir,' said Tracy. 'I see it too.'

'Sight-seeing are we, fellas?'

Potter.

'Where did you spring from, Corporal?' asked Turner as they stood.

Tracy seemed pleased to see his colleague. 'Good to see a friendly face at last.'

Turner held up a cautionary hand. 'Can you get these gates open for us, Potter?'

He shook his head and indicated Cowper's body nearby. 'They're electrified. Don't want you to go the same way as Cowper.'

'He's lying,' whispered Anne. 'We'll take our chances, thanks,' she called. 'Just get them unlocked.'

Potter oozed insubordination. 'No key, sorry.'

Anne was never one to be intimidated, so Turner wasn't surprised to see her stride over to face Potter at the gates.

'Careful.'

'For these gates to release a charge big enough to kill someone, we'd be able to hear the hum. There's nothing.' She turned and grabbed a gate with both hands, then gave a shriek.

Turner and Tracy were with Anne in an instant. But she wasn't being electrified. Potter had a gun to her forehead.

'I did try to be nice,' he said.

Turner moved to reach for his revolver.

'Uh-uh.' Potter smiled and shook his head. 'No, thank you, Captain. I'd rather not blow the lady's head off, so please don't provoke me.'

'What do you want?' Turner asked.

Before Potter could answer, there was the sound of a distant shot and the gates rang to the *ping* of an impact.

Potter turned away from Anne and then staggered back against the gates as two shots caught him in the chest. But he didn't collapse. He stared down at the two smoking holes in his khaki jacket. Then he smiled and glanced at Turner and Anne. The smile became a hearty laugh.

'Something funny?' demanded Sergeant Walters, running towards them all from the cover of nearby undergrowth, holding his handgun out before him. Benton and Wright followed behind, along with a tall man in IE factory overalls. Turner thought the fellow looked vaguely familiar.

Potter stopped laughing and glared at the new arrivals. 'You can't kill me. They've made me invincible.'

The factory worker stepped up to Potter. They eyed each other for a few moments. Wordlessly, the worker grasped Potter around the jaw and slammed his head back into the gate. There was a nauseating crunch and Anne staggered back, spattered with blood.

'Christ on a stick!' said Tracy, placing his hand over his mouth.

Potter's head had been crushed and was wedged between two of the gate struts. The factory worker must have immense strength.

'I'm sorry,' the worker said. 'It's the only way. The conversion process makes us too strong.'

'Us?' said Turner.

The worker nodded. 'I'm the same.' He pounded his chest and produced a solid metal sound. 'Only I seem to have developed a conscience.'

Turner found difficulty justifying that statement with the bloody remains of Potter's head mushed into the gate. With an uncomfortable squelch, Potter's body disconnected from his head and fell to the ground. The base of Potter's neck showed his torn spinal column augmented with components and ripped connections.

'Fascinating!' gushed Anne, clearly over the shock of the attack. 'Someone get these bloody gates open, I want to examine all that.'

In the absence of a key, Walters shot away the lock. The report was loud and unsubtle, but they'd move on soon enough.

'These implants,' said Anne. 'These must be what allows the organic and machine parts to work in harmony. No doubt the head and extremities are fed and nourished by some sort of electrolytic fluid in the same way that blood flows through our veins.'

Tracy moved over to check on Cowper, but Corporal Wright led him away again, his expression telling the newcomers that there was no hope for the soldier.

'Are many of the UNIT force converted like Potter?' Turner asked.

'I only know of him,' replied the man. 'Unless…' He stared at Wright.

'Here, what you bloody looking at me like that for, eh?'

'You've been here the same amount of time.'

'Yes,' Wright nodded vehemently. 'And I wish I'd never been posted here at all. But I'm still me I am, I can assure you of that.' He turned to Walters. 'I hope you don't need to shoot me to find out, Sarge.'

Walters grinned. 'I'll take your word for it.'

Turner was nervous with them all remaining out in the open. 'Let's get under cover somewhere, in case anyone comes to see what all the noises were about.'

'But you must get away again straight away,' insisted the man.

'I can't,' said Turner. 'We're on reconnaissance. I can't go back without incontrovertible proof of what's going on here.' *And news about Isobel*, he added to himself. He looked around at the others. 'But if anyone else wants to go back and try to persuade the powers that be in the meantime—'

There was a strong negative reaction from all, except Wright who said he wouldn't mind.

'Sorry, Wright, we need you,' said Turner as they all moved into the undergrowth at the side of the road.

'We need to get you three neuristors,' said the man.

Anne patted him on the upper arm. 'Way ahead of you there, Enders. I assume you are Simon Enders, brother of our UNIT colleague, Julie?'

Simon nodded sadly.

That's why he'd looked vaguely familiar to Turner. The facial resemblance was strong.

'How is she?'

'Worried about you,' Anne replied. 'The whole family are.'

'I can't go back to them. I'm not… *proper* anymore. I'm just a thing now. We all are, all the factory workers. All partially converted to improve body strength and stamina. And controllability.'

'You mean everyone living in the Community here was a partial conversion?' Turner was appalled.

Simon nodded. 'We were all put on hold when the invasion failed. All waiting for a signal to act again, orders to fulfil. When they finally came, I found myself yearning for my family, wanting to go home, but unable to release myself from Vaughn's bondage. We're all conditioned to stay, you see.'

'We'll help you get home,' said Anne.

The Brigadier entered the sickbay to find Major Branwell in conference with CSM Spring, the deputy MO.

'There you are, Major. I heard you'd gone to sickbay but not the reason why.'

'Checking in with Spring here, sir. Making sure everything's prepared in case we need to support Captain Turner.'

Spring nodded. 'I'm all ready for field duties, sir.'

'Any word yet?'

The Brigadier shook his head. 'No. But they won't have been there long.'

Anne looked on at Simon Enders with a mixture of sadness and fondness, as they concealed themselves in the bushes.

But Turner was keen to press forward. 'Do you know where our platoon is being held?'

Simon nodded. 'Not sure we can release them, though, without an uneven fight.'

'We can leave that until backup arrives. I'd like to get us all armed, at least.'

'Not me, thank you,' said Anne.

Turner appeared to ignore her as he focused on Simon Enders. 'Do you have any idea where Isobel might be held, or Professor Watkins?'

Again, Anne interrupted. 'He's not being held. He's working with Vaughn.'

This time she got Turner's attention. 'Splitting hairs. But if we can get him away, would that damage Vaughn's plans?'

Anne pouted. 'Difficult to say without knowing what they are.'

'So, we need to speak with him. I think we stand more chance of getting answers from the professor than we do from Vaughn.'

On that point, they were all agreed.

'Let me do that,' suggested Anne. 'You focus on rescuing Isobel.'

Turner nodded his agreement. 'All right. A plan, then. First, we check the location of our platoon and obtain additional arms. Then Anne will access the professor's laboratory, with Walters and Wright, while Benton, Tracy, and I find Isobel. Once she's free, we collect the others from the lab, and then try to make our way back to the car.'

'Car?' bleated Wright. 'We'll never all fit in a car.'

'Sir,' said Walters. 'Wouldn't it be best to leave a few of us behind after, keeping watch?'

'My thoughts exactly.' Turner looked pointedly at Wright. 'I was going to suggest as much, but someone interrupted my flow.'

Wright looked away.

'Assuming we all make it back out again, sir,' said Benton – practical as ever. 'How many of your lot are there, Simon?'

'Hundreds. It took a lot to operate this site. We all have an internal tracker. I can monitor their locations, which will help us avoid them.'

'It's almost too good to be true, sir,' said Walters.

'I agree,' Benton said, 'But Mr Enders came to us freely. And I'm not one to begrudge a little good fortune now and then.'

'I'm on your side, Sergeant,' Simon said.

'When all this is over, Simon,' said Anne, 'I'll try to find out why you've been able to resist the control.'

Turner was anxious to get them moving again. 'What's your tracker reading?'

'There's a group heading to the Community gates now. We can head off this way,' Simon pointed, 'without them discovering us.'

'After you, then.'

'Cor,' muttered Wright to Benton as they crept along. 'What I'd have done to have insider knowledge like he's got when I was sneaking around yesterday trying to find you and the sarge.' He indicated Simon ahead.

Benton cast a sideways look at his fellow corporal. 'He's got a robotic body that he doesn't fully understand, Gwyn. Forced on him against his will. Are you really seeing that as a positive?'

'No, but...'

'I'm happier with a straight fight, upfront. All this sneaking around makes me edgy.'

'Quiet, you two,' hissed Walters.

They stopped to allow Simon to focus on his internal tracker.

'Where are we heading?' asked Miss Travers.

'Staff gymnasium, I believe.'

'There are two patrol groups between us and there. We need to circle around to the west and approach the building from the north.'

Vaughn was seated at his desk. He could monitor and control all he needed to from there. The visi-screens on the wall opposite showed transponder signals for all his part-converted ex-factory workers. They were his new army for now, until he was able to suppress everyone worldwide with the professor's machine.

It would soon be ready. The repaired Mark III was connected to the main building and factory PA system, creating a secure barrier against any potential incursion. Watkins, like a giddy schoolboy, was working on the Mark IV, with enough power to cover the Compound. The Mark V would give him the world.

In some ways, he felt he'd been a fool up to now. Plans had taken years to attain their fruition with his allies. He'd been in awe of them, that was clear, and hadn't seen the wood for the trees. Not this time, however. The IE mainframe computer had instigated a plan which, thanks to the groundwork put in place already, could proceed at almost breakneck speed by comparison. And all in secret.

Vaughn watched the transponder signals, zoning in on one group after the other. A solid, dependable workforce, now turned into a solid, dependable security force. There were a few standalone signals. Himself, of course. Chambers. Packer. And one other around the grounds. Potter, probably. No, Enders. There was no sign of Potter.

Vaughn reached forward and clicked the intercom. 'Packer?'

'Yes, Mr Vaughn,' came the reassuringly eager reply.

'We've lost the transponder signal for Potter.'

'If UNIT are here there's been no indication of activity so far.'

'What's Enders doing?'

There was a brief delay. 'If he's not guarding the girl, he'll be out and about around the grounds.'

'Checking on the patrols?'

'Amongst his duties, yes.'

Vaughn nodded thoughtfully. 'Good.'

Anne, Tracy, and Wright were huddled in the lee of an outhouse. Wright looked around nervously. Anne had difficulty thinking of him as Wright, having known him for so much longer as Evans. She understood why he wanted a new identity, a new start, but there was still so much of the old Evans in there, it made her smile. Sometimes, no matter how hard you try, you can't escape who you are, or hide from your past.

The three of them had been left there temporarily, while the others headed to spy on the platoon that was being held captive within the adjacent gymnasium. They weren't gone for long.

Benton looked happier now he was holding a rifle. He had a spare which he passed to Wright, who looked slightly less content brandishing it.

Turner came back deeply concerned. 'They're all catatonic as far as I can tell. There's some low-level suppression field at work in there. I felt an itch at the back of my mind when we went in.'

Benton and Walters confirmed they did too.

Turner continued. 'And this depolariser thing started to vibrate.' Anne looked at Benton and Walters. 'Same for you?'

They both responded in the negative.

'In that case,' said Anne, 'Ours need to be tweaked. We're obviously blocking slightly different frequencies to the depolarisers created here on-site. May I?' She reached out to Benton for his and removed her own. From her bag, she produced a thin probe. It hadn't occurred to her until now to check all the depolarisers were set to the same frequencies.

Turner sounded frustrated. 'Does it have to be now?'

Anne didn't look up but spoke as she closely examined both. 'If it means the difference between keeping our own minds and possibly falling under the control of Tobias Vaughn, the answer should be obvious. This won't take long. I'll do yours next,' she looked up at him. 'Captain.'

She finished hers and passed it to Turner in exchange for his, also returning Benton's.

'Any patrols nearby, Simon?' she asked.

'Not currently, but the captain is right, we shouldn't stay put for long.'

'Done,' she said, looking up with a smile. She fitted it at the back of her neck and opened her palms to the others. 'Ready when you are.'

Turner nodded to Simon. 'Let's move.'

CHAPTER SIXTEEN

THEY ENTERED the main building via a goods-in area at the rear. Simon had made it ridiculously easy for them and Anne was already having thoughts about creating false transponder signal emitters for them all to wear back at HQ. They wouldn't know where everyone else was, but on a scanner, they wouldn't show up as any different from the rest of the IE Factory staff.

They climbed to the third floor via a set of service stairs. Anne was unhappy about them all traipsing around together, waiting to get caught. The idea of separate missions was to try to speed things up. Captain Turner agreed.

'The lab doors are locked,' Simon told them. 'They all are. They'll only release in the presence of...' And he banged his chest.

'Will it be detected when you unlock the door?' asked Anne.

'Perhaps. I'm not sure.'

'In that case we need to be quicker than ever. Surely if you can read the position of everyone else, they can also read your position?'

Simon looked at her reassuringly. 'I've been entrusted with certain duties. I have some... freedom of movement.'

'As long as those duties don't involve leading all of us into a trap.'

'I'm taking advantage of their misplaced trust to help you.'

Anne let her eyes linger on Simon a little longer. He was very difficult to read. His body language was strange, no doubt due to his partial conversion. But he'd been reliable up to now. She nodded.

'Walters, Evans... Wright, sorry, let's go.' Anne looked at Turner. 'There's a lot of advanced technology at play here.

Technology we could use. Make sure it's not all ripped out and binned like in London.'

With that, she disappeared through the door.

'Well, that's me told,' quipped Turner.

Benton and Tracy smiled. Simon nodded at him.

'I'll join you three on the fifth floor,' he said. 'The way up should be clear.'

'*Should*,' said Benton. 'I like that.'

'M Gregory, research.' Anne read the sign on the door. 'I like that. He doesn't even get his own name on his door.'

Simon stepped up to the door and there was a quiet clump noise as the magnetics released.

'I must go,' he said. 'Be quick.'

'We'll see you back at the Community gates,' Anne told him. 'Never mind what Captain Turner said. Get Isobel away as quickly as you can. We'll look after ourselves.'

Without a word, Simon turned and left.

'Look after ourselves, indeed,' grumbled Wright.

'Shut up and get inside,' hissed Walters.

They entered.

'Packer?'

'Yes, Mr Vaughn?'

'Have you had confirmation from our agents at the necessary communications centres?'

'They're all in position ready and waiting.'

'Good, I—

He was distracted by an alert flashing up on a screen. 'The north door to the research laboratory has been activated. By Enders.'

'That's within his remit. I'll take my position.'

'Do so.'

Vaughn sat back and steepled his fingers beneath his chin.

The door to the fifth floor was locked. Benton felt like a lemon standing around waiting. His dissatisfaction must have been coming off in waves.

'For God's sake stand still, man,' hissed Turner.

'Sorry, sir.'

'He can't help it, sir,' said Tracy. 'Benton prefers a straight fight to all this sneaking around.'

'I know. I heard him earlier. We all did. But we're not here for that. This is an intelligence mission. There's no value in any of us getting found and killed.'

They froze at the sound of a door opening and closing below them. Footsteps on the stairs, then Simon Enders appeared, and they relaxed.

'It's locked,' Benton told him.

Simon nodded and approached the door. Something around the frame released and the door pulled smoothly open.

'Is she near?' Turner asked.

Tracy nudged Benton's arm and pointed to Turner. It was the captain's turn to appear fidgety and nervous.

Simon said nothing but walked off quickly. They followed.

Benton couldn't imagine how it must feel for Turner. Or how he'd react himself in that position – except he was dead set on never being in that position. Benton hadn't had cause to doubt Turner's judgment so far. But he was certain of one thing: the sooner they got Miss Watkins rescued and safely away from here, the better.

Simon paused outside a door.

Turner looked at Benton and Tracy. 'You two stay out here on guard. I won't be long.'

Isobel could hear murmured voices and movement outside. She'd been waiting for this. If Zoe had taught her anything it was to seize the moment. She started by seizing the tray on which her food had been brought. Brandishing it with both hands she stood behind the door as it clunked its release and slowly opened.

'Isobel?'

It was too late for her to hear the voice. She was already swinging her weapon with all her might. Crack! It landed on her intruder's head. Smack! She gave a smooth pirouette, bringing the back of the tray around and into the man's face. He collapsed onto the floor, clutching at his head and his bleeding nose.

Amazed at her own success, Isobel then noticed the two uniformed men looking in through the open doorway, aghast. She instantly recognised Benton and Tracy. A quick look down and there was poor Jimmy cowering from her on the floor.

'Oh!' she gasped. 'Jimmy, I'm so sorry!'

As she helped him to his feet, an IE operative stepped into view – one she knew she'd seen before. Her spirits suddenly dropped.

'I guess you're prisoners here too, now?'

Jimmy shook his head, pulling a handkerchief from his pocket.

'No,' he said nasally. 'He's helping us. We've come to rescue you. Are you hurt?'

She brushed his cheek fondly. 'Not as much as you.'

'Then let's go, please,' said the IE operative. 'We should join the others at the lab.'

They headed off.

'What is the meaning of this disturbance?' grumbled Professor Watkins as Anne and the others entered the research lab.

Anne hadn't actually put much thought into what she might do once inside. She stood and stared at her old Cambridge lecturer for some time.

'I'm not ready for more test subjects yet. You can tell Vaughn from me, he needs to be patient. Genius can't be hurried.' He fussed about his work and closed a box out on his computer screen. 'Neither can it be bottled, for that matter. The work will be done when it is done. Go away.'

'Professor Watkins,' Anne addressed him and smiled. 'You may not recognise me after so many years, but I'm—'

'Goodness me,' he gasped. 'Anne Travers! Oh – the house!'

She approached him, waving aside such concerns. 'Professor, what are you doing here?'

He looked at her as if she was dumb. 'I'm working. What does it look like?'

'Still the same line of research?'

'I've made such progress. We have great plans. Let me show you.'

'We? You and Tobias Vaughn?'

He looked over her shoulder at the others. 'Oh. You're with the UNIT people, I see. I had hoped for better from you, my dear. They offered me a position, you know. But I couldn't involve myself with military affairs.'

'Whereas working with a known criminal who tried to

enslave the world is perfectly acceptable?'

'But that's just it, Anne. We're going to make a difference. We're going to make things *better*.'

'For whom?'

'For everyone! What a state the world has got itself into. Wars, unrest, intolerance, *pettiness*. Wouldn't you seize the moment if you could change it all in an instant, make everyone happy?'

'That depends. If I could affect their outlook, make them see reason, then yes. But I'm concerned that your way is a little more heavy-handed than that.'

He nodded. 'People can't be trusted to make up their own minds.'

Wright suddenly spoke up. 'So, you're going to make it up for them?'

'Yes, my lad, I am.'

'That's crazy, that is. You're no better than Vaughn.'

'That's enough, Corporal,' snapped Walters. 'Button it.'

'But—?'

A glare. 'Leave it.'

Anne spoke again, gently this time. 'I'm afraid he's right to object, Professor. You can't force people like that.'

'But if we don't then nothing will ever get better.'

'You're consigning everyone – the whole world – to live according to someone else's view of the perfect society. Doubtless, a society which will make that person the supreme ruler.'

Watkins shook his head. 'That's where you're wrong. With a perfect society, where everyone gets along, you don't need rulers.'

'Only you and Vaughn deciding how everyone acts and reacts.'

'Only in as much as the Cerebreton Mentor will need monitoring. We won't be rulers. We'll be caretakers.'

Anne couldn't resist a dry chuckle at his naïveté. 'Very philanthropic. And you don't see that as a bad thing?'

'Not at all. The satellites are still in position from the aborted invasion. They're just waiting for my signal. It's the simplest thing ever.'

'But you'll be the last, Professor. The last free man. The last scientist. Think about it. Think what you're taking away from everyone rather than what you're giving them. No one else will ever wake up one morning and think, "Eureka!" or, "I could change the world today!" Tell me, did that ever happen to you?'

He paused a moment. Was she getting through to him? 'Yes.'

'And you would deprive others of such moments?'

'Such moments should be unnecessary. There will be no more mistakes to correct.'

'I fear you are making the biggest mistake of all with that assumption.'

At that moment the door opened, and Turner stumbled in, assisted by Isobel, with Simon, Benton, and Tracy following behind.

'What is going on?' demanded Watkins.

'I told you to get away,' said Anne, frustrated. 'We'll manage for ourselves.'

Benton seated Turner and checked him over. 'I think the captain may have a mild concussion,' Benton told her.

'How?'

Tracy indicated Isobel. 'She smacked him over the head with a tray.'

Anne tried to hide a smile. 'I thought you two were...'

But Isobel wasn't paying any attention. Instead, she immediately rounded on her uncle. 'What are you doing here?'

'Isobel, my dear, are you all right?'

He came forward, reaching for her, but she shrugged him off.

'Why are you working for someone you hate? You've been telling me the last few weeks how he ruined your career, tainted your name. And yet here you are again, building your gadgets and testing them out on *me*!'

Watkins looked stung. 'That was not planned. I didn't know you were here.'

'I got abducted on our doorstep by Vaughn and Packer, looking like they'd just dug themselves out of their own graves.'

'We're going to make the world a better place, Isobel. We're going to make it *perfect*.'

'It didn't feel perfect for me.'

'That was only a test.'

'It *hurt*!'

Watkins reached out for Isobel tenderly and this time she

didn't stop him.

'I'm so sorry. But when the levels are perfected, you won't even realise the Cerebreton Mentor is influencing you. If you hadn't come here, you would have remained in blissful ignorance, like everyone else.'

She shoved him away roughly, her face crumpling. 'And that's a good thing?'

Turner was at Isobel's side in an instant, every bit his usual self again.

All eyes in the room were on Watkins. He'd been backed onto a moral precipice. This hadn't gone to plan for Anne at all. If they lost him now, she wasn't sure they'd ever get him back.

'Professor,' she said as calmly and gently as her dry throat would allow. 'We're not the enemy. Come with us. Bring your Cerebreton Mentor. We'll—'

'Never,' Watkins snapped, grasping his machine.

'You must come with us, Professor,' called Turner. He cocked his revolver, his intention clear.

'No! You can't!' pleaded Isobel, turning to block his view of her uncle.

'Leave me alone here,' Watkins growled. 'Or I will turn this on you all.'

Anne glanced at Turner and shook her head. He wasn't going to come with them now. They'd have to do things the difficult way.

'I think perhaps you should anyway, Professor,' said a new voice. Cultured, avuncular. Tobias Vaughn.

Anne felt an involuntary gasp pass her lips at the sight of him. 'My God…'

He was little more than an animated cadaver. His snowy-white hair was lank and lifeless. His eyes dark, sunken, and weeping fluid. His lips moved sporadically with the words he spoke, but it was clear that what he said was not being produced by his own larynx.

'Congratulations on being able to resist our control, by the way.'

All the guns in the room instantly became trained on the newcomer.

'No closer or we shoot, Vaughn,' said Turner.

Anne took Isobel's arm and moved behind the soldiers. 'I'm not sure you can kill a dead man, Captain.'

'Top marks, Miss Travers. But then I'd have expected nothing less from such a distinguished visitor.'

'I never have responded well to flattery. This ends here, now.'

'Yes.' Vaughn gave an approximation of a nod. 'I agree. We just need to connect up the professor's new machine and you're right, it will all end.'

Turner scoffed and the side of his head. 'No dice. We're all immune to your control signals.'

Something that might have been a look of frustration passed across Vaughn's face. 'Maximum power at close range? We shall see.'

'Captain,' said Anne urgently. 'We need to go. Now.'

Turner nodded. 'Simon?'

Vaughn looked towards the door through which they'd entered. 'What's going on?'

'Our trump card, Vaughn. We'll be back. And in force. We'll blow this place to kingdom come if necessary.'

'Oh, really?'

'Problems,' said Simon. 'Multiple groups converging on this position.'

They weren't going to get out without a fight.

Turner looked exasperated. 'Why didn't you raise the alarm earlier?'

'Because my trap wasn't ready to be sprung earlier.'

Vaughn.

A look of pain and anguish crossed Simon's face. 'I'm... sorry.'

'He's been working for me the whole time.'

The Brigadier reached forward and pressed the intercom on his desk. 'Nicholls, any word yet?'

'No, sir, no contact at all.'

Damn it all, what's happening down there? He rubbed his bottom lip thoughtfully. 'Have we still got that chopper in the area?'

'It's at Henlow Downs, sir, awaiting orders.'

'Have it take another look and report back.'

'Sir. Oh, sir?' Nicholls added.

'Yes, Nicholls?'

Her voice lowered. 'He's back, sir. Heading your way now.

Ordered me not to say anything, so I haven't.'

The Brigadier allowed a brief smile to cross his face. 'Of course, you haven't, Sergeant Major. Orders is orders, after all. It's most appreciated.'

As he picked up the telephone and dialled Major Branwell's extension, the Brigadier's office door opened without ceremony and General Ffowlkes-Withers entered.

Vaughn stood to one side, looking resplendent in his assumed victory. All of them together, trapped in one room, their brief glimmer of hope dashed. Watkins cradled his machine and scuttled to join Vaughn, presumably taking reassurance from his proximity.

Anne caught a glance and a nod between Turner and Walters. Clearly a pre-arranged signal because immediate action ensued.

Turner and Tracy grabbed two lab stools and used them to ram Simon Enders into the corner. Wright scuttled away, leading Isobel from the room. Turner and Tracy followed.

'Stay with us, please, Miss,' hissed Walters in Anne's ear. Benton appeared at her side.

'Get after them!' yelled Vaughn as Simon extricated himself from the stools.

As soon as he was gone, Walters vaulted a bench and grabbed Professor Watkins, holding a gun to the side of his head.

'You're gonna open that secret door of yours, Vaughn,' said Walters. 'You're gonna let us through or we hurt the professor.'

Watkins gave a terrified squeal. 'For God's sake, Vaughn. Do as they ask.'

But Vaughn snatched the machine from Watkins and stood firm. 'Kill him then.'

'The machines need more work, Vaughn,' pleaded Watkins.

A look of what might have been frustration passed across Vaughn's death mask. 'All right. But you won't get far. We have all areas covered.'

'We'll see,' spat Walters. 'Move.'

With a stuttered cry from Watkins, the group moved towards the door on the far side. It opened for Vaughn automatically, revealing the inside of a lift. Presumably his personal lift.

Walters growled, 'Down,' but Anne interrupted.

'I think I can manage the buttons, thank you.'

Vaughn withdrew his hand.

'Don't want the wrong thing pressed accidentally, do we.'

There were four buttons, one of which had an alarm bell on it. At a guess, Anne figured the lift would probably call at the basement car park, the research lab and Vaughn's office. She pressed the lowest button and felt the lift descend.

'I'm glad you know where you're going,' said Vaughn.

She gave him a twee smile and hoped he couldn't see her crossed fingers.

'Which side do the doors open?' asked Benton.

'Wait and see,' Vaughn replied.

Benton was in the middle of a frustrated response when the lift stopped, and the doors opened behind Anne. She turned and stepped out into a darkened underground area. She'd assumed correctly. Vaughn's car was adjacent.

'We'll take that,' said Walters.

Benton headed to the driver's door. It was unlocked, but as it opened an armed figure emerged.

'There you are, Packer,' said Vaughn.

If Anne thought Vaughn was cadaverous then Packer was positively putrefying. And the smell!

'Drop your weapons. You lot are surrounded.'

Watkins pulled himself free and scuttled away. Anne wasn't going to try to tackle him herself. They needed to focus on getting away and Vaughn's car was their best option at that moment. Walters and Benton looked around, poised for an attack.

The lift doors closed again behind them, and Vaughn's distant voice called out, 'There's no escape.'

'The professor – damn!'

Anne dismissed the worry. 'They're on their way back up to the lab.'

Benton stepped forward. 'Where's your backup, Packer?'

Packer moved to meet him.

Anne looked about. There were plenty of shadows, but no sign of movement. If they were surrounded, Vaughn's operatives should have taken them all by now.

'It's a bluff. They expected us to surrender immediately.'

'Is that so, miss?' said Packer. 'Well let me tell you this

much, when that lift comes back down it's going to find me and three corpses waiting.'

'Now!' shouted Walters. He raised his pistol and fired at Packer, blasting him in the chest. He staggered back under the impact.

Benton moved in and smacked him in the face with the butt of his rifle, before spinning it and firing at point-blank range.

Anne turned away in disgust as Packer's decaying head plastered itself across the wall and the bonnet of the limousine.

There were sounds of running footsteps from somewhere not too far away.

'Let's get moving,' hissed Anne.

But the headless figure wasn't done with yet. It was now grappling with Benton for his rifle.

'Get in the car, miss,' said Walters, running to assist.

Anne slipped into the spacious rear, while Walters and Benton between them managed to wrestle Packer's cybernetic body to the ground.

Immediately they were both seated in the front of the car. The keys were in the ignition – the car was always ready if needed. Benton reversed out of the space, nearly crashing into the lift in the process. The headless Packer was staggering to its feet in front of them.

'Do it,' yelled Walters.

Benton gunned the engine, slamming into Packer and throwing him some distance away. He then continued forward and drove straight over the body with a double crunch as both front and back passenger-side wheels impacted.

'If that hasn't stopped him nothing will,' said Benton with glee.

'Maybe,' said Anne, 'but let's save the celebration until we're out of here.'

'Assuming I can find the exit.'

Benton swerved and careened around the car park. Shots rang out as other IE operatives arrived. The driver's side rear window shattered and imploded as a bullet embedded itself in the gorgeous leather upholstery close enough to Anne to make her dive into the footwell and hide.

She couldn't see what happened next, but she felt the car begin to head up a steep incline.

'We're outside, miss. No gates!' Benton called back.

'But not out of trouble, yet,' Walters added.

They had indeed left the car park, but now they needed to escape from the grounds. Ahead lay a gated entrance, protected by a UNIT sentry post manned by armed IE operatives. They stood in a line, facing the approaching car.

'We'll never make it through this way,' said Walters.

Benton spun the wheel, taking them off-road until he could get the car back under control. More shots pinged off the bodywork as they drove back past the main building and Anne was torn between the terror of watching what was going on and hiding in the footwell and imagining it.

CHAPTER SEVENTEEN

'PROFESSOR WATKINS was trembling as the lift rose. A combination of anger and fear. 'They could have killed me, Vaughn.'

'My dear Watkins, you're too reactionary. They had no intention of killing you.'

'You're so sure? This is all new to me. Life is precious. I don't have your complacency.'

'If they'd killed you, they wouldn't have had a hostage. Besides which, how do you think your dear niece would have reacted if her friends had done that?'

Watkins knew Vaughn was talking sense, which made it all the more infuriating.

'Thanks to Packer, we don't have to waste time going through the tiresome process of rescuing you, and they can simply be shot in the grounds instead.'

He hadn't expected this. What about Anne? He knew her. He'd taught her. He'd been friends with her father.

'Do they have to be killed? Can't we just leave them until the control wave is fully in place?'

The lift doors opened, and they emerged back into the research lab.

'You're too squeamish. The control wave is covering these buildings and they're already resistant to it.'

'The neuristors they wear. They won't be able to repel a signal strong enough to be boosted worldwide, I guarantee.'

Vaughn looked at him, impressed. 'Very good. How soon will it be ready?'

'Tomorrow.' Watkins took back the Cerebreton Mentor. 'I've nearly finished calibrating this Mark IV for localised use. The larger units for worldwide use are still under development.'

'And that's another thing. You're too candid and open. *The machine needs more work*, indeed. Try to be more circumspect with our enemies.'

'I don't have your level of nerve, Vaughn.'

Vaughn's expression hardened. 'Just focus on delivering the machines as soon as possible and all our troubles, all our cares, will vanish.'

He stepped back into the lift and the doors closed.

Watkins watched them for a moment, thinking about his cadaverous partner. All their cares will vanish, will they? He doubted that would be the case for Vaughn. Watkins wondered when he would admit that his old flesh had died and choose a new body to step into. While the prospect of perpetual life – no, perpetual *existence* (there was a difference) – held a certain scientific appeal, he was only interested at a theoretical level. The prospect of undergoing it appalled him. Watkins found he was glad – not for the first time – that he had not accepted the offer some months prior to undergo conversion.

'Where are the others?' asked Isobel.

They reached a door. 'Through here and be quiet,' said Turner urgently, holding it open. 'They're taking a different route,' he told Isobel as he closed the door behind them.

'It's a dead end, Captain,' said Wright.

Turner frantically gestured for him to be quiet.

They all stood and waited, trying to calm their breathing. Outside there was the tread of booted feet thundering past. Hopefully Simon Enders. Turner waited until he was sure they had gone, then peered out again.

'Let's go.'

'We're running blind now, aren't we,' grumbled Wright.

Turner rounded on him. 'Yes, but so are *they* now that we don't have anyone traceable in the party. So, I'd call that evens, wouldn't you?'

Wright didn't get the chance to reply.

'Go, now.'

They headed down the stairs as quickly and as quietly as they could. They'd been on the fifth floor, so it was a fair old trek to the ground. At the bottom of the stairs was a fire exit door. Turner opened it cautiously and peered out. He couldn't see anyone about, but it was quite a distance to reach cover.

Several floors above them a door banged. Footsteps followed, heading their way.

Behind the base of the staircase was a low, sheltered area – the only suitable hiding place Turner could see. He urged everyone over to it, crouching or bending to get in.

'Why didn't we just run for it?' asked Isobel.

'I was thinking the same thing,' grumbled Wright, unhelpfully.

Turner explained. 'There's a wide, open space outside and someone following us inside. We'd have never made it to cover before they'd got to the door and spotted us.'

They all fell silent as a number of IE operatives trundled down the steps and out through the fire exit they'd specifically left open.

'Oh!' gushed Isobel after the last operative had left and the doors remained open. 'They now think we're somewhere out in the grounds.'

'Yes.'

'Which we will be anyway, shortly,' observed Wright.

Turner was fast losing his patience with the Welshman. 'But now we don't have a group of them tracing us from behind. I'm just trying to play the game with the best odds I can. Now, Wright, you know these grounds well.'

'Do I?'

'You've been here the longest.'

'Yes, but...'

'You lead. And no dawdling.'

Turner practically threw him out ahead of the others.

It occurred to Benton that they had been somewhat fortunate again. The patrolling IE operatives across the Compound didn't automatically fire on the limo. Presumably, their first thought was that it was taking Vaughn somewhere. This allowed Walters a number of free shots and helped them get quite far before word finally got ahead of them and they began to encounter proper resistance.

They were also fortunate that he was an excellent driver, but he wasn't going to brag about that – at least not until they'd got away safely.

'Is it much further?' called up Miss Travers from the back.

'Don't ask me,' he replied. 'I'm only the driver.'

'Nearly there,' said Walters, firing another round ahead and forcing the IE staff to break ranks.

'No sign of Captain Turner's party,' Benton added.

Walters gave a curse. 'I'm out of ammo.'

Benton saw the Community buildings ahead. He accelerated again, slaloming through the IE operatives and trying not to slow as he approached the gates. He could see Potter's cybernetic body leaning collapsed against the gate. What remained of his head was still wedged in between two of the struts. Simon had done that. *Why would I have done that if I was working for Vaughn*, he wondered.

'Brace yourselves.'

At the last second, the gates parted enough for Benton to drive through. He was so surprised, he slammed on the brakes to find out what had happened. In the rear-view mirror, he could see Simon Enders running after them. Benton immediately slipped back into gear and reached for the handbrake, but he found Anne's hand stopping him.

'No, wait.'

'But Miss Travers – he'll give us away again.'

'He's just opened the gates for us. At least hear what he has to say.'

Walters' window was still down. 'What do you want?'

'I'm sorry. I didn't mean to – I had no idea I was under Vaughn's control until it happened.'

'Convenient.' Walters didn't sound convinced.

'Thank you for helping us, Simon,' Anne called from the back seat.

He acknowledged her words with a gesture. 'Go now,' Simon continued.

'We were trying to,' Benton pointed out.

Simon waved the words away. 'This car is too recognisable. Change to your staff car for the rest of the journey.'

'Is that it?' asked Walters, curtly.

Simon nodded and Walters wound his window up.

Benton quickly pulled away. 'Shall we, Sarge?'

'I don't reckon we should,' said Miss Travers. 'If we take that, Captain Turner has no hope of getting away.'

'True,' agreed Walters. 'But he's got a fair point about this beast. It'll be very easy to track.'

*

Chambers laid Packer's shattered form gently on the floor of Vaughn's office. Their cybernetic bodies were strong and resilient, but not in the face of repeated and extreme trauma. Chambers stood up, reverently. But inside he was thrilled. This was the moment he'd been waiting for. The reward for all his lonely dedication and service, maintaining activities by stealth at the Compound during Vaughn's period of deactivation. Recruiting and converting Potter. Chambers would now step into the vacant position at Vaughn's right hand.

But Vaughn was acting strangely. He was crouched over Packer's remains, touching and stroking them tenderly as a mother would a deceased infant. And he was talking to the body in an affectionate voice.

Chambers wondered if he'd completely misunderstood the relationship between the two. He felt uncomfortable, exposed to something that shouldn't be witnessed by others. He began to back away, respectfully.

As he did so, Vaughn looked up.

'Don't leave us, Chambers.' He'd never heard Vaughn sound so vulnerable before. 'Now Packer has met with this… unfortunate accident, I have greater need of your services.'

Ahh, what he'd been waiting for.

'You will have the honour of being the first.'

First? 'First what, Mr Vaughn?'

There was something in his hand as he stood. A circuit.

'You will remove your motherboard,' he said, his voice hardening.

'I—' But Chambers found that he was compelled to obey. This hadn't been what he'd expected at all. And even as he performed the act, knowing he'd been betrayed, he did so willingly. For Vaughn.

There was something going on around the grounds, that much was clear. Gunshots could be heard periodically from various directions. IE operatives were running about the place, not necessarily looking for Turner and his band. They remained concealed, just in case.

'Hopefully, that's the others driving everyone crazy,' said Tracy with a wry smile.

Whatever it was, it was working in their favour. They were

slowly making their way towards the Community, finding cover wherever possible.

Suddenly there was an explosion ahead of them. Somewhere around, or near the edge of the Community. They saw a cloud of black smoke and debris emerge over the tops of the trees. Turner blanched.

'Only one thing that could have been,' he hissed. 'Our staff car. Must have been booby-trapped by the IE lot.'

Wright looked at him aghast. 'Then... the others?'

Turner licked his lips. 'All the more reason for us to succeed. Let's keep moving.'

The noise on the road behind them was little more than a dull crump, but the smoke and debris told Anne what had happened.

Walters twisted in his seat. 'Was that—?'

'Our staff car? I think so,' said Anne. 'Must have been a timed detonation from when we passed through the gates. Are you glad we didn't waste time swapping cars now, Sergeant?'

Walters faced the front and didn't answer. His shoulders slumped very slightly.

While they had driven through the Community, Anne had argued that speed was more important to them, and all they needed to do was reach a telephone box. Swapping cars seemed a pointless exercise.

'Enders' brother again,' said Benton, shaking his head. 'Helping us with one hand and trying to kill us with the other.'

Anne sat back thoughtfully. Benton was right. But how much of Simon's behaviour was premeditated and how much was it him fighting against the control? She wasn't certain they would ever find out.

'Packer?'

Packer opened his eyes. His eyes? They felt like they belonged to him and yet simultaneously they didn't. He recalled his mother saying something similar when she'd had her dentures fitted. His throat began to gag in expectation of his stomach churning. But he had no stomach. He waited for the feeling to pass.

He saw something like an image from a Hammer horror staring down at him quizzically. His memory took a little while to align with his thoughts. He knew the face, despite the decay.

He knew the man. Revered him. His employer. He'd do anything for Tobias Vaughn. Arguably he already had.

'Yes, Mr Vaughn.' The voice was his. That helped a lot. Not only that, but it came from his mouth and didn't sound distant and electronic.

Vaughn helped him to sit up and handed him a mirror. The face of Chambers was reflected back. Older than Packer had been, a little baggier, and wearing a moustache. As he watched himself, Chambers' mouth – his mouth now – gave a smile that morphed into a sneer. Just like his old self. That was reassuring.

He stood up, experiencing a momentary wooziness as he adjusted to his new height and weight, finding his new centre of gravity. He remembered the final moments of his previous body. The shot, the car, the curious lack of pain or sensation. Was this how living would be for him from now on? Without true feelings or sensations? His body merely a conveyance for mobility, nothing more?

Vaughn spoke again. 'Take your time adjusting. This is, I believe, the first time someone has changed bodies in this way.'

Packer tried a few more expressions in the mirror and found the muscles automatically falling the way they had in his original face. It didn't quite match his new one, like a dodgy police photofit. But it was comfortable, it was *him*. Unlike the decaying remains of Vaughn.

'Almost your old self.'

'Where is… Chambers?'

Vaughn indicated the micro-monolithic motherboard on his desk. What must it be like for Chambers? Would he be aware? Packer noticed his own shattered remains on the floor and looked away again quickly. That way madness lay.

Vaughn was keen to get on. 'How's your tracker?'

Packer concentrated on his internal systems. The tracker had recalibrated following the insertion of the replacement motherboard – him, basically. He told Vaughn as much.

'Good. Can you detect Enders? The car has exploded so that's one group dealt with. Operatives have been monitoring the position of the group containing Watkins' niece from afar. They won't be expecting you. Head there now and get them back under lock and key. I need to find out how my new partner is getting on. Although if he doesn't hurry up, I may have to rethink the arrangement.' He paused and smiled. 'After the world is ours, of course.'

*

'There!' cried Anne, pointing. 'Pull in over here.'

They almost missed the telephone box. Its red livery was tarnished, and it was set back within the line of bushes at the side of the pavement. Thankfully Anne had caught a glimpse as they approached, and Benton was able to react in time.

'Stay alert, Benton,' said Walters as he opened the car door. Anne joined him.

'Where now, sir?'

Turner looked at Wright, then at the others. He lingered longer on Isobel. She'd been through a hell of a lot already and she wasn't cut out for this sort of thing at all. She should have been photographing beachwear models in Bournemouth, or something.

Isobel smiled at him encouragingly.

'I still think the Community is our best and easiest way out,' he said.

'But the explosion,' bleated Wright.

'Damage done,' said Turner grimly. 'And we should probably check to see if anyone was involved.'

'Sir,' said Tracy, holding up a palm to interrupt. 'I thought I heard—'

'You did.'

The voice was Packer's, and the bearing, but Turner recognised the face as Chambers. He appeared from within a nearby bush.

'Throw down your weapons and come quietly.'

Turner's lip curled. 'And if we don't?'

All around them the bushes moved, and IE operatives appeared.

'Sergeant Walters!'

The Brigadier was almost up and out of his seat with excitement. 'Are you all right? Where are you?'

Walters' tinny voice emerged from the telephone handset. 'A public phone box at the side of the road somewhere near Hurst Green. Any word yet from Captain Turner, sir?'

'No, we've heard nothing from anyone.'

'They blew up our staff car. We've stolen Vaughn's limo.'

'What's going on? Do you need backup?'

There was some background muttering, then Walters came back on the line.

'Hang on a moment, sir. Miss Travers wants to—'

'Give me that.' Anne's voice.

The Brigadier allowed himself a wry smile.

'Brigadier?'

'Anne. What the devil's going on?'

'As I thought, Watkins is collaborating with Vaughn. They're going to use the IE communications satellite array and broadcast emotional manipulation waves to control the population of the entire world.'

'How's he going to do that?'

'He's controlling the factory buildings, possibly the whole Compound, through his public address system. The platoon you sent here are all under his control. I imagine there'll be something similar on a broader scale for the whole world.'

'But we destroyed the radio telecommunications controls on-site.'

'Vaughn's had operatives working under our noses for weeks. Don't assume it hasn't been repaired.'

'I'll get onto Geneva, get them to check the communication centres that were previously taken over by IE operatives worldwide. They may be our last line of defence.'

'And it may come to that – I really don't know how much time we have. We're wearing neuristors so we were all right, but there's no point in us returning to the Compound. We'll never defeat Vaughn without extra muscle.'

'We're pinpointing your location now. Stay there and we'll collect you *en route.*'

'I do have a plan to help us. Well, it's more of an idea at present. I think I can set up a kind of counterwave to protect larger groups of people, on the same frequency as the neuristors.'

'I see.'

'I'll need the mobile lab.'

'Anything else?'

'Corporal Enders, please.'

The Brigadier paused momentarily. 'Are you sure that's wise?'

'Imperative.'

'As you wish. We'll be with you as soon as we can mobilise.'

The Brigadier replaced the handset and turned to General Ffowlkes-Withers seated opposite. 'General, you heard the situation. I need those men. Now. We know what's going on at the Compound and we need to act immediately.'

'And what is going on, Brigadier?'

The Brigadier pressed the intercom on his desk. 'Nicholls? Full mobilisation, immediately. Contact Geneva and New York. Immediate action required to confirm all marked communications centres are secured. Deploy the mobile lab unit for Miss Travers. Skeleton staff only to remain behind, under Major Branwell.'

He looked up at Ffowlkes-Withers, his words only now registering. 'Sir, this is an emergency. We need to deploy now.'

'And I need to understand what you believe is going on.'

Very patiently, the Brigadier said, 'Tobias Vaughn is planning to take over the world. Again.'

'From his factory in the country?'

'That appears to be his base of operations, yes. With respect, sir, we don't have time to discuss this. It's a matter of national – not to say international – security. We need to act in tandem with Geneva and New York.'

'I'll decide what action takes place in the British Isles, Brigadier, not some Johnny Foreigner.'

'Sir, really—'

'You're not putting the frighteners up the British Armed Forces, or the Government, anymore. Show me this compound and this dead man walking and then we'll see.'

The Brigadier stood and gathered his thoughts. The general's pig-headedness left him little choice. 'By delaying us, you could hand the country – even the world – to Vaughn. We'll take what men we can muster, but I will have to let my superiors know of this in Geneva.'

Ffowlkes-Withers smiled and headed for the door. 'You do that, Brigadier. You do that. I'll wait for you in the vehicle bay.'

The Brigadier watched him go and momentarily fumed before he reached for the Geneva hotline.

'Can't I beat them up a bit first?' There was a plaintive edge to Packer's request, like a spoilt child deprived of that one final treat.

'They're no good to us damaged,' Vaughn replied. 'Besides, what would such a display of aggression prove?'

'It would give this new body a workout.'

'Packer, you've got to stop judging by appearances. Your body has been manufactured to a consistent specification. Only the organic components are different.'

'Yes, but… It *feels* different. I need to break it in.'

'Not on the UNIT soldiers.'

Captain Turner and the two corporals stood motionless before them. One of the corporals – Wright, was it? – was recognisable from the skeleton crew left there when Vaughn had first arrived. The three neuristors removed from the soldiers lay on Vaughn's desk. Without them, they had instantly fallen under the control of Watkins' Cerebreton Mentor.

Vaughn looked at Packer again. 'The girl?'

'Back in her cell. Regular home from home.'

Almost as a second thought, Packer plucked another neuristor from his pocket and placed it with the other three.

'Good.'

Packer looked at him oddly and Vaughn realised that last word had come out sounding filtered, electronic, as Packer's voice had been previously. Vaughn thumped his chest and pretended to cough.

'Anything else?'

That sounded like his proper voice again.

'Where d'you want these three held?'

'They're no danger to anyone like that. Take them to join the rest of their men. A platoon without a commanding officer is never going to convince anyone, after all.'

CHAPTER EIGHTEEN

MAJOR BRANWELL intercepted the Brigadier outside his office. He opened his mouth to speak but the Brigadier got there first.

'Any word from Geneva yet about the international effort?'
'Only that our agents have been activated, sir, that's all.'
'R/T with any updates while we're gone.'

Branwell nodded. 'Sir, are you sure you should be leading this mission?'

'How do you mean, Major?'

'Well, sir. You're the CO. Don't you see yourself in more of a strategic role back here?'

The Brigadier smiled. 'Looking for a bite of the cherry, eh? Top man. Ordinarily, I'd agree with you. However, I've got first-hand experience of the area and the enemy. Plus...' He looked around surreptitiously and lowered his voice. 'General Ffowlkes-Withers is up to something and I'm not about to risk anyone else in his firing line but me.'

Branwell stood to attention. 'As you wish, sir. Best of luck.'

The Brigadier gave a knowing smile. 'Thank you, Major. I have a feeling we're going to need it.'

The order had caught Lieutenant Lefebvre unawares at first. She had simply never expected it to come through. The assumption was that she'd remain at her posting for a few months, then be recalled to Geneva for deployment elsewhere.

She was the lucky one, too. Some of her associates had received postings halfway across the globe. Compared with them, the Swiss Alps was almost on her own doorstep. Lefebvre set aside the canvas she'd been painting and removed her smock. Underneath she was in full uniform.

Outside Monsieur Pépé's artists' retreat, a little further up the mountain, was an international communications centre. It was mainly used for directing telephone calls and the fledgling video links used by top brass and governments. Lefebvre had been painting an Impressionist version of it for the past month – a simple way of keeping it under observation (as well as providing a potential Christmas present for her least-favourite aunt).

Covert no more, she strode out, leaving the impassioned protests of Monsieur Pépé behind. Across the mountainside, Lefebvre had the distinct impression that all was not as it should be. Certainly not as it had been on her last recce early that morning. The booted foot of a guard lying just inside the entrance was evidence that someone had forced their way in. Someone who wasn't supposed to be there.

Lieutenant Lefebvre drew her weapon and cautiously entered.

Captain Norman Schlesinger found himself disconcerted by the bright lights inside the Alaskan comms centre. He never expected such a remote outpost to be so harshly lit. He chided himself. Everywhere in Alaska was remote.

A security door was hanging open. Schlesinger upgraded his disconcertion to concern. It looked like he was too late and enemy agents were already in control. Brandishing his pistol, he stepped through into a bustling operations centre – and relaxed. Everything looked to be proceeding as normal. He somewhat sheepishly holstered his pistol inside his jacket. The two staff there glanced his way and nodded or gestured. He didn't think he was known there, but maybe they were simply receptive to the uniform.

'Everything all right, you guys?'

'Sure.'

'You, uh, you know that security door is open?'

One of the guys – as much a man as he was a moustache and glasses – approached with a toothy grin.

'Yeah, we been meaning to get that fixed for a while. Hinge is busted.'

Schlesinger nodded and looked at the big screen. It showed a satellite array above the Earth. Nothing unusual there. But

a logo near the bottom of the screen caught his eye.
IE.
Next to it scrolled some rolling text.

TRANSMISSION PLOTTED.
READY TO RECEIVE.

'Hey, what—?' he began, but stopped when he heard footsteps behind him. He turned to look as a fist swung his way.

'You should not be here.'
'Please, I am lost.' Captain Singh tried to sound vulnerable.
A voice from the operations room called out, 'In Mumbai, this should be no surprise to anyone!'
Singh pretended she was too distracted to hear the comment.
The person blocking the entrance did not share his colleague's light-hearted approach.
'Seek your help elsewhere,' he said. 'This is a private installation. How did you get in?'
'The door was o—'
Singh gestured behind, only to find another man there.
'—pen,' she finished, dragging the word out as she assessed if the man behind her was going to move or not. It was clear he was not.
Singh was grabbed very firmly, making it impossible for her to struggle. The other man stepped forward and tore at her dhoti and kurta, revealing her uniform beneath. Then he tugged at the false beard she was wearing. The glue held in several places, but not enough to prevent the men from understanding she was a woman. She doubted it would make any difference to how they would treat her.
'You're too late,' said a voice at her ear.

Second Lieutenant Sandberg felt helpless as he reviewed the world map on the screen before him. All the monitoring resources they had on station had been deployed. But there had been no news, and the situation was becoming critical.
So focused was he that the comm buzzer made him jump when it activated.

'Monitoring.'

'Any update?' said his Flemish senior officer.

He licked his dry lips. 'Nothing to report, sir. No change on all locations. Still imperative that Mission Control London take out the primary centre.'

'Unless we bomb them.'

'That's a lot of crucial infrastructure we'd be taking out, sir. And the loss of life. Can we justify that action?'

'To save the world?' He gave a derisive snort. 'I should hope so, Lieutenant. Especially as this is the second time in as many months.'

'London might... what is the phrase? Pull it out of the bag, though, sir.'

'I wish I had your faith. I'll have air patrols standing by, just in case. Keep monitoring and report immediately any changes.'

'Sir.' Sandberg did have faith. But he reached for his depolariser anyway. Just in case.

General Ffowlkes-Withers was playing a game, that much was clear. Whether or not this was a game sanctioned by the minister, the Brigadier couldn't say. But Ffowlkes-Withers was clearly looking to wrong-foot him and show him up as incompetent. The inane questions he asked on the drive to the compound were indication enough that he was out to test everyone's patience.

The Brigadier was confident enough in his own abilities – he'd been doing this job in one form or another for a number of years now, often facing senior-level scrutiny. But this was a different ball game, especially at such a crucial operational stage.

When this was over, assuming they succeeded, Geneva would have to do something about Ffowlkes-Withers. UNIT couldn't function effectively with such an obstructive, obstinate liaison. And if he wanted the Brigadier's job, Ffowlkes-Withers would have a hell of a fight on his hands.

He realised his mind had wandered and he'd missed another comment from Ffowlkes-Withers.

'Sorry, General, did you speak?'

Ffowlkes-Withers smiled indulgently. 'Thinking ahead were you, Brigadier?'

'Always, sir.'

'I simply asked if there was catering. Always enjoy a bit of field scran myself. Nothing like it.'

The Brigadier paused before answering. Ffowlkes-Withers didn't waver in his look.

'If we succeed, sir, I'll make you a bacon sandwich myself in Vaughn's canteen.'

The edge of Ffowlkes-Withers's mouth twitched. 'I may hold you to that, Lethbridge-Stewart. Of course, if we don't succeed, according to you, we'll all be wandering around like dummies under Vaughn's control.' The final words were absorbed into a chuckle.

No, thought the Brigadier, *I won't respond.* Ffowlkes-Withers would have to try harder than that to get him ruffled. However, it may not do any harm to make the general think he was getting somewhere.

'Keep an eye out for Sergeant Walters,' he snapped at Lamb, the driver. 'And step on it, Private, we haven't got all day.'

Benton hated being idle. But he had little choice right now. He'd checked over the car, discovering a few snazzy features internally. When he'd popped the hood, Walters had joined him for a good look around. Walters was impressed, but it was as Benton had expected. There were no brow-raising amendments or additions, just a beautifully made and carefully maintained engine. All very down-to-earth.

'How much longer, I wonder?' he mused.

'Eager to get back into the fray, are you, Corporal?'

Benton wasn't sure. What he did know, though, was that he was hungry and thirsty. To try to take his mind off it, he looked to see what Miss Travers was up to.

She was sitting to one side, cross-legged on the grass verge, holding a pencil poised above a notepad. There was already plenty of scribbling evident, along with crossings out and small diagrams or sequences. At least she was able to get on with her job while they were waiting.

'Anything we can do to help, Miss?'

'Yes,' she replied without looking up. 'Leave me in peace.'

Benton felt even more useless until she glanced up and gave him a little smile.

'Thanks, all the same.'

Very dedicated, just like her fiancé, Bill – his old mate at the Green Berets. It was Bill who got him the post at UNIT, of course. No, Benton told himself. He wasn't going to get caught up thinking over old times. He needed to stay focused. When backup arrived, he'd be expected to jump into action again immediately.

Benton returned to the driver's seat. He noticed a lever for the boot. They hadn't yet checked in there. Always interesting what people kept in their car boots. He pulled the lever and heard the crump as the boot released. He walked around to the rear. As he raised the boot lid, arms flung out from within and grabbed for his throat.

'Sir!' said Private Lamb. 'Is that them ahead? There's something going on.'

Indeed, there was. The Brigadier could see – was it Benton? Grappling with an assailant in IE uniform behind a parked car on the other side of the road. Sergeant Walters was trying to help but the attacker was clearly very powerful. Anne was there too, waving at them as if they needed encouragement to stop and assist.

'Pull over in front of them, man, and quickly!'

As soon as they did, Ffowlkes-Withers was through the door, the Brigadier close behind him. He could see the problem immediately. Walters couldn't use his gun for fear of hitting Benton.

'You men, quickly,' the Brigadier called, summoning relief from the troop transport as it pulled up behind.

Benton's assailant was overwhelmed and pinned to the ground.

'MO,' barked the Brigadier.

'I'm all right,' wheezed Benton – which was what the Brigadier expected.

Thankfully Sergeant Major Spring was already on the case.

'Check the others over as well, Spring.'

'Sir.'

The Brigadier turned to Ffowlkes-Withers. 'Some proof for you, sir, that we are not dealing with the ordinary here. Come and look at this fellow we've captured.'

The IE operative was not struggling.

'Co-operate, and we'll go easy on you.'

There was no response.

'Lance Corporal Enders?'

'Sir?' she was with him in a moment.

'Is it—?'

'No, sir,' she shook her head for emphasis. 'I knew straight away.'

The Brigadier turned back to the prone figure. 'Open his uniform at the chest, someone.'

They did, revealing a body composed of metal, plastic, and circuitry.

'There, General.'

Ffowlkes-Withers peered down at the figure. 'It's a dummy.'

Unbelievable. 'Sir, you saw it attacking Benton as we approached.'

'I saw something going on. I've seen similar things on stage. People manipulating dummies to make it look like they're being attacked.'

Anne strode over. 'General, that's ridiculous!'

The Brigadier held up a hand to stem her flow. 'One moment.' He turned back to the prone figure. 'What's your name?'

No answer. No movement whatsoever.

The soldiers suddenly realised they were holding down a corpse – or possibly a dummy after all. They moved back. The head and hands of the IE operative had started to dissolve before them, leaving only a cybernetic body, legs and arms behind.

The Brigadier looked at Anne again. 'How do you account for that?'

She was shaking her head in wonder. 'Even if the men hit something vital and – for want of a better term – *deactivated* the poor fellow, corruption of the bone and tissue elements shouldn't happen that quickly.' Anne looked up at the Brigadier and Ffowlkes-Withers. 'If I didn't know better – and at the moment I don't – I'd say that disgusting display was deliberate.'

The Brigadier turned away. 'Sergeant Walters, get the men and the vehicles ready to move out again.'

'Sir.'

The Brigadier stepped closer to Anne. Ffowlkes-Withers was also hovering nearby.

'Deliberate? How so?'

'My theory is that the cybernetic body is designed to function as an organic body would, providing the flesh parts with whatever is required. Perhaps, then, there is a failsafe built in, like a sort of dead man's switch. Chemicals are released which cause the organic parts to dissolve, to avoid capture.'

'They effectively commit suicide?'

'Yes – unless…'

'Go on, Miss Travers,' said Ffowlkes-Withers.

'Unless the decision is taken for them, remotely, if they can be tracked.'

Ffowlkes-Withers burst out laughing. 'Stuff and nonsense! Really, you two. You're going to have to try harder than this. Fellow was a dummy from the start, spring-loaded into the back of the damn car. Clearly a setup. Let's get on to the IE Compound and put a close to this ridiculous charade – and UNIT's manipulation of everyone – for good. You two.' Ffowlkes-Withers pointed to Spring and Benton, who was still insisting he was all right. 'Drop the pretence and get that dummy back in the boot.'

The Brigadier nodded silently, and they obeyed.

'Don't worry,' whispered Anne. 'There'll be plenty of proof he can't deny when we get to the Compound.'

If we're not too late, that is.

'Well?'

Packer observed the readout. He disliked technology. He was a man of action and was suspicious of words and numbers. However, in this instance, there was no doubting what the data was telling him.

'Dead.'

'Good. Interesting these features we are only now learning. Almost as if the Cybermen were deliberately hiding things from us.'

'Will it have been enough?'

'Oh no, they'll still be on their way. But it should have been enough to increase the scepticism of that fool Ffowlkes-

Withers.'

Packer was nervous. 'You sure it's not an act?'

Vaughn's decomposing features twisted into an approximation of an expression Packer remembered well. 'There's no indication he was aware of the monitoring circuit. He simply moved into Rutlidge's old office and picked up where his predecessor left off. His conversations were candid enough. We know what he thinks of UNIT. And Brigadier Lethbridge-Stewart. And the minister too, for that matter, the naughty boy. He's given us ample to play with. We'll keep manipulating the situation as much as we can to slow down any official response until the tiresome professor finally completes his work.'

'Yes, Mr Vaughn.'

'Which reminds me, is the general's next... obstacle in place?'

'They're in position now.'

'Good, Packer. Very good.'

It didn't take the UNIT convoy long to reach the primary entrance to the IE Compound. Sergeant Walters had explained how they had escaped through the Community. However, the presence of the car bomb showed they had that area monitored and the Brigadier felt there was little to be gained by trying to enter surreptitiously.

It was only as they arrived that the Brigadier remembered that this had started out as a UNIT roadblock, to manage site access immediately after the thwarted invasion. It appeared to be manned by UNIT personnel still, much to General Ffowlkes-Withers's derision. Even when a warning shot pinged off the front vehicle.

The convoy screeched to a halt.

'Oh really, Brigadier,' he scoffed. 'You could at least have had them wearing a different uniform if they're pretending to be the enemy. That's clearly Captain Turner.'

The Brigadier looked on in concern. 'Yes, it is, isn't it?'

Before he realised what was going on, Ffowlkes-Withers was out of the vehicle and striding across to the roadblock.

General Ffowlkes-Withers could barely contain his joy. That idiot Lethbridge-Stewart had played right into his hands. He knew all this guff about Tobias Vaughn was nonsense and a UNIT-manned roadblock at the entrance to the so-called enemy's lair simply confirmed that. By the end of tomorrow, he'd be given command of UNIT himself and then he could bring those johnnies in Geneva into line. He'd show the world once again that Great Britain was a force to be reckoned with and not a puppet of the United Nations.

'Captain Turner,' he barked. 'What's the meaning of this treachery?'

Turner wasn't moving. None of the UNIT operatives were. They all watched Ffowlkes-Withers as he approached the roadblock. If he hadn't been so jubilant in his victory, he might have found it disconcerting. He couldn't hear anyone leaving the convoy to stop him. Ffowlkes-Withers stepped right up to the barrier and leered in Captain Turner's face.

'I'll have your commission for this. You'll be rank and file quicker than you can say—'

Ffowlkes-Withers stopped as if he'd hit an invisible brick wall, suddenly unable to say whatever it was himself. There was a nagging at the back of his mind. Had he forgotten something important? No. He was feeling... different somehow. Saddened. Saddened by everything that had been happening of late. What a state the world had come to.

But it was all right, because Tobias Vaughn had returned from the dead, risen again like a new Messiah, to lead humanity into a bright and bold future. And Vaughn needed to be protected. Protected from UNIT and the rest of the world. It was his duty. As yet no one else understood the new truth. They would soon understand, like him. But until then, General Ffowlkes-Withers would join Captain Turner and the others in protecting the compound.

He had to – he must – obey.

CHAPTER NINETEEN

THE BRIGADIER watched from the roadside as Ffowlkes-Withers fell under Vaughn's control. His body language altered, becoming slack and submissive. He didn't need to see Ffowlkes-Withers's face, but when the general crossed the line and stared back at the Brigadier, he looked like he'd been deactivated, switched off. Just as Captain Turner did, next to him.

'What's going on, sir?'

Walters and Benton were at his side in moments.

'We've lost General Ffowlkes-Withers, I'm afraid,' he told them. 'Marched over there to confront Captain Turner and immediately fell under Vaughn's mind control.'

'The captain doesn't look right, that's for sure,' said Benton. 'He looks like he's... empty.'

'Emotional manipulation or suppression. He must have lost his depolariser.' None of them had heard Anne join their group. She continued. 'He's no longer a fully functioning human being.'

Walters turned to her. 'Then what is he?'

'He is... lacking. That's all. He's almost there, but not quite.'

'Like some of the wasters my kid sister's dated,' quipped Benton.

'And if we don't get in there soon and stop things, Benton,' said the Brigadier, 'that'll be the only type your sister will be able to date.'

'But, sir,' objected Walters. 'We can't open fire on our own men.'

'Of course not. Anne, over to you. How soon can you produce the counterwave and get us in there?'

Anne stood in the mobile lab and looked at the mess sprawled around her. She was having to work fast and incautiously, which was both a huge thrill and a huge risk. She was starkly aware that with a wrong connection here, or a misguided assumption there, she could accidentally help the enemy and broadcast their signal further.

At least everyone the Brigadier brought with him was fitted with a neuristor. Everyone except Ffowlkes-Withers who had, she was told, flatly refused any such nonsense. They'd be protected, but that wasn't the point – she needed to counteract the emotional control signal and free others without the need for bloodshed.

She was extending the work done during the recent invasion and also pulling on all her experiences before that. The plan was to extend the effect of the depolariser and somehow transmit or broadcast it. If the emotional signal could only be overridden at a distance of a few yards, there was no way she could avoid bloodshed.

The door opened and Corporal Enders stepped inside. 'I was told you wanted me here, ma'am. Is that to assist you? I've only got general science O-level, I'm afraid.'

Anne beamed at Enders' innocent willingness. 'Julie – may I call you Julie?'

Enders appeared nervous. 'Yes, ma'am.'

Anne pulled a face. It was like being back Stateside. 'Please, just call me Anne.'

Enders relaxed and smiled. 'What can I help with?'

'You're wearing a neuristor?'

'Yes.'

'Good. When we break through the roadblock, I want you to try to find your brother and bring him back here to the lab. He's been under some stress and is questioning his loyalties. I think you're what's needed to tip him over fully onto our side. I think Simon can then help me help the others who have undergone the same... stress. Is that okay?'

Enders' hand flew to her mouth. 'You've seen him?'

'Yes. I'm sorry, I thought someone would have told you by now.'

Enders shot forward and her threw her arms around Anne. 'I'm so relieved!'

After a moment, Anne separated herself, and offered a brief smile. 'Okay, since you're here, hold these two wires for me while I solder this join, will you?'

Enders took them in her right hand.

'And don't let them—'

There was a spark, a fizzle, and a whiff of ozone.

'—touch.'

Enders smiled with embarrassment. 'Whoops.'

The Brigadier eyed Captain Turner and General Ffowlkes-Withers warily. They showed no expression, no recognition. They, and the other soldiers behind them, simply stood impassively. Stalemate? Or simply delay tactics? Perhaps Vaughn wanted to see just how desperate they were to gain entry. But firing on his own men would have to be – could only be – the very last resort.

Walters appeared at his shoulder. The Brigadier noticed Benton a little further back. The pair of them had most likely been planning. Benton was known to get restless if left with nothing to do for longer than a few minutes. And they'd been there nearly an hour.

'Should I take some men around to another entrance, sir?'

'No reason to think we'd find it any easier anywhere else, Sergeant. We'd like to avoid bloodshed if at all possible – especially where our own men are concerned. Likely the rest of the platoon will be manning the other roadblocks, and we've only got a squad.'

'Yes, sir. Sorry, sir.'

'Miss Travers will come good, I'm sure.'

'If you say so, sir.'

The Brigadier turned and looked Walters directly in the eye. 'I do, Sergeant Walters. I do.'

'What are they doing, Packer?'

'They're just standing there. Waiting.'

'Waiting?'

'That's what it looks like.'

'Waiting for what?'

'Reinforcements?'

Vaughn shook his head. 'Not without Doubting Ffowlkes-Withers, and he's already joined our side. They're planning something, I'm sure.'

'Shall I go and find out how the professor's doing?'

'Yes. The longer UNIT stands around waiting, the closer we get to absolute victory.'

Enders showed the Brigadier into the mobile lab. He looked around, his moustache bristling at the mess.

'Progress?'

Anne gingerly stepped forward through the organised chaos. 'Yes, although there's a problem I'm unable to solve in the time available.'

'We don't know how long we've got.'

'Precisely, which is why I don't think it's worth me going there.'

The Brigadier nodded. 'All right, what *have* you got?'

Anne held up a small box with an aerial. 'This. Think of it as an amalgamation of the depolarisers we're wearing and the yeti control device we developed in the Underground.'

'Will it work?'

'At very short range, yes, I hope.'

'And I assume the range is your problem?'

She nodded, sadly. 'Yes. It's a question of power – there just isn't sufficient power in something portable like this.'

'What about this lab? It's mobile, after all.'

Anne's eyes widened as the Brigadier's suggestion sank in. *Brilliant!* 'It wouldn't be able to transmit too far. But it could be moved to where it's needed while others try to stop Vaughn and Watkins, for sure.'

'Then that's what we'll do. Good work, Anne. You too, Enders.'

Enders smiled and blushed.

'Hang on,' said Anne, holding up the handheld device. 'I need to test that this works, first. Did you bring spare neuristors?'

The Brigadier looked around, somewhat disheartened. 'Yes. In here. Somewhere.'

Professor Watkins could see the UNIT roadblock in the distance through the large window in his – Gregory's – research lab. He watched them for a while to see if anything was going on. When it didn't seem to be, he returned to his work, on the bench. It was almost complete now. One of several much larger versions of the Cerebreton Mentors that were currently hooked up to the PA systems and controlling anyone venturing within range. Such as the UNIT convoy that had recently arrived.

He thought about Anne Travers, and her poor father. Now there was a man who'd taken on a lot in his life, and what had he to show for it? Following his daughter to America, by all accounts. He thought about Captain Turner – a fine young man, which brought him to his niece, Isobel.

He owed it to his late brother and sister-in-law to look after Isobel. To love and care for her *in loco parentis.* Yet what had he done here? His hands dropped to his sides. He cursed his egregious passions.

And yet... something *had* to change. Civilisation couldn't continue along its current self-destructive path. He owed his family, but he owed the world more. He glanced out the window again. If only he didn't have to see it all.

The door opened and a figure entered. Chambers, one of Vaughn's chattier goons.

'It's done,' he said, gesturing at the series of large creations on the workbench.

The figure looked at it curiously. 'Looks a mess.'

Watkins ignored the slight. The voice was Packer's, which explained the cocksure stance. 'What... have you done?'

'I had an accident. Chambers found he was surplus to Mr Vaughn's requirements going forward. I wasn't. It's also a handy way to hide from people, don't you think, Professor?'

Watkins' mind reeled at the possibilities. 'You could go on moving from body to body in perpetuity – as long as there are suitable bodies in which to be transferred.'

'That's right.'

'One of man's oldest and deepest yearnings, answered by electronics. How does it feel?'

Packer clearly wasn't as excited by the concept as Watkins. He was a doer, not a thinker, after all. 'Like putting on a new suit.' He gestured at the workbench. 'How are we supposed to transfer this lash-up?'

'It was impossible in the time available, and with the resources available, to build a single machine with sufficient power. I had to build several machines. They will operate in sequence, to allow the power to grow to the required output.'

'And you've done very well, Professor.'

Neither of them had heard Vaughn enter. Watkins looked

at him and recoiled in horror. The decay was increasing rapidly.

'Gather a team immediately, Packer,' Vaughn continued. 'I want the professor's machines carried safely to the radio communications controls, connected up and activated.'

'Yes, Mr Vaughn.'

Despite his more imposing physicality, Packer still seemed to scuttle off to attend to Vaughn's orders, just as he had done in his original body.

Watkins looked at Vaughn as he stared out through the window at the UNIT convoy. 'What now?'

'Now? My apotheosis, Professor. Victory.'

Anne cautiously approached the roadblock. The Brigadier was close behind, but not too close. They didn't want Anne to look threatening. Just in case. However, the possessed soldiers remained impassive.

'Hello, Captain Turner, General Ffowlkes-Withers. How are you feeling?'

In her hand, she held the small counterwave control box. She activated it and stepped up close to the barrier. Immediately Turner and Ffowlkes-Withers sagged, as did the UNIT soldiers behind them.

'Now!' yelled the Brigadier.

The squad jumped into action, with Benton at the forefront. They vaulted the roadblock and moved in on their colleagues. But they didn't attack, they quickly and efficiently fitted neuristors before dismantling the roadblock.

'Now listen, everyone. You've been under the control of Tobias Vaughn, but with the neuristors fitted you should be immune. We're going to take control of the site. There may be resistance from IE operatives. We need to do what we need to do to secure the site and protect the nation. But a lot of the people we encounter won't necessarily have chosen to obstruct us. Aim to incapacitate where possible. Understood?'

'Sir?' said Captain Turner, stepping forward. 'What's been going on?'

'I'll explain as we go, Captain. Did you find Miss Watkins?'

'Isobel! Yes, she was with us, but then...' He tailed off as his memory failed.

'We'll find her again, don't worry.' He turned to Ffowlkes-Withers, who was holding his temple. 'General?'

Ffowlkes-Withers looked as though all his Christmases had suddenly been denied him. 'Brigadier,' he muttered. 'I'm... sorry. I think I may have misjudged things.'

'Are you all right, sir?'

'I was aware the whole time, yet seemingly trapped within myself. There were... feelings I couldn't explain.' He seemed to reach a snap decision. 'Tobias Vaughn is alive and a real threat. I need to get you reinforcements.'

'I'm not sure there's time, General. We need to take control of the Compound with what we've got.'

But Ffowlkes-Withers wasn't listening. He dashed to the nearest Land Rover and quickly took off, away from it all. Turner ran several paces and called after him, but he continued to speed away from them.

'Let him go, Jimmy,' said the Brigadier before turning to look for Anne. 'Ready to move in now?'

Anne nodded and returned to the mobile lab.

'Sir,' yelled Benton. 'Looks like we've got company already.'

In the distance, a large number of IE operatives were approaching. Some of them were armed.

The Brigadier urged his troops on. 'Forward, everyone. Don't let them hold us back.'

'They're inside the boundary!' snarled Vaughn, still looking out through the research lab window. 'How is that possible?'

'The UNIT organisation is very resourceful,' said Watkins with a shrug.

Vaughn rounded on him. 'Is this your doing?'

Watkins looked affronted. 'Not at all. I was simply stating the fact.'

'They don't have the Doctor. They don't have *you*. They can't possibly have the knowledge or skill to prevent us.'

'Yet they're inside.'

The door opened and Packer led a team inside, saving Watkins from a further lash of Vaughn's tongue.

'Take that.' Packer pointed at the professor's creation. 'You know where.'

'Packer. Your timing is excellent, as always. The second wave has just moved into position at the main entrance.'

Packer rushed over to join Vaughn and the professor at the window. 'Did they shoot their own men?'

'No. They're up to something. Do find out what, there's a good fellow. And make sure they get no further.'

Packer swallowed hard. 'Yes, Mr Vaughn.' He turned to the nearest member of the team. 'You, with me. And you lot, I want that in place and connected up in fifteen minutes.'

'Yes, sir.'

Simon Enders left the others to it and followed Packer from the lab at pace.

'Have a rest, Professor,' said Vaughn as he headed for the door to the lift. 'I'm sure you've earned it. I shall be in my office, waiting to address my new subjects. All over the world.'

The door closed behind Vaughn, cutting off his words, but Watkins was no longer watching or listening.

'You think you're a god, Vaughn,' he muttered, 'because you've been granted a form of eternal life.'

He looked across at the empty workbench, then down at his own hands.

'Well, you're not. You're simply a user. I'm the creator, Vaughn.' He turned to face the closed door. '*I'm* the god!'

CHAPTER TWENTY

THE UNIT mobile lab pressed forward through the roadblock after the vanguard of soldiers. Within, Anne was frantically plugging connections into a bank of sockets on the wall. The shouts from outside, and the occasional explosion, simply reiterated what she already knew: the IE Operatives were very difficult to take out.

The radio sounded and Enders answered. It was Captain Turner.

'There's too many of them, they've got us surrounded. We need that counterwave – now!'

Anne slid the final jack into place and nodded to Enders. 'Brace yourself, Captain.'

Anne threw the lever and connected the circuit. The whole lab started to hum and vibrate.

'Are we safe in here?' asked Enders, sounding like she was trundling down a flight of stairs.

'Probably,' Anne replied.

Enders looked out through the window.

'Is it having any effect?' It was difficult to speak.

Enders nodded.

'Probably a good time for you to start your mission, then.'

'What should I do if I find him?'

'*When* you find him, bring him here – wherever we are at the time.'

Enders snapped to attention and staggered to the door.

'Good luck!' Anne called. She wasn't sure if Enders had heard her or not.

Captain Turner nodded to the Brigadier, who called for

everyone to get down. Anne had said it wasn't necessary, but he decided it would help them if there was any effect on the IE operatives.

And there was. Almost immediately those closest to the mobile lab, engaging with the soldiers, simply slowed and in some instances stopped as if they'd paused for thought. With those further back, the effect was less marked – a sort of mild confusion – but enough for the UNIT soldiers to take advantage. Several operatives at the rear of the group simply fled.

The Brigadier was about to yell for them all to proceed on towards the main building when Anne came over the radio. He sent Captain Turner into the lab, while he led the men onwards on foot.

Corporal Enders jumped down from the mobile lab, into the field of battle, and almost ran into Captain Turner. They didn't stop to talk. She had her mission.

Enders immediately ran to all the prone or confused IE Operatives. None of them were her brother. Several were running off in the distance. Checking her neuristor was in place, she set off after them.

'It's still localised, but the effect is much wider using the lab.'

Anne looked at Captain Turner, who was clearly struggling with the contradiction in what he'd just said.

'That was always the best we could hope for, sorry. I'll deactivate for now. Don't want to fuse anything.'

They both staggered momentarily as the lab lurched forward, on the move once again.

Anne smiled. 'It's all right as long as we stay on the roads.'

Turner didn't look convinced.

'Hey, Jimmy?' Anne grabbed a spare neuristor from the bench and threw it to him. 'In case you need it for Isobel.'

He smiled and nodded, then made his way back to the door. They weren't travelling that fast, needing to keep pace with the men, so Turner was easily able to open the door, jump out and then close it again.

Left alone, Anne moved to the lab's solitary window and looked out. She could just see the main office building in the distance. *Do they have enough time*, she wondered?

*

An alert sounded from Vaughn's desk. One he'd not heard before. It took him some time to locate it. It was connected to the detector showing him the positions of all his operatives. A number of them were showing irregularities or part-failures.

'Impossible,' he hissed. 'How could they…?' He knew the neuristors could block the emotional signal, but there was a world of difference between blocking something and counteracting it.

He made to contact Packer, then stopped. Packer was supervising the connection to the radio communications. The satellites were already aligned. That would give them victory, no matter what. In the meantime, his remaining operatives must hold out against whatever secret weapon UNIT had devised. They must! Ultimate victory was *so* close at hand.

Enders was frustrated. She'd quickly lost sight of the IE operatives. They must have a special mode of movement. As she paused and looked around, regaining her breath, she spotted a line of figures carrying curious-looking equipment. They were heading eastwards, towards what looked like an older part of the site.

She had her mission, but instinct told her following them would be far more important. She set off after them at a distance.

'Sir.' Captain Turner jogged to keep up with the Brigadier.

'They've fallen back, Jimmy.'

'But we should assume our cover is blown and they now know we can affect them.'

'Yes, the mobile lab will be a prime target. Let's hope all they have are the small arms.'

'I wonder where the rest of our men are? Perhaps at the other roadblocks? No sign of Wright or Tracy.'

'They may send them out against us. But we'll cross that bridge if we come to it. We need to secure the main building and the radio communications area in the old factory complex. There's enough of us now for a two-pronged attack.'

'My thoughts exactly, sir.'

'You've been in the main building more recently than me. Take a squad there, do what you need to do.'

Turner gave an appreciative nod.

'I'll take the rest to the radio communications array, try to stop whatever's going on there.'

'What about Miss Travers?'

'Yes, what about me?'

Neither of them had heard her approach.

The Brigadier. 'That trick of yours will be useful for us both.'

She looked at him askance. 'Hardly a trick, Brigadier.'

He'd already made up his mind. 'I'll take the handheld device you built. You go with Captain Turner.'

Anne was sceptical. 'Isn't securing the radio communications controls more important?'

'Potentially,' the Brigadier agreed. 'But my squad will be trying to destroy the radio communications controls, to be certain. We can afford to be a little less discerning in our attacks. I'm sure the handheld device will suffice.'

Anne gave a half-smile. 'There's a mantra for us all to live by.'

The Brigadier ignored the facetiousness. 'Let's move out. Good luck. Benton, you're with me – and bring that bazooka.'

Isobel Watkins was seated in a corporate waiting area. There were stylish modern soft furnishings that looked a lot more comfortable than they felt. A potted palm stood next to her in the corner, growing dusty. It was manufactured – easier to maintain. She'd seen them often enough in photographic studio lobbies and picture galleries.

Isobel stared ahead in silent discontent. She knew that all was not right with the world. Her feelings were telling her that a new order was needed. Her uncle was right. Humanity had reached a point of no return unless… unless everyone submitted willingly to Tobias Vaughn – the man who had saved them from the invasion, the man who had given her uncle hope once again when all around him the scientific community had turned their backs. The man who…

There were others. Invaders. An organisation. She knew one of them. Knew him well. Her… dolly soldier? He had to be stopped. They all had to be stopped, or they would spoil everything for everyone. All she wanted was happiness and to serve. To serve Tobias Vaughn.

*

Anne stood by the lever once again. They had run into another bunch of IE operatives. There had been another, short, pitch battle with firing and explosions. In the corner of the lab, Fred Spring was tending to a wounded private, making the best of things without a field medical facility to hand.

'Hold on to something,' she said, as Turner's signal came through.

The lab began to vibrate again.

Vaughn received the report from one of his operatives as he tried once again to silence the alert from his desk.

'Concentrate on that vehicle – I want it destroyed. It must be the source of the interference. Leave the other group to Packer. He'll know what to do. Just don't let them progress to the main building.'

'Yes, Mr Vaughn.'

'And send someone back here to my office. I'd like a bit of rearguard support.'

'Yes, sir.'

'And collect Professor Watkins on the way. I'd prefer him to be... close by.'

'As you say, sir.'

The comm link went dead.

Vaughn felt his sense of urgency wane. Calm swept over him as the chemical imbalance was corrected. The increase in simulated heart rate and adrenaline caused by his thought processes at least reassured him that he remained more than a machine.

The operative's final words echoed within his thoughts. He responded – to no one and yet everyone.

'Yes. As *I* say. That will be so from this day forward. My word, my will.'

He pressed another comm link. 'Packer? You'll be getting company. How soon until you've completed?'

'We're just connecting the devices now, Mr Vaughn.'

'Then UNIT is too late. The world will be *mine*.'

Corporal Enders found it easier to hide from the group she was trailing when they entered the complex of old factory buildings, but also more difficult to keep track of them. She'd been able to close the gap without risk of detection, but when she emerged again, they'd vanished.

Probably entered a building – damn!

She paused and listened. There were indistinct noises in the background, but nothing she could pinpoint.

And then Enders spotted it, at the first-floor level – the patch repairs to the walls and roof, the warped metal door. That had to be the radio communications array control room.

Sure enough, immediately after, a door across the far side of the flat roof opened and the troop of IE operatives marched out with their odd cargo.

'Why have you been following us?'

The low voice, right behind her, was totally unexpected. Enders spun on the spot.

'Simon!'

'Vaughn? Is it time?'

Vaughn turned from the window and acknowledged Watkins as he entered with an operative.

Watkins recoiled from the sight. 'Good god, man, have you seen yourself?'

Vaughn's mouth slowly opened. A dribble of black bile ran from the corner. 'Such things are unimportant. When the time comes, I know what I need to do.'

He checked the readouts on his desk. A panel began to flash. He gave a jubilant cry and ran to the panoramic window, his arms flung wide.

'The control beam is activating. Professor, once the signal is received, we will control the entire world!'

Watkins' head began to spin. At last, after all his work, he had finally achieved something. He could manipulate mankind to his own agenda, make them into better people. So why was he feeling nauseous all of a sudden?

Julie Enders looked at her brother. It was Simon and yet he seemed different. She realised how utterly unprepared she'd been for this moment. She hadn't a clue what to say or do.

He smiled. 'Don't I get a hug, at least?'

She almost sobbed with joy and flung her arms around his neck. He felt oddly cold and hard, like cuddling a mannequin.

'What are you doing here, Jules?'

She pulled back from him a little. 'I came looking for you.

I want to take you home. Mum and Dad are beside themselves with worry.'

He looked away.

'What's the matter? Don't you want to come home?'

'My life is here now, Jules. My life is International Electromatics.'

'International Electromatics is no more.'

He shook his head. 'Right now International Electromatics is becoming the world for all of us.'

Enders followed his gaze toward the makeshift building where his colleagues had entered. Realisation dawned. 'No, we can't let them.'

'You can't stop them.'

'The Brigadier can. Come on, I've got to take you to Anne – she needs you.'

'Anne Travers? Which way?'

'She was heading for the main building.'

'Good. I need to… Facing Vaughn is the only way we're going to stop him.'

Enders frowned. 'You just said IE was your life.'

'I…' He seemed to falter, and his shoulders slumped. 'I can't explain the dichotomy, sorry. Just trust me on this. I'll go and find Anne, you stay here and show the Brigadier what he needs to destroy – and tell him he needs to do a proper job this time.'

Simon turned and fled.

Enders decided she might rephrase that last recommendation.

All around the world, ordinary people suddenly stopped doing whatever they were doing. Then, just as suddenly, they started again, but this time slowly, ponderously, seemingly without zest or vigour. Except where there had been fighting. Now there was no more fighting, no more aggression, no more criminal attacks. People put down their weapons. They simply turned and walked away from whatever had been going on. They would continue to live their lives, but without the need to fight, or argue, or dominate. Pacified.

Enders watched Simon disappear behind a building. He'd moved surprisingly fast – she wasn't sure he used to be able to sprint that quickly. As she turned back to face the repaired radio communications building, the edges of her mind began to shimmer. Everything slowed.

What...? What is happening?

She became aware that the Brigadier, Corporal Benton, and a squad of soldiers were now with her.

'What the devil are you doing here, Corporal? I thought you were assisting Miss Travers?'

Some of the soldiers were beginning to be affected as she was. She clasped her head. 'Brother,' she managed to say. 'Gone to find Anne.'

The Brigadier staggered.

Benton dropped the bazooka. 'What's happening, sir?'

The Brigadier clenched his fists and stood firm. 'It... must... be... the professor's... machine.' He was gasping the words out. 'Signal... is... too strong... for the... depolariser. Must...concentrate... harder.'

Enders pointed up to the repaired radio communications building. 'There. Destroy... it.'

Benton staggered forward, trying to bring the bazooka to bear across his shoulder.

As they looked up, Corporals Tracy and Wright emerged from the radio communications building. They wore a glassy expression, as the others had done at the roadblock.

Wright spoke robotically, displaying none of his usual eccentricity. 'Turn back. Give up. You no longer have any choice.'

'I think I'll be the judge of that, Corporal,' the Brigadier called out, gritting his teeth against the psychic onslaught. 'Since I'm your commanding officer.'

'We follow Tobias Vaughn,' intoned Tracy.

'Do you now? Let me show you something.' He turned to Benton. 'Try to resist it, Benton, and be ready to act on my signal.'

'Sir,' hissed Benton beneath beetled brows.

The Brigadier walked forward, slowly, maintaining a very narrow focus to try to filter out the interference. He reached the nearest fixed ladder and made his way carefully up to the flat roof. The metal balustrade was bent out of shape. He could almost imagine Vaughn swinging from it still.

Vaughn. He must obey. No!

He wiped a hand over his eyes. Wright and Tracy were there to meet him.

Perfect.

'I need to show you this.' The Brigadier reached into his pocket and pulled out the handheld device from Anne. As he activated it, not only did the controlling influence leave the two corporals, but he felt his own head clear also. Tracy pitched forward. The Brigadier caught him. Wright, however, staggered to the side.

'Look out!' A yell from below, but it was too late.

The drop was about ten feet. The Brigadier heard the thud as Wright hit the concrete. He gazed down at the crumpled figure and cursed under his breath.

With Tracy over his shoulder, the Brigadier returned to the others and activated the device again. Those near him quickly recovered.

'Enders, help me with Corporal Tracy. You four, move Corporal Wright as carefully as you can and then get a stretcher party. Benton, once they're clear, destroy that building.'

Enders looked up from the unconscious Tracy. 'What about the IE people, sir?'

'What IE people?'

The metal door flew open and three operatives emerged. They jumped from the roof, landing firmly, and began to attack the soldiers attending to Corporal Wright. The Brigadier dashed forward, the counterwave device still in his hand. The IE operatives all spasmed and collapsed. A fourth suddenly emerged and made a run for it, vaulting off the edge on the far side of the roof and disappearing into the shadows.

'Let him go,' ordered the Brigadier. 'Let's get these men clear and blow this place up for good.'

CHAPTER TWENTY-ONE

THE MOBILE lab rocked under fire once again. The window shattered and the background hum cut out.

'That's the counterwave deactivated,' yelled Anne. 'Let's get out of here. We're probably safer outside.'

As she did so, Anne understood immediately what was happening. Vaughn had activated the Cerebreton Mentor worldwide, and the neuristors on their own were not capable of protecting them against the boosted signal.

'Try to focus on something nearby,' she yelled, her face creasing under the strain. 'It will help your minds fight the control wave.'

'And find cover,' added Captain Turner. 'We're still under attack.'

'Physically and mentally,' said Anne. 'Let's hope the Brigadier is having more success than we are.'

A familiar figure stepped towards Anne.

'Simon! We need to get into the main building, try to end this. Can you help?'

'I think so.'

'"I think so" isn't good enough for me,' said Turner, joining them. 'Based on your record to date. I ought to shoot you in the head.'

He was right, of course, but they were also low on options.

Anne held up a hand. 'I think it's as good as we're going to get.' Another blast rocked the mobile lab, taking out one of the tyres. 'We need to get into that building.'

'Surrender,' said Simon.

Turner raised his pistol, but Anne stayed his arm, gazing into Simon's eyes, searching for truth. 'Then you escort us inside as hostages?'

Simon nodded.

'Anne, you can't—'

'In lieu of anything better, Jimmy,' she briefly clutched at her head, 'and the strain we're all under, I think we have to.'

Turner holstered his pistol and raised his hands, as did Anne.

'Cease fire!' yelled Turner.

There wasn't much firing at present anyway, but what there was ceased.

'We surrender.'

The nearby troops looked at Turner through a haze of confusion and strain. A few trained their rifles on Simon but at a subtle shake of the head from Turner they nodded and lowered them again.

Simon took both Turner and Anne by the collar and led them forward, through the lines of armed IE operatives and up through the entrance of the main building. Once they were well inside, he released them.

As he did so, Anne felt the strain in her head reduce. Either the building was screened somehow, or the Brigadier had done his work.

'I can't believe we weren't challenged,' hissed Turner.

'We're not there, yet.' Anne indicated ahead.

There, standing before them and clearly not herself, was Isobel.

Benton felt smug. His bazooka had done most of the work, but the Brigadier ordered half a dozen grenades to be used too, just for good measure, which took out much of the structure below the radio communications control as well. Tracy had been fitted with a depolariser and was almost his old self. Wright was conscious, and bleating away on his stretcher to CSM Spring, predictably making a meal of it.

'I don't know what you're looking so pleased about, Benton,' snapped the Brigadier. 'We've still got to deactivate the local signal and take out Vaughn.'

Benton tried not to let his shoulders drop as much as his spirits had.

All around the world, ordinary people suddenly woke up as if from a fleeting dream. They had the strangest sensation that, for a while, things had been… *different*. As if they'd not been in full control of their actions, or their thoughts, or their lives. A mass hallucination. It was written on everyone's faces.

And life carried on.

There was a distant rumble like thunder, and Watkins could see a pall of smoke rising into the air in the distance, over Vaughn's shoulder. Immediately afterward, lights flickered and faded on the panel on his desk. Vaughn turned from the window, his decomposing face approximating anger.

'My signal!' moaned Watkins. 'It should have been too strong for their neuristors to repel.'

Vaughn stabbed at a button with uncharacteristic agitation. 'Packer? Come in.' Silence. 'Damn you, Packer, where are you? What's happened to the radio communications control?'

Vaughn looked at the IE operative standing guard, as if to order him to find out what was going on, then appeared to think better of it and simply turned away again, frustrated.

'So close,' he muttered, balling a fist. '*So close.*'

'Isobel, it's me.' Turner approached her with caution. 'You know me, don't you?'

Anne held back, keeping half an eye on Simon – just in case.

'You are with the UNIT organisation.' Isobel sounded drugged.

'Yes,' said Turner. 'And we're here to help you.'

'We don't need help. The world will be a better place under the rule of Tobias Vaughn.'

'We don't have time to debate this, Captain,' Anne reminded him.

'I know,' he hissed. 'Isobel, you need to let us pass.'

She shook her head robotically.

He stood before her, holding his hands out placatingly. 'Isobel—'

In a flash, she grabbed his throat and began to throttle him. 'You will not pass.'

Anne grew more and more anxious. Turner wasn't fighting back – or he couldn't. He sank to his knees.

Anne marched forward. Isobel looked up at her without taking her hands from Turner's throat. In one swift movement, Anne punched Isobel in the face, sending her staggering back into the wall where she slumped to the floor.

Anne rubbed her sore knuckles. 'Ow.'

'Thank you,' croaked Turner, massaging his throat. 'I just couldn't bring myself to—'

'I know, but come on, we've still got a lot of work to do.'

'This way,' said Simon, pressing on ahead.

Anne cast a quick apologetic glance at the unconscious Isobel and followed.

Packer made his way through the IE grounds. Things had taken a sudden turn for the worst. He knew Vaughn had underestimated UNIT yet again. Or overestimated Watkins. He had to get back to the main building. He had to reach Vaughn before UNIT did. There must be some way out of this for them. There *had* to be.

'The Compound's PA system is in here.' Simon indicated an unmarked door much like any other door.

Anne reached for the handle.

'Wait,' said Turner. He had his pistol to Simon's head. 'Let him do it, just in case it's another trap.'

'All right,' agreed Anne.

Simon turned the handle. The door swung open. There was nothing unexpected.

'Satisfied?' He sounded miffed.

'Move,' growled Turner.

'How are you doing it?' Anne asked.

Simon stepped past her into the room and pointed to Professor Watkins' Cerebreton Mentor, wired up to the public address system.

'Through that.'

Anne rolled her eyes. 'Not *that*. How are you managing to maintain such self-control?'

'If I try to work out why, I am worried it may stop,' he replied.

Anne gave a dry chuckle. 'Faith, in a word.' She flicked the off switch on the PA console. 'Let's end this whole thing while we've got the chance, then we need to find Vaughn.'

'And the professor,' said Turner, who had positioned himself to keep watch in the doorway.

But Anne didn't respond. Seeing the Cerebreton Mentor in

operation for the first time, she looked upon it with a mixture of distaste and wonder. It was, quite literally, brilliant – and yet appalling at the same time.

'Anne? What are you waiting for?'

She held up a hand to stay him. 'I'm just... This is... Not only does it affect emotional responses, but it also *implants* fixed ideas connected to those responses. That must be how the teaching side of it works. More of an experiential trigger data recall system than a true process of learning. Grossly Dickensian, at the end of the day.' She disconnected all the machine cables and a background hum she hadn't previously noticed died away.

'What, you mean like getting the cane in order to remember your five times table?'

Anne smiled. 'At a basic level, yes.'

'Destroy it!'

She fixed Turner with a harsh gaze. 'I can't. We need to know how it works to make sure it's like is never developed again. It's deactivated so we're safe, but that's as much as I'm prepared to do.'

Turner was already urging Simon back through the door. 'Come on, let's deal with Vaughn.'

'The compound PA system, too?' Watkins noticed another section of Vaughn's desk deactivating.

'It's not over yet. Enders has some of their leaders. That's my ticket out of here.'

'What about me?'

'Come as well if you can keep up.'

Watkins licked his lips nervously. He hadn't bargained on trying to escape from the authorities. That was never in the plan.

'Where will you go?'

But Vaughn wasn't listening. He stabbed at the comms button. 'Packer? Packer! Where is he?'

A crackled response emerged. 'I can't get through, Mr Vaughn. There's too many of them and the signal's been lost.'

'Withdraw. You know where to go.'

Vaughn whirled to face Watkins. 'This is all your fault! If you hadn't taken so damn long to build your machines, and if the signal had been strong enough, we'd have had everyone under our control days ago.'

Watkins set his jaw and puffed out his chest. 'I am a craftsman, a specialist, a perfectionist, and most of all, a genius. You would do well to remember that.'

'You're an imbecile!'

'Whereas you, Vaughn, are nothing more than an egocentric cadaver who's lost all sense of their humanity.'

'Humanity is nothing. I shall survive. I shall achieve my goal. Mark my words, Professor. I shall be a god among men.'

Vaughn's self-eulogising was interrupted as the office doors were activated. An IE operative stood in the open doorway.

'Enders. You have the hostages?'

Enders stepped into the room, revealing the presence of Captain Turner behind him.

Watkins noticed the circular screen on the wall to the right of the doorway begin to flicker, but it quickly died. He thought no more of it as Turner stepped into the room and drew his revolver.

Vaughn seemed momentarily confused, before his natural self-control once again took hold.

'Captain Turner. You really are far too easy to manipulate.'

Turner grimaced. 'You've had your time, Vaughn. More than your time. I'm here to end it. For good.'

'My dear young man, you are my ticket out of here.'

'What do you mean?'

Turner glanced at Enders. A look of confusion gripped the operative's face.

Vaughn spoke slowly but firmly. 'Enders? You know you can't resist in my presence.'

Watkins kept his distance. Vaughn's guard stepped forward.

Turner tried to cover everyone in the room with his gun. 'Stay back or I'll fire.'

'Go ahead,' Vaughn taunted. 'You can't actually kill any of us, except the professor there.'

Now he'd been spotted.

'That's as may be,' said Turner. 'But I'll have a damn good try.'

Then several things all seemed to happen at once.

Vaughn's guard threw himself at Turner. Before the UNIT officer could respond, Enders intercepted the guard and the two of them struggled together, each as immovable as the other.

Turner fired at Vaughn, repeatedly. Watkins watched in terror as Turner sank round after round into the decomposing figure of IE's CEO.

It'll be me next, he thought, panic rising.

Anne Travers then appeared in the doorway.

'Anne! Save us!' Watkins yelled.

He wasn't certain that she heard. As Anne entered, she paused, raising a hand to her temples before screaming at Turner to stop.

Distracted by Anne's presence, Turner stalled. Immediately, Vaughn's guard tackled Turner to the ground.

Left alone, Enders moved to the prone form of Vaughn, kneeling over him, presumably picking up where Turner had left off.

Watkins wondered what he should do. The door to the lift was closed and he needed an IE transponder signal to open it. There was a discarded micro-monolithic motherboard on the desk. Presumably from that Chambers chap. He reached out to grab it.

Anne had been cautious in following after Turner and Simon. Turner was a dedicated officer on a mission. She'd seen that look in many a soldier's eyes over the years. Not unreasonable, necessarily, just incredibly focussed. Nothing was going to stop him from achieving his goal.

She finally caught up with him in Vaughn's office. Anne had felt a little discomposed walking through the doorway. She put it down to the room being shielded somehow. Turner was firing repeatedly at close range into the decomposing remains of Tobias Vaughn, who was sinking under the assault. She noticed Professor Watkins cowering to one side, and Simon wrestling with someone.

If they were going to deal with Vaughn properly, they'd need to remove his micro-monolithic motherboard. She called out for Turner to stop. He did, but was then thrown to the ground by the IE operative who had previously been wrestling with Simon. Vaughn was down, he could wait. Anne tried to help Turner, but even together they were no match for the sheer strength and manoeuvrability of the augmented operative.

'Professor, help,' she called out, but Watkins remained where he was.

Simon stood up from near Vaughn's body, holding something in his hand. It was a micro-monolithic motherboard. He placed it on the floor and stamped on it, before striding over to remove the operative who was giving Turner a beating.

In one swift move, Simon flipped the operative over, ripped the chest of his overalls and removed his motherboard, too.

'No, don't!' Anne yelled, just in time to stop Simon stamping on that also. 'I need to study it intact.'

Simon nodded and kicked it across to her, then intercepted Watkins on his way to the secret lift, leading him back to the others.

Anne approached the remains of Vaughn. His face, head and hands were in such an advanced state of decomposition that the bullets had met with little resistance. His cybernetic body still smoked where the bullets had entered. Some remained lodged within the surface metal. There was a gap where his micro-monolithic motherboard had been. She looked at the broken circuit remains on the floor nearby and sighed with deep relief.

'Is he...?' croaked Turner from the floor.

Anne nodded. 'Very much so.'

Tobias Vaughn was dead. At last.

'Can anyone explain what's going on?'

Anne turned to find Isobel standing in the still-open doorway.

'Help him, Isobel, if you can,' said Anne, indicating Turner who was slowly trying to pick himself up off the floor.

There was a sudden loud, sharp sob from Watkins. 'Isobel. I'm *so* sorry.'

Isobel looked across at her uncle, her fiery glare saying more than words ever could. Then she ignored him and tended to Turner.

'The IE lot suddenly stopped fighting outside,' said the Brigadier as he arrived. 'We were able to walk right in.'

'Probably because of that.' Anne indicated Vaughn's corpse.

'Are we sure he's dead this time?'

'Take a look for yourself. I watched Simon Enders destroy his micro-monolithic motherboard.' She began to collect up the broken pieces.

'Ahh, yes, good idea,' said the Brigadier. 'Better make sure it doesn't fall into the wrong hands, even in that state. Good grief, look at the state of him. How did he keep going?'

'He was being sustained by the cybernetic part, but presumably it couldn't halt the organic decomposition once it started in earnest.'

He looked at the prone operative. 'Where's Packer?'

'We don't know. But that could be him.'

'How do you mean?'

'The brain pattern is held on the motherboard. It can be transferred from body to body if needed. Packer could be anyone.'

'No,' said Captain Turner, joining them. 'Packer is Chambers, the union chap.'

'Why didn't Vaughn change bodies as well?' the Brigadier asked.

'Vanity?' Anne suggested.

The Brigadier's lip curled. 'Hmmm. Miss Watkins, I hadn't expected to see you again quite so soon under such circumstances.'

Isobel smiled. As she did so, the evidence of Anne's punch began to show on her upper cheek.

'Looks like you've both seen some action,' the Brigadier told Turner and Isobel. 'Spring is outside with a makeshift medical unit. Go and get yourselves checked over and cleaned up.'

'Isobel!' Watkins called, as he saw her about to leave.

She looked at him again, blankly, and then followed Turner from the room.

'She won't listen,' Watkins moaned.

'I think that runs in the family,' Anne told him.

'Right,' barked the Brigadier. 'Let's get this place cleaned up. And keep an eye out for that Chambers chap.'

'We should check in with Central Command and see what the situation is globally.'

The Brigadier nodded. 'Major Branwell's already onto that back at HQ. There's just one more thing to do here first.' He drew his revolver and marched over to Watkins, who cowered with fear.

Anne was at his side again in an instant.

'Brigadier, you *can't.*'

'I must. Professor Watkins. You are to consider yourself under arrest for crimes against humanity.'

Watkins only answered with a sharp squeal.

Several armed soldiers moved in to surround him.

A little later, Anne spotted Lance Corporal Enders tending to her brother. She appeared concerned.

'He won't speak to me, Anne. What's wrong with him?'

Simon was looking shell-shocked. He did his best to smile, but it really seemed to be a lot of effort. Anne nodded sympathetically and led Julie away.

'I think we're seeing the after-effects of him breaking...' she searched for the word, 'conditioning, I guess. Do you know about Asimov's prime directive with robots?'

'He's not a robot!'

Anne held her palms up apologetically. 'You're right, he's not. But his cybernetic body was programmed to obey Vaughn. Simon managed to resist that, somehow, and operate against it at the end. If he hadn't, we'd never have succeeded. He's a hero, Julie. But it seems to have come at a cost. This is how it's left him.'

Enders looked bereft. 'Just when I've finally found my brother, it seems I've lost him again.'

'He should recover. It might just take a while, that's all.'

'Thanks.' She wandered back over to her brother.

Anne didn't think she sounded convinced.

CHAPTER TWENTY-TWO

'CHAMBERS ISN'T among them, sir. Packer, I mean.'

Benton finished his report and stood back, expecting the Brigadier's wrath. Instead, he looked at Miss Travers.

'Is there any way of checking amongst the dead... Deactivated?'

Miss Travers shook her head. 'I didn't find any with the motherboard intact. Your grenades and shells saw to that.'

'It was the only way we could take them out, Miss,' said Benton.

'Yes, thank you, Benton,' said the Brigadier.

'They didn't have a choice, Corporal,' Miss Travers told him. 'The only one that managed to resist control ended up a psychological mess. By the way, where is Simon?'

'I've given Corporal Enders a few days' leave. She's taken her brother to the family home, see if that helps bring him out of himself.'

Anne nodded. 'Best thing for them all, I'm sure. And the other IE operatives?'

The Brigadier took a deep breath. 'They're being held at a secret government location at present. All good and proper and above board, I can assure you. We've rounded up IE's international operatives as well. They'll all be housed together. Thorny issue, this. Ethical nightmare. I don't know what will happen to them in all honesty.'

'They all have families, most likely. Can't we let them try to live normal lives again?'

'Sorry, sir, miss,' said Benton. 'But what about Packer?'

'We'll just have to hope he's one of those being disassembled in the morgue right now.'

'Yes, sir.'

The Brigadier continued. 'And if he's not, we'll have to deal with that when it comes up. As you were, Corporal.'

Benton saluted and left.

'How's Major Branwell?' Anne asked after Benton had left. 'Still miffed that you kept him out of the action?'

The Brigadier smiled. 'Just fine. He was doing sterling work in support back here. He's getting some fresh air now, though. Since Captain Turner took a beating, I've put Branwell in charge of operations at the Compound. We're decommissioning the whole area. I'm not waiting for instructions this time. Too much of a risk.'

'But Vaughn's dead now. Properly so.' She indicated her bag. 'I've even kept the bits with me, just to be sure.'

'All the same. Decision's made.'

'Try not to have everything destroyed this time.'

'As much as possible will go to Wood Lane, don't worry.'

There was a knock at the door. Turner entered, his face still looking very much the worse for wear.

'I thought you were convalescing, Captain?' The Brigadier sounded unfairly harsh.

'I can't just lie at home with a bag of frozen peas on my face, sir, sorry, There's too much to do.'

Something about the image he'd conjured made the Brigadier smile and relent.

'All right. But light duties only. How's Miss Watkins shaping up?'

Turner glanced briefly at Anne. 'Sore, but unharmed, sir.'

The look was not lost on the Brigadier. He raised an enquiring eyebrow at Anne.

She cleared her throat. 'She was under Vaughn's control. Needs must and all that.'

'I see,' he said with a wry smile.

'She says she's more upset about losing the agency work than anything. Personally, I think it's more to do with her uncle.'

'That's my other thorny issue,' admitted the Brigadier.

Anne pursed her lips. 'Is he here?'

'Yes. Down below, under armed guard. Been through a full gamut since we locked him up. Tears, repentance, denial, rage, indignance.'

'Sleepy, Sneezy and Doc,' Anne finished. 'What are you going to do with him? What *can* you do with him?'

'We need to consider our options. For a start, do we have any actual proof that he willingly assisted Vaughn?'

'He designed and built those machines, surely that's enough?' Turner asked.

Anne gave a long slow sigh. 'Vaughn held Isobel hostage, though. It could be claimed he did it under duress.'

'Yes,' continued Turner. 'But we know—'

Anne stopped him. 'Circumstantial evidence, strong supposition, but mainly our word against his.'

The Brigadier nodded. 'That's the problem. I don't think we have enough to make a case. And I'm not about to do anything underhand.'

'Even though he tried to take over the world?'

He looked at her disappointingly. 'Anne.'

'I know, I know. Justice is justice at the end of the day.'

'Isobel knows,' said Turner. 'But, I suppose it's only her word. And even then, she's not entirely convinced herself that he wasn't under some sort of influence or control.'

Anne thought over the correspondence she'd seen back at the house and had an idea. 'Maybe that's our key. Without Vaughn, how much of a threat could the professor possibly be?'

'None, I shouldn't think,' the Brigadier replied. 'There's no evidence to suggest he instigated anything.'

'There you go. On his own he's harmless.'

'Sir,' said Turner. 'Why don't we send him off into the country, somewhere quiet, to convalesce and rethink his life? We could maintain covert surveillance, watch how he behaves, just to be doubly sure.'

'Nice one, Jimmy. Private Wright's our man.'

'You mean Lance Corporal Wright, sir?'

The Brigadier looked slightly pained. 'I'm taking away his stripe. Evans has under-performed in several areas since transferring to UNIT, and before come to that. And he was given the authority at the Compound over other lance corporals, and a hell of a lot went on right under his nose, and we didn't know anything until it was too late. I expect the best from all of us here at UNIT. He let us down.'

Anne knew more of their shared history than most. 'Then why give Wright this mission?'

'Chance to redeem himself, of course. Plus, he needs to recover from that fall, so let's put him somewhere where he's not going be entirely useless.'

*

CSM Nicholls reached for the internal telephone. 'Ops room.' She paused while the Brigadier gave his orders. 'Yes, sir. Immediately.'

As she replaced the handset, Corporals Benton and Tracy entered. Tracy held out a folder. 'Yesterday's daily reports, ma'am.'

She looked at them scathingly. 'And about time. Takes two of you to carry them, does it?'

'I'm just here for moral support,' said Benton.

'Well, you're in luck. The Brig wants to see the prisoner in his office. You two fit the bill perfectly for escort duty.'

Tracy pulled a face. 'We were off for a NAAFI break.'

'Then this will help you build up more of an appetite. Now move it – at the double.'

'Come!' barked the Brigadier at the sound of the knock.

Benton and Tracy entered, with Professor Watkins between them. The professor was looking a lot older and more world-weary than when he'd last been there.

'Thank you. Wait outside.'

The two corporals snapped to attention and left.

The Brigadier watched the unkempt Watkins who slowly became aware that there were others in the room. He looked at Turner and Anne with watery eyes.

'Captain Turner, my lad.' His voice was dry and husky. 'I'm… sorry, I'm so, so sorry.'

'Have a seat, Professor,' said the Brigadier.

Watkins eased himself down gingerly.

'Your leg still playing you up?'

'I've not slept well for days. My body is protesting under the strain.'

'I've received reports that you've not been eating properly, either.'

'I've not been hungry.'

'Tea?'

He nodded. 'Thank you, I would like that.'

Turner popped his head around the door and issued instructions to Benton and Tracy.

'What's going to happen to me, Brigadier?'

'You know that what you've done is wrong, I'm sure.'

'I've spent, I don't know how long, telling my guards how much I've repented my actions. It's made no difference.'

'It's not within their gift, that's why. Professor, we're not your judge and jury, but I need to know that you can and will be a constructive member of society going forward.'

'It's all I've ever tried to be. I've only ever wanted to better mankind.'

Anne was unable to contain herself. 'Yes, but your view of what would make mankind better doesn't tally with everyone else's.'

'I realise that—'

'So,' interrupted the Brigadier. 'Being a constructive member of society is more about you not continuing with your previous lines of research and not trying to enforce your personal crusade on others.'

'That's easy enough,' Watkins admitted. 'No one in the scientific community will touch me.' He glanced up at Anne. 'I already know as much.'

They were interrupted by the arrival of a tray of tea things. The Brigadier noted that there were only six biscuits on the plate instead of the usual eight. He'd catch Benton and Tracy out later for that. He waved Turner away and poured himself, serving Watkins first.

'We have operatives at your house as we speak, packing up your scientific notes.'

'What—?'

'They're being confiscated. Your previous research is considered too dangerous.'

'I see. I'm being silenced.'

'Professor, you're very lucky you're not being tried in a Court of Law.'

He sat and silently stewed.

'Your niece is being moved into a flat. The rest of your affairs are being placed in storage temporarily.'

'Am I to be kept here indefinitely?'

'Not at all. But you were only caretaking the property while Miss Travers was abroad.'

Anne pulled a face at the term 'caretaking', and said, 'Besides, we've agreed that my house will be best served by UNIT personnel for now.'

Watkins nibbled at the edge of a biscuit. 'Then what is going to happen to me?'

'You've been through a lot of late. I'm not sure you ever properly recovered from the IE business the first time around, getting shot and all that. I suggest some time in the country, to convalesce.'

'You *suggest*?'

'I *strongly* suggest, yes. Do you have any relatives you can visit?'

'I have a sister in Dorset.'

'Splendid.'

'She's an objectionable old hag.'

'I see, but—'

'We don't really get on.'

'Yes, that much is clear. But take some time out there. Enjoy the countryside, read some Thomas Hardy and relax. See what comes of everything.'

'I think I'd be happier staying locked up here.'

The Brigadier could feel himself reaching the end of his patience. 'Captain Turner will make any necessary arrangements.'

Turner nodded. 'Yes, sir.'

'As soon as you can, please.'

'He's a good lad,' said Watkins. 'And you, Anne.' He turned to face her. 'You're quite brilliant. Give my regards to your father.'

Anne looked momentarily stumped for words. 'Uhh, I will, thank you.'

'Someone said he'd died, but that doesn't sound like him at all.'

The Brigadier stood and ushered Watkins from his seat to save Anne any more discomfort. Turner opened the door and Benton and Tracy entered.

'Corporals, if you could escort the professor back to his room and fetch him a good meal from the NAAFI. Captain Turner will be taking care of him in a short while.'

'Yessir.'

'And thank you for the tea. I would have offered you both a biscuit but there weren't quite enough to go around, for some reason.'

He noted the awkward glance that passed between Benton and Tracy.

'Thank you, sir,' said Tracy. 'I'm sure we'll be able to grab one in the NAAFI.'

They turned and started to leave.

'Tracy...?'

He turned back to the Brigadier.

'Make sure that's all you grab.'

Anne gave a broad grin at the chastened look on Tracy's face as he left.

EPILOGUE

THE BRIGADIER had hoped he wouldn't be walking the hallowed corridors of Whitehall again quite so soon, but here he was, on a ministerial summons. This was not unexpected in light of the recent conversations he'd had with UNIT Central Command in Geneva and the various reports that had been submitted. He hadn't heard anything of General Ffowlkes-Withers since he'd fled the IE Compound. The Brigadier hoped he wasn't about to be stitched up again.

He was given a pass and immediately shown through the reception area like a VIP.

I could get used to this, he thought.

'Brigadier!' The minister greeted him warmly with a handshake and a glass of single malt. 'I appreciate you making yourself available at such short notice.'

He was almost lost for words.

The minister showed him to a seat.

'The Government is…' he began, clearly unsure of his words. He swirled his drink. 'Ice?'

The Brigadier held up a hand. 'I prefer mine straight.'

'Good man,' said the minister, adding two cubes to his own with a pair of ornate tongs. 'It seems there were international repercussions. But, thanks to you the whole matter is… That's twice this summer. Is this how it's always going to be?'

'I hope not, Minister. And I'm hoping we'll continue to receive the support we need from the British Armed Forces so UNIT can perform to the best of our ability.' *Worth getting that in straight away.*

The minister didn't answer, simply downed his whisky

and licked his lips. 'Tobias Vaughn. He is *actually* dead, now, isn't he?'

'Indeed, sir. My report should have made that clear.'

'There is concern. This... cybernetic technology, keeping corpses alive. It's more than a man can bear after an internal committee luncheon.' The minister's distaste was evident.

'Even if there was a chance of anything resurfacing, sir, I've taken the decision to strip the IE factory compound. In the interests of both national and international security.'

'Yes, of course. After all, we have a duty to the other UN member states. I understand your superiors in Geneva have spoken to the PM.'

The Brigadier hadn't been aware of this.

'I... must apologise for what occurred under General Ffowlkes-Withers. There was a... misunderstanding. I've told the PM as much. I feel that perhaps we may have let you down somewhat. Made things more difficult for you. But this isn't a free hand, Brigadier. I'm not giving you *carte blanche* to... whatever. The safety of the general public must come first. And to protect the British Government.'

There was actually no pleasure in watching the minister squirm. The Brigadier tried to move the conversation on. 'How is the general, sir? I've not seen or heard anything of him since he left the IE site.'

'Arrived back here in a hell of a state. Babbling nonsense. Just after everything had gone very strange the world over. I was here in my office the whole time. Damned odd business. Like going through the motions in a dream, but the whole time thinking what a splendid fellow Vaughn was and how he'd be the perfect leader for us all. Problem with artificial food colouring, that's the story going out this end. We'll recall a few products, but everyone will have forgotten about it by the time the schools go back, I'm sure.'

'I'm sure. And the general?'

'Nervous breakdown, mental strain. Quietly retired. I've roped in an old friend to act as your liaison with the regulars – temporarily, of course, since he's just about to retire. Someone who fully appreciates your remit. I believe you might already be familiar with him. Air Marshal Gilmore.'

The Brigadier grinned a broad grin. Perhaps the future was shaping up well for UNIT after all.